BUCK'S
LOOT

An Autumn Leaf Adventure

**Clarion County
Historical Society
17 South Fifth Avenue
Clarion, PA 16214-1501**

HEATH NEELY
FROM
MOM + DAD
~~2005?~~
2006?
2007?

BUCK'S LOOT

An Autumn Leaf Adventure

HANK HUFNAGEL

IBSN 0-9743881-0-6

Published by
Hufnagel Software
PO Box 747
Clarion PA 16214

Manufactured in the United States of America

Acknowledgments

This novel is set in Clarion, Pennsylvania, a place that I have called home nearly all my life. In the course of writing this book I met many people who provided me with information useful in creating my fictional account of a very busy week in town. Among those to whom I am indebted are:

Judge Chuck Alexander who talked to me about the workings of the legal system and the law as it relates to lost treasure.

Don Stroup who told me of the early history of Clarion's Autumn Leaf Festival.

Clay Williams for a tour of the fire hall and for his explanation of how the place works.

Edward Reighard who talked to me about Boston Buck and whose book *The Clarion County Horsethieves* was a valuable mine of information.

Joyce Zuck who let me examine one of Buck's counterfeit silver dollars in her possession and who related interesting local tales of the famous outlaw.

Phil Sarver, owner of *Sarver Coins* who helped me calculate weights and values, and who showed me how to spot a counterfeit.

Matthew and Pete Megnin who talked with me about the diseases of trees.

Joe Dolby who told me about old dumping spots in Clarion County and directed me to a whopper.

My wife, Pam Hufnagel, who helped with water balloon experiments and in many, many other ways.

All the kind people who proofread the various drafts of the novel.

Author's Note

This is a novel. Its characters and its scenes are imaginary. The histories of families and places mentioned accord well with the general history of the Clarion area, but all particulars are entirely fictional. Comstock's Coins does not exist. Bear Run does not exist. The Grit Farm and Sweetlands do not exist.

Boston Buck did exist, and his activities as described here are as true as the old newspapers from which the information originated. However, Lou Sweet and the rest of the Sweet clan never existed.

Some locales used in the novel do exist. The Clarion County Courthouse and the Hahne Building are physically as described. The Autumn Leaf Festival, its events and its history, are much as described here. However, the people of this novel — all officeholders, employees, tenants, attendees, functionaries and event participants — are completely imaginary.

Troop 51 is a real Boy Scout troop located in Clarion, Pennsylvania. Indeed, I was Scoutmaster of that troop from 1996 to 2002. However, the Scouts and Scouters described in this novel are completely imaginary; the campout on Bear Run never happened. Sadly, there are no Mouse's Mice.

PROLOGUE

Clarion County, Pennsylvania
3 a.m., October 16, 1885

The shouts of the federal agents died away. They were city men, used to bright city streets, and Lou thought they had little chance of catching him in the forest at night, even without the storm. The wind and rain, the thunder and lightning just added to his confidence that, once again, he would escape the law, though his progress was anything but swift.

He was following an Indian path that trailed east through the hemlock woods toward his old home, and with each flash of lightning was able to hobble along another ten or fifteen yards toward his destination. When he became unsure of the way, he would stop and wait in the dark for the next flash, listening to the cold, black rain tumble down onto new fallen leaves.

Lou was wet from topknot to toes, but that didn't bother him all that much. He had spent most of his 83 years outside and was used to wet clothes, numb hands, and tired feet. Still, he thought, tonight was no picnic. In all his years as hunter, trapper, and horse thief, he could only recall a couple of times worse than this, and those were decades in the past, back when he was considerably more spry. Not for the first time that night he thought, "I'm gettin' too old for this crap."

Lou's wide brim hat kept most of the rain from his face, but emptied the water it caught down his front and onto his boots, making them all the wetter. His old mangled hip pained him every time he put weight on his left foot, so it made sense to keep the saddlebag on his right shoulder. The bag weighed about 20 pounds and he shifted it around from time to time to ease the bite of the strap, but under his sodden coat, it had still rubbed his shoulder raw and painful. The old bag was all he had managed to get away with though, and he meant to keep it.

He kept moving while the lightning lasted. When the storm finally grumbled away to the east, he stopped. This was no time to get lost. He knew exactly where he was headed, but the end of the journey would have to wait an hour, wait for the first of the morning's light to show him the path home. He felt his way in under a big bushy pine and faced around when he found its trunk. Dropping the heavy bag, he leaned back, rubbed wearily at his raw shoulder and rested. Only a couple miles to go, then he could sleep. Until then, he had best stay wary.

Lou dozed a bit, cursing mildly when he came awake again. It wasn't that late, just before dawn, so it wasn't like he'd wasted much daylight, but still it irritated him — never would've happened when he was in his prime.

He picked up the heavy bag and shuffled off down the dim path. The wind had died to nothing, and clean, starry sky showed through the tops of the trees. A half-hour later, he stepped out into the high pasture. Forty years before, this had been home. The stars were dimming now with the coming of full dawn, and he could see the country for miles around. Below was the old farmhouse and barn. At sight of it, the hate came rolling back, even after all the years away. Forty years ago, he had sworn to her he'd never come back, and he still meant to stick by that. She could keep the damn place, burn it down. He didn't care. Even after all the years away though, he still felt lousy about leaving the kid behind to grow up with the shrew. It was either that though or something worse. What kind of a man had the kid grown into? Was he down there still? Then Lou saw the farm was broken down and abandoned. The fields were full of weeds and wrist-thick saplings. The barn had a used up, swayback, out-of-kilter look. Slates were missing from the roof of the house. His boy didn't live here anymore. Where was Jakey now?

The valleys beyond the farm looked the same, full of fog and mystery. That's where Lou longed to be, hidden away in a gray, cottony cloud. The path slanted down through milkweed and goldenrod, burdock and thistle — the old path that had been here long, long before any white man had ever seen this hillside. He followed it down toward the barn, but as he went, he noticed something new. It poked up from the yard at the front of the house — an oil derrick. That meant a drilling crew and unwanted questions. The place looked deserted at this early hour, but Lou was a cautious man, and so he sloped off to the left through fields filled with rain-wet goldenrod. He slouched and moved as fast as he could; the pasture could be seen from a long ways off, and he would stand out like a beetle on a bed sheet if anyone was around and happened to look up this way.

When the house and barn fell back over the curve of the hill, Lou changed course again and plowed downhill through the weeds until he struck the old road. He remembered it as a brown gash leading from his farm to the furnace. It was brown no more, but plants grew poorly where heavy wagons had once compacted the earth, and the going was suddenly easier. His feet were numb stumps, his hip ached wearily and the shoulder that carried the bag seemed on fire. As he limped along he noticed chimney smoke coming from the old Hammerman place across Bear Run, heard the way-off moo of a cow. Who in his right mind would choose to live at that ramshackle old place? He'd take woods and streams, the freedom of the road, new places, new people; anything was better than a life spent milking cows and tending crops. He still missed the kid though, missed the early years of his wife's company, back before she had turned bitter and hard, full of bad moods and complaint.

The road fell gently into the valley until it came to the lip of the ravine that held Bear Run, then it swung sharp right, went steeply downhill and was soon lost in a slowly rolling wall of fog. Down there, a five-minute walk away, was Toby Creek and the old furnace. How many times had he gone down into that fog, felt the cold whiteness of it on his face? Not today though.

He left the old road where it turned, and stopped to peer down into the sharp-sided valley. It was still dark down in there, and he could only just see Bear Run as it churned over a dozen small waterfalls and made its last run for Toby Creek. There was the old Indian path again. This bit had always been steep and treacherous, but today wet leaves and fallen nuts would make it even more dangerous. Worse, some fool had used this handy bit of steep hillside as a place to dump unwanted machinery, and the way down was littered with dark rusting shapes.

Lou could still barely feel his feet and knew his steps would be anything but light and sure. He paused, his resolve fading away like the darkness around him. Maybe a visit to the loft of the old barn might be a better plan. He turned and looked unhappily back the way he had come, and very quickly gave up that notion. Far off, a man was walking down the road toward him. Damn. Lou couldn't make much of the distant stranger, but he could see he was a large man, wore a long dark coat and had a plug hat perched on his head. Not a countryman then, looked a lot like a detective. No help for it, down he must go. At least the fella was alone. Lou smiled grimly; he could just about handle one man in this particular valley, even if he was weak as a squirrel.

Lou wound the strap of his old leather bag around both hands and lowered it until it nearly touched the ground between his feet. Then, taking two short steps, he planted his boots on the slippery slope and started to slide down into the darkness. The ride was smooth as grease for twenty feet, but then he started slowly rotating to the right and his speed increased alarmingly. He was just about down when, sideways and going full tilt, he plowed into an old horse rake. He fell then, landing painfully on his sore shoulder just where the path turned right to run down beside the roaring stream. He lay there stunned for a second, very glad the hill was behind him. The bag had hit top first and coins had splashed out to dot the leaf-strewn ground with dull gleams of silver. Lou pawed with raked fingers to gather them in and quickly shoved them back into the bag. As he stood, a lone coin rolled from his clothing. He stooped painfully to pick it up, shoved it deep into a pocket and set off down the run as fast as his trembling legs would carry him. It wasn't far now.

The rhododendron bushes had grown some and hid the side of the hill. They didn't fool Lou though. He knew just where to look. Fifty feet downstream from where the slide had dumped him, he turned up and scrambled low through fat green leaves. There it was — the entrance to the mine. The head beam had rotted and given way some. One good shove and it would let go altogether, but this was no time to be picky, he'd just be very careful. Hunkering low, he eased in under the beam and into the dry of the old shaft that ran 100 feet back under the hill. Just let any city Johnny find this particular hidey-hole!

Thirty feet in Lou felt with his hands for the ledge on the right. It was still there and, as he hefted the bag up and on to it, he thought of the countless times he had put his lunch up here back in the '40s, back when his crew was digging this shaft. In some strange way, the old man felt he had completed a long looping trail. It had taken forty years, but now he was home, back where it had all started. He would sleep the day away, and then that evening, he'd slope over to Startown and get some grub, maybe a bottle. First, though, there was the detective. Better get ready, just in case he was better than he had looked.

Lou felt stiff and tired as he moved slowly back to the entrance and huddled down against the rock wall near where the weak beam dripped and sagged. Entry would be difficult here, and as dirty as he was, he'd blend right in, becoming invisible to eyes fresh from daylight. If the big detective managed somehow to find the entrance to this long lost place, Lou would be on him like a bobcat backed against a wall. Lou was content now, starting to warm up a little as he sat quietly waiting for the man who likely wouldn't come. It was good to be done with the weight of the heavy bag, good to just sit in the dry, and wait, listening to the drip of the trees on the leaves outside, the nearby crash of the stream…

His eyes didn't close, they never did when it mattered, but soon the weariness and the pleasant splash of the water swept him away and, eyes still staring, he slept.

It might be he slept 10 minutes, maybe half an hour; whatever it was, something changed, and he was suddenly awake again. His old eyes widened a bit when he saw the silhouette of the lawman against the brighter day outside, not much though. Not for nothing had he been a hunter all those years. He waited, cursing silently. He should have tended to his back trail before dozing off. Now his tracks at the entrance would lead the man in. When he came, Lou would spring, like a cat on a rabbit. No, more like an old wolf at a large buck. He had to be careful. Surprise was his only weapon. Just let this detective get his back under that weak beam, though, and Lou would settle him good.

The intruder was reluctant, evidently not liking the look of the rotten beam or the night-dark hole beneath. He was examining the ground again, putting off the inevitable. How had the man found this place? Must be a decent tracker, much good it would do him.

Finally, the detective bent low and moved forward, leading with his head, his hat pushed back. Lou stopped breathing and tensed his leg and back muscles, waiting, waiting for the right moment. Then the dark man's back was under the beam, and Lou uncoiled hard and fast. He grabbed hold and strained to push and twist. The detective was very heavy, and Lou didn't move him much, but somehow it was enough.

The soggy beam quietly parted and the whole entrance to the mine started to slowly crumble down on them both. Lou was ready, he had expected this and so continued his motion to push out from under the detective as the man fell, out and up toward daylight. If the man had not gasped that one word, Lou would have gotten away clean. The short, short word was shocked greeting, cry of fright and plea for help all rolled in one, and Lou was suddenly frantic to release his prey from the trap he had just sprung. Was it too late?

Desperately Lou turned, grabbed the man and pulled. No use. He was not near strong enough to pull him free. Dirt and rocks, leaves, clumps of ferns; it seemed the whole hillside was sliding down to bury them both. The hand he pulled on went limp, but Lou would not let go. There must be a way. He couldn't just let him die. Lou struggled up, set his feet, pulled, and pulled harder. It was useless. Then a great moss-covered boulder came rolling and sliding down at him. He tried to step to the side, but still it reached out and struck him a smashing blow as it tumbled on by. He felt ribs break and he fell, but his two-handed grip on the dead hand never slackened, and suddenly the man's head and upper body slid free of the cold earth.

The boulder was the last of it. Now the hillside was still, the entrance to the old mine gone forever.

Lou crawled back up and looked into the man's face. Was he really dead? If he wasn't, he was sure hurt bad. He had to get help; maybe a doctor could save him.

Lou tried to stand, but something was wrong inside. He tasted blood, but there wasn't much pain. What he wanted most was to curl up and sleep off the damage. Instead he started crawling — through the green bushes, down into the ravine, through the icy stream and then up the long hill to Hammerman's.

He fights the weakness of his limbs and the desire to sleep. He keeps crawling on and on, up and up; his mind whirling with that one awful word. It rackets round his head as he makes his slow way, and the sky above brightens, and he nears the top. That one word, uttered as the world fell down around them. That one word the man chose as his last. Lou's delirious mind shows him that moment again and again. He smashes upward into the stranger. The beam parts. The man falls, and then he breathes that single terrible word — "Pa."

MOUSE'S MICE

Bear Run Campground
Saturday, October 5, 2002

1

Mouse Monroe woke when the snoring stopped and a different kind of commotion began. He was surprised he had slept at all, after lying awake into the wee hours of the night listening to Pig's snore, thinking what a bad bargain he had made. Now Pig was rooting around and everything in his duffle seemed to be involved; pieces of mess kit clanked; a canteen sloshed; something heavy, like a Boy Scout Handbook, thumped to the ground. What was he up to? All Mouse could see was a vague outline, black-on-black. Then the shape moved toward the door, a zipper unzipped, and Pig was crawling out.

"Where are you going?" Mouse asked quietly.

"I'm hungry. Gonna get something to eat."

"Wait for me!"

Mouse squirmed up out of his mummy bag and felt around for something warm to put on. He had to hurry or Pig would just disappear like last time. Then there would be trouble, and not just for Pig but for himself as well, since he was Pig's semiofficial minder. The kid just wasn't responsible.

Lying flat on his back, Mouse pulled himself into damp jeans and yesterday's socks, then knelt and felt for his shirt. Pig's rooting had disturbed Mouse's neat system for arranging his gear and it was a half minute before he found his shirt, crowded against the side of the tent. It was wet from the condensation that covered the inside of the tent on this cool morning. It was wet, but it wasn't soaked, and it would just have to do. As Mouse felt in his pack for his old green camping sweater, he wanted to call out to make sure Pig was still close by, but was reluctant to disturb the rest of the camp at this early hour and so just concentrated on getting dressed as quickly as possible. He had accepted this job only because of the deal he had made with Paxton. Pig was legendary for loud snoring, extreme messiness, and for his strange and solitary ways. The other Scouts were overjoyed when Mouse volunteered to bunk up with him, but that did not stop them from promptly naming their tent the Animal House. So funny. Not!

Mouse pulled on his jacket and exited the tent, making sure to zip up the door behind as he stepped out into the cold, gray predawn camp. Now if he could just find Pig. He shuffled over to where the rest of the troop's tents were pitched in a cluster and on past to the supply tent. He opened the flap of the big old canvas monster and could dimly see the stacks of tools, the duffle bags full of gear and the crates filled with food, but he saw no sign of Pig.

"You lookin' for me?" came a voice at his ear. Mouse jumped a foot.

"Yeah," he whispered, "Don't sneak up on me like that."

"I didn't want to wake the rest of the camp," said Pig.

Mouse turned to look at the roly-poly 15-year-old boy. He was dressed in a red barred hunting shirt buttoned askew over top of baggy army fatigues that looked like they belonged to a much bigger man. Unlaced army boots completed the outfit and Mouse thought he looked more bum than woodsman.

"Want some?" asked Pig, holding out a plastic Tang container.

"Are you eating that stuff raw?" asked Mouse incredulous.

"Yeah, why mess around with mixing. Just eat it and when you've had enough you take a big drink of water and it gets mixed up just fine in your stomach. No fuss, no mess, no cleanup."

So saying, he tilted the container to his mouth and gave it a tap. His cheeks bulged as he chewed at the Tang. "Good stuff," he mumbled through lips coated with orange powder.

"How can you eat the stuff like that?" said Mouse.

"Don't knock it till you've tried it. Come on, take a little."

Normally Mouse would have said no, but the Tang did smell pretty good, was making his mouth water, so he reached into the container, took a big pinch between thumb and index finger and dropped it on his tongue. It was like a citrus bomb going off in his mouth. His eyes got big and started to water; he nearly choked. Then his saliva dissolved the powder into a paste, then into a liquid and finally into nothing but a strong aftertaste. "Hey, not bad!"

Together the two polished off the rest of the can and went in search of some water to complete their early morning snack. It was still well before dawn when this phase of operations was complete, and Mouse was thinking about stirring up the previous night's fire to get warm, when he turned to see Pig was gone. No, wait, there he was striding off across the campground. Rats, he felt like a baby sitter or something. Still, to hold up his end of the deal he had to make sure Pig showed up on time for breakfast. Hurrying to catch up he tripped and fell over a tent line, but scrambled to his feet and soon came up beside Pig.

"Where are you going?" Mouse asked.

"Out for a walk. There are lots of animals out this time of day."

"Wouldn't you rather start a fire and get warm?"

"Naw. A good walk will warm me up just fine. You wanna come along?"

Mouse thought a second. It sounded like Pig was going with or without him. At least if he went along, he could keep an eye on the time, so he said, "OK," to Pig's already retreating back and followed along behind.

They went close by the part of the campground where all the adults were sleeping — "Camp Snore" the Scouts called it and with good reason. The sleeping men were very, very loud. Pig's snores were small and puny things by comparison. Mouse supposed that with some practice he could probably tell who was in each tent just by the style of the snore, its pitch and its volume, but he was content to leave that line of investigation for someone else to explore.

The snoring faded as they walked past Mr. Ellsworth's pyramid-shaped tent and left the large clearing that was Bear Run Camp. In a few seconds, they were in the woods. Pig seemed to know just where he was going, and Mouse was content to follow along twenty feet behind. He noticed Pig's feet somehow magically managed to move through the leaves, twigs, downed branches, logs and clutter without making a sound. He tried to do this himself, but he could not get the knack of it. As Pig silently stalked the forest floor, he may have looked like a goofy lumberman, but he moved like an Indian. Every once in a while he would look back to make sure he had Mouse's attention and then point at a log, or a pile of leaves in a tree, or at one of the large boulders that littered the landscape. When Mouse got to the same spot he would look closely, but all he ever saw was a big log, a pile of leaves or a dark gray boulder. "So what?" he thought in frustration.

Now Pig came to the rim of the valley. This was brim full of fog and Mouse was concerned about both visibility and the steepness of the hillside as it fell toward a stream he heard far below. No way did he want to go down in there and get lost.

"Pig! Stop!" and Mouse went chugging up to stand with his Indian guide. "Let's not go down in there. I'm not against a little hike, but I want to be able to see things. We'll never see any animals down in there."

Pig considered for a second then said, "Well, we've been doing all right so far, haven't we? I think we could maybe find a flock of turkeys down there this time of day."

"What do you mean, 'We have been doing all right?' We haven't seen a single thing so far."

24

Pig's eyebrows rose. "I've been pointing all kinds of stuff out to you."

"Yeah, real interesting logs, fascinating piles of leaves, riveting old rocks. I thought we were looking for animals."

Pig smiled unbelievingly; he was plainly puzzled. "You really didn't see the rattlesnake under the log, or the squirrel in the leaves? You didn't see that porcupine?"

Mouse didn't believe any of it. "How could I have missed a porcupine?"

"Well, all right, maybe I didn't *see* the porcupine, but couldn't you smell it hiding up under that rock?"

"No. Are you sure you're not just making this stuff up?"

"Why would I lie? Look, how about we go up instead of down. We can get up on the hilltop in time to see the sunrise. How's that for a plan?"

"That would be fine," replied Mouse.

"Yeah, that will be better anyway. As noisy as you move, we'd never get close to a turkey. Maybe we'll see some deer or a bear from up there."

"That would be fine," said Mouse, not believing he would see anything, but anyway relieved that they would be headed up into the dawn instead of down into fog as thick as night.

Pig turned on his heel and set off across the bench they had been walking along, then up the hill on the other side. Soon they came to a dirt road, and Pig stopped and pointed. Mouse came sliding up beside him as quiet as ever he knew how. He followed the point, and then leaned close and very softly said, "I don't see anything."

"It's a dirt road," was Pig's whispered reply. "Careful, don't spook it."

Mouse gave him a shove, and they were both giggling as Pig led the way along the road 30 feet and onto a path that went up the hill again. Mouse looked back down the road as they turned and was not surprised to see cars parked along its edge in the

25

distance. That would be the campsite. Anybody could get back from here. He followed Pig, and soon the woods disappeared on the left to reveal a wide meadow that rolled up to the hilltop. No way could he get lost here either. Pig stopped and pointed. Mouse came up alongside, suspicious of more tricks. Pig was pointing at a tank of some sort. Nearby was a large, old-looking metal mechanism that reminded Mouse in some vague way of a grasshopper. Running from tank to mechanism and then on to disappear into the ground was a thick pipe, its various connections covered with some thick, black ooze.

"Oil well," said Mouse, looking at Pig to see how this answer would be received.

"You're getting better," said Pig with ill-concealed glee. "Come on, we have to hurry now or the sun will get there before us." So saying, he stepped out, hurrying up the path.

Mouse was hard put to keep up as the path swung out into the field. He was breathing hard by the time they reached the top of the hill. They stopped there and turned to face the sunrise, but Mouse saw that the path continued on along the ridge top and off into another woods headed for who knows where. Now he gazed off to the east, where the sun was just peeping over a far distant horizon of dim, dark-green trees. It was wonderful. They stood quietly and watched the dawning of a new day. The landscape slowly changed from a confusion of dark blobs to a fascinating mix of hills and valleys, forests and fields. In the far distance, Mouse could just see the courthouse tower over in Clarion. He walked past that every day on the way to school, and it seemed strange to see it now, way out here in the wilderness. It was somehow exciting to stand here and look over to where his mother was still fast asleep in her bed. He felt sorry for her that she was missing something as beautiful as this sunrise.

The river valleys were full of clouds, and it seemed the shine of the sun was warming the clouds, shifting them about. The tops of the valleys were mostly covered with pine trees that looked dark and remote. The hills, though, were a million shades of orange, red, purple and, most of all, yellow. What a great fall day it was going to be. It would be easy to get Pig back to breakfast on time, and then, based on that success, he would finally be accepted as one of the old hands in the troop. No longer would he be counted a kid, a beginner, a tenderfoot — a mouse. From this day on, he would be one of the old Scouts.

Pig nudged him and pointed to the northeast. "I live over there about three miles."

"So that's how you know so much about the country."

"Yeah, my dad and me walk all around here in hunting season. Down there in the ditch is Toby Creek, over there towards town, that's the Clarion River."

"Got it. That thin bit of fog down in there to the left must be Bear Run then."

"Right," said Pig, satisfied that Mouse could read the land at least a little. "Look up further to the left there. What do you see over there?"

Mouse's response was guarded. He had been tricked before. "I see a farm and some fields across from where Bear Run comes up along the base of this hill."

Mouse paused. He sensed Pig's impatience at the reply. He looked again, looked harder, then with a smile, he said, "And I see the herd of deer."

"Good," said Pig, "and you haven't even managed to scare them away yet." Then he got serious. "Say, what's that?"

"Where? I don't see anything else."

"There, about 100 yards to the left of the deer. See the man? See how he is moving slow and low? See the gun?"

Suddenly Mouse did see. And, there was something wrong with what he saw. If the man stood up and fired down toward the deer, the bullet would just about line up with the campground down at Bear Run. Somebody down at camp could be hurt! They had to stop him, were too far away to shout. No time to talk about it. They had to move now before it was too late.

"Come on," said Mouse already running, "We've got to stop him before it's too late."

With that, Mouse took off on a beeline for the deer herd. Coming up the hill, Pig may have been a little faster, but headed down, Mouse's long legs were a distinct advantage. The air whistled in his hair as he almost flew toward the woods along Bear Run. Adrenaline spurred him on as he rushed through the trees, down across the small run and up the opposite hill. Pig gained some near the end, but it was Mouse alone who raced out into the field, straight for the deer.

The peaceful animals looked up, spooked and then bounded away in great arcing leaps from the yelling, arm-waving creature that has so suddenly burst from the quiet forest. Then they redoubled their pace as two massive explosions ripped the morning calm.

Behind them, Mouse fell heavily to the ground.

2

Abby Grit crouched among the sunflowers and waited. It was nice to be out here so early in the day, and she was pleased her father trusted her to help. Suddenly she heard shouting up over the top of the hill, followed almost immediately by two loud explosions from her father's shotgun. She smiled and got ready, watching the skyline intently for any movement, scanning right and left. Then she saw it, the horned head of a buck bouncing up and down as it fled the noisy gunfire. It had a 12-point rack and so would know all too well that gunshots meant danger. Abby watched fascinated as the rest of the herd bounced into view behind the buck. They were coming toward her fast. She wet her lips with a quick flick of her tongue, took the safety off of her old 16-gauge and waited, a little nervous. The world seemed to slow as the deer effortlessly bounded over the rows, headed for the woods. She imagined they thought themselves safe now that the man with the gun was back over the shoulder of the hill. Little did they know.

When the big buck was just 30 feet away, Abby stood up and quickly brought the gun to her shoulder. She pulled the trigger and the gun went off with an enormous roar, much louder than she was expecting. The buck paused for an instant, its eyes wide at this new threat so near at hand, and then leaped sharply left and flew on toward the woods. Abby let loose with her second barrel and then screamed, "Get!" as loud as she could. The deer herd entered the woods and was almost immediately invisible, except for wildly bouncing white tails that looked like white handkerchiefs waving good-bye as the deer flew away down over the hill toward Bear Run. Abby smiled. That should keep them away from the farm for a few days!

Remembering the shouts, she slid out from among the flowers and headed up to find her father. Soon she came over the brow of the hill and was greeted by the strangest sight. There, as expected, was her father, but oddly, there were two other people with him. One she immediately recognized as Pig Hammerman from across the valley. He looked even worse than he did in school, wearing a red plaid hunting shirt, rumpled khaki pants and half-tied boots that had once been black. His hair was every which way. He looked like he had just crawled out of a dryer and needed folding. Pig was standing a little away from her father. They were both looking at a third person lying on the ground, and Abby was suddenly afraid something terrible had happened. Then, as she got a little closer, she noticed Pig was smiling. A glance at her dad showed he was more irritated than concerned. As she walked up to stand beside Pig, her father glanced at her then returned his entire attention to the figure lying on the ground.

"Get up, boy," he said in his sternest voice.

The boy rose slowly, his full attention on the gun in her father's hands. Abby doubted he was even aware she was there watching. The boy held his hands half in the air as if under arrest. Abby knew him. It was Mouse Monroe! He too was dressed for the woods, but if Pig looked like he had been rolled down a long hill, Mouse looked as neat as if headed off to school. He wore jeans and a dark blue jacket over a green sweater. His curly brown hair was unmussed, and he held himself straight. He looked fine, she thought, except for the fact that he had been face down in the dirt and now seemed to be under arrest. Abby could not help cracking a smile — Mouse Monroe, outlaw. A quick glance to the side, and she saw Pig was now actually grinning.

Abby's dad was not at all amused, "What do you have to say for yourself, boy? Just what did you think you were doing screaming and chasing that herd of deer?"

Mouse was silent, silent so long that Abby began to worry he was deaf from the shotgun blasts. Finally, though, he spoke and it seemed as if he was forcing each of the words from his mouth. "I... I was trying to stop you... stop you from shooting into our camp."

"You're camping down at Bear Run?"

"Yes. When I saw... I saw you hunting those deer I... I knew that when you shot your bullets... your bullets might fly down there and hurt somebody."

Mouse paused, took a deep breath that sounded almost like a sigh, then continued more steadily. "The deer were closer, so I figured if I scared them you wouldn't shoot. It didn't work though, and when you shot I dropped to the ground so I wouldn't get hit myself. I hope no one got hurt down at the camp."

Her father considered the boy's statement and Abby could see his irritation growing. She had seen that look before.

"You're a fool," he finally said. He was now just plain angry. "This is a shotgun not a rifle, as anyone can see. I couldn't have shot as far as Bear Run if my life depended on it. And, worse than a fool, you are an idiot to run in front of my gun no matter what the reason. If I had been really gunning for those deer you could have been shot. All you had to do was cup your hands and yell, 'Stop.'"

Her father paused as if waiting for some response, some argument. Then when Mouse wisely remained silent, he concluded by saying in a disgusted tone, "Put your hands down, and get the hell off my land!"

"Yes, sir," came the slow, almost stuttered reply. Then Mouse turned and saw Abby standing there.

Suddenly she was sorry for the trace of a smile that still lingered on her face. Mouse looked so unhappy. His great act of heroism had gone all wrong. He had been called a fool and an idiot. She felt sorry for him, but all he had seen was the last of her smile, and his face was suddenly sun burnt with embarrassment. Wheeling on his heel, he started walking toward the hilltop across the run. Where was he going? That wasn't the way to Bear Run Camp. She looked at Pig, her eyebrows raised as if to ask a question. He answered with a little wave and then hurried off. When he caught up with Mouse, Pig tapped him on the shoulder and pointed off sharply to the left, "Camp is that way, Mouse," she heard him say. He said it quietly, with a kindly voice, but Amy could see Mouse's shoulders slump, and somehow she knew just what he must be feeling. His mortification was now complete. His grand act had turned out to be a fool's notion and now he had to be led off back home like a child found lost in the woods. She felt so sorry for him.

As Abby and her father walked back to the barn to stow the shotguns, he was inclined to make a joke of it all.

"Did you see that kid's face when he stood up? He was white as a sheet. It was like he thought I was a highwayman or something. I was surprise he spoke at all, as scared as he looked."

Abby was unhappy with that assessment. "He was just doing the best he could. He didn't know we were out there to scare off the deer. If you had really been going to shoot, he would have been a hero. He was scared because of your gun. Why didn't you tell him it was only loaded with powder and no shot?"

"He probably wouldn't even know what that meant. The kid is a menace and a fool," said her father definitely. "He has no business running around in the woods trying to save the world. I know that, you know that, even his friend the Hammerman kid knew that. I saw the two of you laughing at him. Maybe I was tough on the kid; so were you. Next time though, he'll think twice before he runs in front of a gun."

Abby blushed. She had laughed.

They walked on in silence and then her Dad said, "You know him, don't you."

"Yes. His name is Mouse, Mouse Monroe."

Her father snorted, "Good name for him."

Abby was surprised to feel her eyes tear a little, and she looked away, embarrassed. She wanted to defend her classmate, but kept her arguments to herself, suddenly tired of discussion. As she walked on beside her father up to the farmyard, she thought, "Mouse Monroe may have been foolish, he may have been ignorant, he may even have become confused, but he was also very brave. That should count for something!"

* * *

Pig had led the way, keeping to a faint set of wheel tracks that ran between the tree line and the large field. Mouse followed behind, silent, brooding on recent events. He felt the eyes of the farmer and his daughter on him as he walked away in disgrace. At the corner of the field, the road had turned left, but Pig turned the other way and entered the woods. They followed a scratch of path down into the ravine. Down and down it went. They threaded their way through a curious boulder filled glen, crossed the stream, came to a much better path — tamped earth covered with moss in places and running right alongside the stream — and followed it down toward Toby. Pig finally stopped at a place where the stream flowed smoothly over a waterfall and peered down. Mouse came up beside him and stared into the churning white where the smooth water hit the rocks ten feet below. It was soothing to watch it cream off of the rocks. The air was filled with the loud, liquid sound of splashing water. He liked this place. His mood began to lift a little.

Still looking at the water, Mouse asked, "What do you think that farmer was doing up there?"

Pig replied seriously, "He was scaring the deer out of his crops by shooting off powder charges. Abby was down over the hill to

33

give them a second dose after Mr. Grit had spooked them down her way."

Mouse winced. "How was I supposed to know that? He could have been a hunter. When we first saw him across the valley, that's what I saw — a hunter who was going to shoot at some deer, and maybe miss and hit someone down at camp. Anyone could make that mistake!"

Pig smiled just a little, "Well, maybe somebody who lived in town, somebody who never hunted."

That irritated Mouse a bit, "What do you mean? What did *you* think when we first saw him across the valley?"

Pig started walking downstream along the path. He didn't say anything and after a dozen steps, Mouse realized he wasn't going to. Mouse came up beside him, saw the small smile remained and was irritated. "Come on. Tell me!"

Pig looked sideways at him, then back at the path. When he spoke, it was in a quiet, sort of sad, voice. "Well, first of all, the man was dressed as a farmer, not as a hunter. Most hunters don't wear bib overalls and big straw hats. Also, there is a law you have to wear orange if you're hunting. The man didn't have on any orange.

"The next thing was that the man was carrying a shotgun, not a rifle. Some people might hunt deer with a shotgun, using pumpkin balls, but it's not very common. Also, this particular man was on the Grit farm and looked like Simon Grit, so I figured it was Simon Grit. Simon Grit is the game warden around here and a real stickler for the law, so I figured he wasn't trying to kill those deer. They were grazing his field, so I figured he was going to make a little noise and scare them away. That's what he did."

Mouse felt like a tenderfoot. He had seen a disaster waiting to happen; Pig had seen a farmer trying to shoo away some deer. How could he have known though? What did he know about farmers and shotguns and pest control?

They came to a place where a thin trace left the main path and went steeply up over the hill. The path continued but it was no longer very pretty. The stream still churned and chuckled in its bed, but to the right of the path, the whole steep hillside was covered with old refrigerators and ovens, heaps of rotting paper, tangles of wire, mangled lawn chairs, broken farm implements, bald tires, crushed TV sets and other junk of every description. Good-sized trees grew up here and there, and the steep hill had the look of a long-ago environmental disaster.

"What's this place?" asked Mouse, almost in awe.

"Used to be the dump a long time ago, back before I was born," replied Pig. "At least that's what my dad told me."

"It sure is ugly," said Mouse with feeling.

"Yeah, but you can't see it from the road."

Mouse looked down past the dump and saw that something, a storm probably, had pulled the roots of a huge tree free from the rocky hillside. The tree had fallen to make a sort of natural bridge that went from one side of the ravine to the other. They wouldn't have any trouble getting under it though, and it really was time to be getting back. "We better get moving, Pig. They will be up and looking for us by now."

So saying, Mouse started on down the path. He heard a small whistle behind him and turned to see Pig shaking his head and pointing up the small side path. "Camp's up there."

Mouse shook his head in disgust and followed along behind as they scrambled up the steep slope. At the top was the road, and across the road was their campsite. Mouse was impressed. Pig really did know his stuff in the woods.

As they crossed over toward the campsite, Mouse was amazed to see that the sun was not yet up down here in the valley. It was as though they had lived through an entire day that had been but an hour long, full of its own adventures unrelated to the Boy Scout camporee. Sunrise had come up on the hilltop, then there was the sad adventure with the gun-toting Mr. Grit. The walk down into the valley had been like night falling. The waterfalls and the dump were like dreams, good and bad. Now it was sunrise again and another day. He was pleased with the notion and hoped this day would be better than the short one just finished.

They were walking side-by-side across the dirt road at the edge of the camp when a last question occurred to Mouse.

"Pig, if you knew all that stuff up on the hill, why didn't you stop me?"

Pig laughed, "Man, you were down that mountain like a deer running from hunting season. I couldn't catch you and had no wind left to yell. You're the fastest mouse I *ever* saw. You ought to go out for cross-country or something."

3

Mouse was amazed at how little had changed at his troop's campsite during their absence. He had expected breakfast to be well under way, expected to find Paxton fretting over what had become of Pig and him.

"Not a creature is stirring, only a mouse," said Pig. "When are these guys going to get up? I don't think we'll get breakfast until it's time for lunch."

"Camp Snore is awake, anyway," said Mouse, nodding in that direction. "Mr. Ellsworth won't let them sleep much longer."

The men over at Camp Snore had three burners fired up. Eggs and potatoes were being fried. Coffee was on the boil. Steaks were being grilled. The troop camps were less busy; the Scouts seemed to be shy of emerging into the crisp morning air. Still, at each of the other campsites, a few hardy souls had appeared and were obviously getting breakfast started. Only Troop 51's campsite remained silent.

Mouse thought about waking Paxton; he was senior patrol leader, and it was his job to get things moving. Maybe waking him would get Mouse a pat on the back, or maybe Paxton knew just what he was doing and would not appreciate being rousted. Better just leave it. He had Pig here on time. That was all Paxton had told him to do. Why push his luck?

Mouse looked around, suddenly anxious. Pig! Where had Pig gotten to? Maybe the food tent again. He couldn't be far. He had been here a minute ago.

"You lookin' for me?" came Pig's voice at his shoulder.

Mouse jumped, "Quit doing that! Where were you?"

Pig held out a large economy-size bag of mini-marshmallows. "I was hungry. Want some?"

"Thanks."

As Mouse dug out a handful of the tiny marshmallows, he saw that the bag was nearly empty. How had Pig managed to eat that many marshmallows in so short a time? He must have inhaled them. Suddenly he had a vision of Pig's insides — stomach, lungs, heart and head all crammed tight with tiny, puffy, white marshmallows. He shook his head to clear the disgusting image.

"Let's get the fire going," he said. "Those other guys will be cold when they finally do get up."

Together they gathered dry needles from under a nearby pine, taking some of its smaller twigs as well. With these, they made a sort of a mat over a warm spot in the fire pit where it had burned until late the previous evening. Mouse would have gotten some matches then, but Pig never even considered the idea. Leaning close he began to blow softly on the mat of needles. Shortly a faint ribbon of smoke emerged from the pile and this gradually grew in size to be more like a thin, twisting rope. Taking a deeper breath, Pig pushed a hard, thin stream of air down into the pile of tinder and suddenly a small flame burst to life. Quickly Mouse built a teepee of small pine sticks and then over that another of thumb-sized bits of hardwood hastily gathered from the nearby forest floor. In less than five minutes, they had a tidy little campfire going. It was only the size of a bucket, but it made a pleasant sound, pushed out lots of heat and smoked hardly at all.

Mouse was pleased. Here at least was something that he did know about. Pig seemed content to watch Mouse scurry in the latter stages of the fire building. He had done the hard part by breathing the fire to life, so now he sat rocking on his heels by the fire, busily stripping the frosting from a half dozen donuts he had acquired somewhere.

Mouse went for his canteen and then ate what was left of the donuts. He was feeling good, sitting by his warm fire, filling his stomach with the uneaten parts of Pig's donuts. Looking around he could see that the other camps were now going strong. Knots of Scouts clustered around campfires and portable grills making the meal that would supply the energy for the morning's games. Mouse was getting uneasy. Maybe he had better wake Paxton after all, get this show on the road.

He was about to rise when he saw a car and a pickup truck arrive to park with the other vehicles by the roadside. The pickup was red and had four American flags waving from its fenders and bed. Without any doubt, that was his grandfather's truck. Mouse's dad said that many flags was overkill, but at least it made Grandpa Mike's truck very easy to spot.

He watched as Mike got down out of the truck. Then his cousin Chuck appeared from the passenger side and Mouse's mood soured. What was Chuck doing here? He had thought Chuck dropped out of the troop after Mr. Ellsworth scolded him at summer camp for filling Bobby Carfield's canteen with dirt. Still, it made sense that if he ever was to return he would show up with Grandpa Mike along to sort of protect him. No matter what Chuck did, Grandpa would chuckle and smile and say, "Boys will be boys." Mouse liked his grandfather just fine, even if he was a bit partial to Chuck. Chuck though, with Chuck it was a different story.

An old man got out of the other vehicle and joined Mike and Chuck for the short walk into the camping area. All three were dressed in Class A uniforms — pressed green pants, khaki shirts bedecked with patches, and red neckerchiefs. The old man's uniform was of a different style though. It looked old fashioned, or maybe it was just the man's hat. It was one of those enormous broad-brimmed things you sometimes saw in pictures of old-time Scout troops in *Boy's Life*. As the trio strolled over toward Camp Snore, Mouse could see his grandfather knew the older man well. Who was the elderly gentleman? Might that be Baden-Powell? Naw, but he could tell from the way his grandfather treated him that the man was somebody important.

Chuck soon left the two men and came walking over to where Mouse and Pig sat beside their campfire.

"Hello there, little Mouse. I see it's just you and the pig man." Then he turned and grunted in Pig's direction. Pig didn't bat an eye, but Mouse was outraged that one Boy Scout would act this way toward another. He didn't say anything, though. The tense moment would pass if he just didn't make a fuss. He was an expert at dealing with his cousin.

Chuck took a quick look at the campfire. "Hey, that fire is way too small. You've got to have a big one to warm a whole troop." He scooped up leaves and logs that were lying near by and dumped them on the small blaze, knocking the neat pyramid flat.

He chuckled, "That ought to be a rip-snorter in a few minutes."

Mouse thought, "Yeah, if it doesn't go out altogether," and suddenly he was very sad. It was always this way. He wanted to say it aloud, wanted to protest, but he felt frozen, afraid of confrontation, just like with Mr. Grit earlier that morning. His big cousin never failed to irritate him, but he intimidated as well. The best plan had always been to just clam up and wait it out, or get away somehow.

Feeling like a coward, Mouse finally said, "Hey, Pig, come on. Let's get into our Class A uniforms."

"I was going to tell you to do that," said Chuck. "I'll go wake Paxton. Which is his tent?"

Mouse pointed silently and then walked away, Pig trailing reluctantly behind.

"Come on, Pig," Mouse said irritably. "You know we have to wear Class A uniforms at the opening ceremony."

He sent Pig into the tent first and waited outside, talking to him through the fabric.

"I think he probably put out our fire," said Mouse morosely.

"It'll catch all right," replied Pig. "It was a hot little blaze while it lasted. Did you see the stuff he put on it though?"

"Yeah, wet leaves and damp pine logs. If it does catch, it's going to smoke like a house on fire. You would think he would know better."

"Why didn't you say something to him about it then? He's *your* cousin."

"He may be my cousin, but he's not my friend. All my life he has been there. Two years older, two grades further along in school, involved in sports that I was never any good at. You know he likes to talk, loves to get people's attention. If I ever say six words around him, he just cuts in like I'm not there. A long time ago, I just gave up trying to talk when he was around. I guess it's just gotten to be a habit."

Mouse could hear much rooting around inside the tent and raised long-suffering eyes toward the sky, thinking of the mess that would shortly greet him.

Then things got quieter and Pig said, "But you don't talk much to anyone. I always figured that's why they call you Mouse."

"That's what everyone figures, but they figure wrong," said Mouse, thinking how unjust his nickname was. "It was my grandpa that started the whole thing. He saw Chuck chasing me around the backyard with a foam bat trying to kill me, when I was six. He thought it was cute, said it looked like a cat chasing a mouse in a cartoon. From then on, he took to calling me Mouse and somehow the name just stuck. I don't know why. I hate it!"

Pig emerged from the tent. He was a strange sight to see. His green pants had evidently been stuffed in a hole somewhere, he had missed a button when fastening his shirt, and he wore neither

41

neckerchief nor belt. "I don't know what you're complaining about; my own mother calls me Piggy. She thinks *that's* cute."

"My mom says she calls me Mouse for the same reason. But, so does my dad. He says it's better than calling me Albert."

Pig grinned, "Well it is! I'd sooner be a Mouse than an Albert any day. My dad calls me George."

Mouse entered the tent. It looked like Pig had just kept throwing things up in the air until his uniform came down on top. Moving Pig's stuff over to one side, he was relieved to see that his own gear had not been much disturbed. Lifting his sleeping bag and air mattress, he found that his plan for pressing his Class A uniform had been a success. It looked almost as good as if it had been hung up on a hanger. "So why do they call you Pig? I always thought it was just because you were such a slob."

"Yeah, everybody thinks that. Actually, it's a family name. A long time ago, there were two brothers that moved out here. One of them owned part of an iron furnace and the other was a lumberman. They were both very big men and sort of famous back then, I guess. One was nicknamed Ax Hammerman and the other was called Pig Iron, or Pig for short. My full name is George Pigiron Hammerman, the Fourth."

"Wow, that's a mouth full of words."

"Tell me about it. I couldn't spell it all until I was eight. My Dad is 'the Third' and goes by George, so I got stuck with Pig."

Mouse put his jacket back on, since the morning was still cool, and stepped from the tent looking like something out of a Boy Scout recruiting poster. His pants had razor sharp creases, his shirt looked freshly pressed, his belt buckle was shiny and his neckerchief was crisp and clean. Pig took it all in with a look of awe, like he had just seen some sort of magic transformation. Presto chango.

"Well," he said, "you sure don't look like a mouse at the moment."

"Thanks." Then Mouse laughed and gave Pig a shove, "Unfortunately you do look like a pig. Here let's see what we can do to straighten you up a little."

After working on Pig's appearance a bit, the two strolled back toward the center of camp. Chuck's "improved" fire was huge and cast great gouts of smoke in every direction. They stood at a distance and shook their heads, watching it roar. Four younger Scouts were playing a game running around it, trying to get in close for the warmth while at the same time avoiding the choking smoke. Chuck was with a bunch of the older Scouts over near the food tent. Paxton was there too. They all were sixteen or seventeen and tended to hang out together. This was the group that Mouse hoped to be a part of for the games, though seeing Chuck among them took most of the shine off that idea.

Mr. Ellsworth and Grandpa Mike came marching over to talk to the older boys, and suddenly things got very busy indeed. Mr. Ellsworth took Paxton off to the side and had a few sharp words with him. Mouse could guess what that was about — "There is no sign of breakfast. It's almost time for the opening ceremonies. Get a move on!"

Grandpa Mike came over to tell the younger boys to get into their Class A's and ready their tents for inspection, then he waved Mouse and Pig over.

"I see at least you two are ready. You're about the only Scouts in the whole troop who are — you guys and Chuck.

Mouse waved a timid hello then said quietly, "We... We were up early and went for a walk and then started the fire."

"That's good, Mouse. What's the point of coming if you're going to sleep all day?" Then, looking skeptically at the fire, he added, "Your fire building skills need a little work though."

Mouse wanted to say it wasn't his fire, it was Chuck's. He wanted to say how they had built a great little fire, hadn't even used a match to start it, but Chuck screwed it up. He wanted to explain, but knew he couldn't get it all out without stuttering and making a fool of himself. Anyway, if he did manage to stammer out the truth, his grandfather would not be happy to hear it. So he just stood there, sort of looking at something else, and didn't say anything at all.

Finally, when Mouse didn't answer, his grandfather felt the need to continue, "Yeah, next time make it smaller and use hardwood, not those rotten old pine logs you find around here. You ought to have gotten some help from Chuck or one of the older boys. They know how to lay a fire, at least most of them do."

The younger Scouts were starting to reappear and were now heading for the food tent. Mouse and his grandfather, with Pig a step behind, walked over that way too, Mouse raging silently at his grandfather's opinion. Chuck was the guy to go to if you wanted to learn how to build a small fire? Chuck was the guy who knew good wood from bad? No way! He looked back to see what Pig thought of the statement; he saw the raised eyebrow, the crooked smile, and read the message — "And, that's why they call you Mouse."

Enough of this thought Mouse angrily. Let's talk about something else. Anything else! And so, he abruptly changed the subject as they came up to Chuck and the other Scouts milling around waiting for some sign of breakfast.

"That's a neat neckerchief slide you're wearing, Grandpa." It was, too. Mouse didn't remember ever having seen it before. It was a very big and old-looking coin mounted on a loop of leather.

"Yeah, it's a good one all right. I've had it a long time. I always wear it when we come to Bear Run to camp. I found the coin right here, you know, down over the hill there," he said pointing toward Bear Run.

"What was it doing down there?" Mouse asked.

Chuck immediately interrupted, "I'll bet it was lying down there. What else would it be doing?"

"Well, actually, I was lying down there, too," chuckled Mike. "See, I was playing *Capture the Flag* back in the '50s, back when I was about Chuck's age. Ox Cockerson was chasing me and I went flying over this steep hill to escape. All of a sudden, I was going full-speed through this big, old dump. I couldn't get stopped, it was too steep, and I went bouncing down through the trash. I just about made it too, but right at the bottom, I tripped over a refrigerator and ended up smacking my head into the ground just where the dump ended by the stream. I didn't feel all that good, and my leg had gotten twisted pretty bad, so I stayed put and Ox went for help. While I was lying there, all crumpled up with my ear in the ground, I noticed this little gleam of silver. I scratched at it some and up comes this old coin."

"Did you find any more?" asked Pee Wee Barnstaple, one of the first year Scouts.

Mike grinned, "I wasn't in any too great shape for treasure hunting. Mr. Sweet and the guys showed up pretty soon and hauled me off to see Doc Myers. He gave me a tetanus shot, fixed up my leg and sent me home to bed. One coin was all I needed, anyway. I epoxied a leather loop to it and have had it ever since."

Mike looked around at the Scouts listening to his story and frowned. "Just exactly when, do you think, will breakfast be served?"

"I'm working on it," came Paxton's edgy voice from the tent. "Something has gotten into our food supply. The marshmallows are gone, the donuts are gone, even the Tang is gone."

"Sounds like raccoons," chuckled Mike.

"Yeah, right. Tang-eating raccoons. I guess we'll have to settle for Pop Tarts and cocoa."

Pig, at least, was pleased with the suggestion, "Now that sounds like a great way to start the day. I'll take four of the strawberry and a big mug of cocoa. Are you sure you don't have any marshmallows?"

4

Mouse neatened, folded and fiddled until his side of the
tent looked like a page from some fancy camping
catalog. Pig had a different strategy. He just stuffed his
duffle bag full of everything he owned, until it looked like a
lumpy, green punching bag. He finished up by placing it at the
head of his sleeping bag and saying, "Good enough."

Mouse shook his head. It would be impossible for Pig to get
at things stuffed deep in the bag. Still, the inspection would be
over in an hour. Then, the first time Pig needed a snack, his other
shoes, dry socks or a drink from his canteen, he would dig it out
of the duffle and his mounds of stuff would reappear to once
again take possession of half the tent.

At the sound of a whistle, they walked back to the center of
camp, where the fire was quickly doused and Paxton organized
a sweep to check for litter. He formed the Scouts into a line at the
edge of the clearing, then they marched abreast across the
campsite toward the road on the other side. The sweep turned
up some interesting stuff — a Tang container, an empty
marshmallow bag and a couple of tent stakes. It was little Pee
Wee Barnstaple who found the marshmallow bag, and he was
very excited to see the imprints of teeth in the plastic where it

had been ripped open. "Look at the size of them! They're way too big to be from a raccoon!" He tore off the part of the bag with the teeth marks and stuffed it into his pocket. "I'll look these up in my field guide later and find out what really ate the marshmallows. I bet it was a bear or a coyote, something like that."

Pig found the best thing — half an arrowhead that he said had been littering up this campsite for a thousand years. He handed it to Mouse who examined it with interest. It was broken at the haft end, but the point was perfect. It was made of some hard, white stone and Mouse was fascinated by the flake marks that showed how it had been formed.

"Can I have this, Pig?"

"Sure, if you want to collect litter that's OK with me."

Mouse shoved it into his jacket pocket, pleased to have a nice souvenir of the camping trip. Maybe he would make it into a neckerchief slide sometime.

A bugle sounded. Paxton formed up the Scouts and they marched out to join the other troops for the opening ceremony. Half way there, he turned to survey his Scouts. He seemed satisfied at first, but then his look darkened.

"Pig, where is your neckerchief?"

Pig looked a little nervous, then mumbled, "It's back at the tent."

"Well, go get it and hurry up!"

Pig was reluctant, "I'm not sure where it is."

"Just go get it, Pig, and be quick about it," was Paxton's sharp reply.

Pig hurried back the way they had just come, and Paxton glared at Mouse, like somehow Pig's mistake was his fault. Mouse didn't think that was fair. The deal was that he would sleep in Pig's tent and make sure he showed up on time. If he did that, Paxton had promised, he could be a member of the Eagle Patrol during the contests. The Eagles were what the older guys called

47

themselves, and Mouse badly wanted to be one of them. They just might win the competitions, but, even more importantly, Mouse hoped to show them that he was no longer a kid, that he could contribute something to the patrol. He had kept up his end of the bargain. Now he expected Paxton to do the same. It didn't seem fair that all of a sudden he was getting dirty looks just because Pig looked sloppy. Pig always looked sloppy! To fix that would require a team of professionals working around the clock for days.

The troop arrived at the ceremonial circle and formed up facing a makeshift flagpole. There was some small delay in organizing a color guard, and the boys stood and talked quietly among themselves. Mouse stood alone, though, staring hard at Paxton's back and thinking about what he would do if Paxton tried to weasel out of their deal. He really, really didn't want to get into an argument with Paxton, but if he didn't stand up for himself this time, that would prove to everybody that he was just a mouse, like his nickname implied. Maybe this was the time he would finally have to make a stand. That, or just give up and accept the fact that he really was a wimp.

Pig came chugging up all out of breath. He had made it back in time. His neckerchief was around his neck, but it seemed, he had forgotten his neckerchief slide. Paxton glared at him. The others were staring, too. There were some smirks.

"I couldn't find the slide," said Pig very quietly, not liking so many eyes pointed his way.

Mouse felt sorry for him, then he had an idea. "Pee Wee, do you still have that strip of plastic with the tooth marks?"

"Yeah, here it is."

"Would you lend it to Pig for an hour?"

Pee Wee was a little reluctant. "I suppose. What does Pig need it for?"

For answer, Mouse took the piece of plastic and used it to neatly tie up the tails of Pig's neckerchief. When he was finished,

48

the biggest of the tooth marks were on prominent display and the thing looked just fine.

"Neat!" said Pee Wee.

Pig looked relieved. Paxton gave Mouse a grim nod, then the bugle finally sounded and the Clarion County Camporee was officially under way. The color guard made a hash of raising the flag on the rough pole, but at least they didn't drop the thing in the dirt. Roll was called and, when it was their turn, Paxton took a step forward and boomed out, "Troop 51. All present or accounted for, sir!" A tall, thin man with a very large and droopy black mustache stepped forward and led the group in a short prayer. He then introduced Mr. R. M. MacFarlan, the camporee chairman. An extremely round man stepped forward. He wore a bright, red wool shirt over his uniform, and this was covered with dozens of patches. Everyone knew, with just a glance at that shirt, that this fat guy was a pro. Maybe you wouldn't want him along on a twenty-mile hike, but in camp, he would be full of odd stories and, if his waistline was any indication, he was a good cook as well.

"Good morning, Scouts!" said Mr. MacFarlan loudly.

"Good morning, sir," came the surprised response. Why they were surprised was a mystery to Mouse. These things always started the same way. It was stupid.

"I can't hear you. Good morning, Scouts!" came the very predictable reply from the fat man.

"Good morning, sir." The Scouts were louder now, but Mouse knew there would be one more repeat. There always was.

"I still can't hear you! Good morning, Scouts!"

This time the Scouts responded with gusto, and their "Good Morning, Sir!" caused an echo to return from the far banks of Toby Creek. Many of them grinned, pleased with their last effort. Mouse, surprised by the effect, smiled too. Neat, but now it was over. They always did it just three times, as if it was written down somewhere in a book that this was the only way to start a speech to a bunch of Boy Scouts.

Mouse was unsurprised to find he had been right. The man began to speak, and, if his legs were unlikely to move his massive person any great distance, his jaw at least was in prime condition.

"Today, Scouts, we are gathered once again at Bear Run Camp for another weekend of brotherhood and Scouting fun. Many of us have been here before. This camp has been used by Scout troops ever since 1912 when Jacob Sweet helped start the first troop in Clarion County. Ever since that first campout, over 90 years ago, the Sweet family has not only allowed Scouts to use this beautiful place, but has also contributed sons and fathers to the movement. With us today is the current owner of this beautiful campsite, Judge Theopholis Sweet!"

The old man with the hat who Mouse had noticed earlier stepped forward and the Scouts gave a big cheer. He smiled and, perhaps, would have spoken, but Mr. MacFarlan had only been catching his breath.

"Judge Sweet, myself and all of your leaders will be the referees during today's competitions. I am sure that you have read the rules and have been practicing for weeks, so I won't bore you with details, but let's just go over some of it again..."

Mr. MacFarlan spoke of the camp inspection that was now underway and of the four skills contests. He stressed that safety was very important, and that points would be subtracted or teams eliminated for unsafe behavior. He said there would be eight patrols competing, two from each troop. At the end of the day, there would be awards for the best campsite and for the winners of each of the four contests. A grand prize would go to the overall winning patrol. Instead of the more usual round robin, here only one contest would take place at a time. This would allow the patrols to compete directly against each other, instead of just against the clock, and this would add excitement to the day's proceedings.

If Mr. MacFarlan had stopped there, the Scouts would have walked away pleased with him and excited about the coming contests. Instead, he did just what he had earlier said he would not do. He described each contest in great detail, with many warnings and asides. Mouse glazed over as the man talked on and on and on. It was all in the signup sheets they had read and reread, but that didn't matter at all. Finally, MacFarlan reached the last event and talked about the string burn and fire safety. The Scouts breathed a sigh of relief, at last the talking was over. But no! The round man then summarized what he had just said. Then he summarized even his summation, finally finishing with, "Have fun! Be safe!"

The Scouts had wilted under the torrent of words. They had not come out into the woods to hear a long-winded and very repetitive speech. They had come to camp, to explore, to play and, most of all, to have fun. Why were there always these rambling speeches? Right at the start, most of the adults had left to do the campsite inspections, and Mouse suspected this man's real job had been to keep yakking until those were complete. But man, his ears were numb. There must be some other way to fill the time that didn't involve hearing the same stuff repeated again and again. Anyway, the opening was over, and now the fun would begin.

They walked back to camp to change into shorts and troop T-shirts. Mouse was pleased. Now all his hard work with Pig would pay off, and he would join the older guys in a day of fun and adventure that would change the way they looked at him forever. He smiled. Just wait till they saw the trick he had thought of during the speech. It might win them the string burn. They would love it!

They entered camp. Mr. Ellsworth was standing there waiting. He did not look happy. The Scouts split off to go to their tents, but Mr. Ellsworth motioned for Paxton to stay behind. Mouse felt sorry for the older Scout. Anyone could see Paxton was going to get chewed on again. Things were just not going well for the senior patrol leader.

Mouse strolled down to his tent, Pig bringing up the rear. The flap was already open and Mouse ducked down to enter, then he stopped. Something very bad had happened since he had last seen the place. Something or someone had emptied Pig's duffle and thrown his stuff all over the tent. It looked like a bomb had exploded, or some wild animal had been ripping around looking for Pig's food supply. Mouse heard footsteps and looked around as Mr. Ellsworth and Paxton walked up. They stooped low and looked inside at the rummage of possessions. Mouse suddenly noticed the expression on Pig's face, noticed the rumpled, red neckerchief around his neck. The parts of the puzzle fell into place. "Uh, oh."

Mr. Ellsworth looked at Paxton, "So you were telling me how you checked all the tents to make sure they were ready for inspection. Tell me then, how did this one get past you?"

"I did check them, all except this one," Paxton explained desperately. "The bugle had already blown for the opening and we were late. I didn't get to this one because it was off from the rest. Anyway, I knew Mouse was in this tent, and everyone knows he's as neat as an old lady. He and I had a deal. He was supposed to look out for Pig, keep him out of trouble. I trusted him to hold up his end."

Mr. Ellsworth's response was surprisingly mild, "Trust is good, but seeing is believing. If you had not spent the morning sleeping and talking to your buddies, you would have had time to check *all* the tents."

"Yes, sir. I'm sorry, you're right. Once you get behind in this job it's awful hard to catch up."

Mr. Ellsworth smiled, "True, very true. If you have learned that one lesson this morning, then your day has not been wasted. That little lesson will serve you well all your life. 'Haste makes waste' is the old proverb, and it is still true today. Now see if you can't catch up and make something of this troop the rest of the time we are out here. Remember, you are not here this weekend

52

to pal around with your buddies. You are out here to lead a Boy Scout troop. Now, get your patrols formed up and make sure they are ready for the contests."

With that, Mr. Ellsworth walked away toward his tent.

As soon as he was out of earshot, Paxton wheeled around to face Mouse.

"Thanks a lot, Mouse!" he said bitterly, "Like I don't have enough problems without doing your job for you."

Mouse was indignant. He was supposed to insure Pig's presence, not nursemaid him. Where did Paxton get off, saying it was his fault? It was Paxton who had screwed up. He started to speak, but his lips wouldn't move. His tongue seemed frozen to the roof of his mouth. What did Paxton mean when he said "like an old lady?" Is that what everyone thought of him? Mouse was screaming mad inside but no sound escaped. In the end, he just stood there, furiously trying to keep the tears back. He *was* a wimp.

Paxton swung around to face Pig, who looked decidedly uncomfortable.

"And you, Pig, are a slob. You have always been a slob, and I think you always will be. You think you're special because you know the woods. Well, you are not. If I tell you to clean up your tent, I expect you to do it — do it or don't come camping next time," he paused. "Yeah, that's the answer. Why are you in Boy Scouts, anyway? If you aren't going to act like one, maybe you ought to think about getting out of the Boy Scouts!"

Who could read Pig's expression? His face was blank, and it was obvious he would say not one word in his own defense. Mouse though had had enough. Strangely his tongue came unstuck, his mouth opened. Damned if he would let Paxton speak like that to Pig.

"Hey, Paxton, it wasn't all his fault, you know."

"Oh, so the Mouse can speak."

"Yes and what I say is 'It was your own fault the tent got trashed.'"

"No way."

"Yes way. The whole tent was neat and ready for inspection when we started for the opening. Then you had to go get excited and send Pig back for his neckerchief. Remember how mad you were and how you told him to hurry? That is what caused this mess. He was hurrying. And for what? What you should have done was just put him in the back row where he wouldn't be noticed."

"That's what I should have done?" said Paxton with a defiant tone. "That's what you think based on your years of leadership experience?"

"That's what I would have done," said Mouse. He wasn't backing down now. "And also, I don't think you should be telling Pig to quit the Boy Scouts. He may be sloppy, but that doesn't mean he can't change. And even if he never changes, there is nowhere it says you have to be neat to be a Boy Scout."

Paxton looked surprised, but then his expression turned thoughtful. "Well, maybe you're right about that, anyway. I'm sorry I said that about you quitting, Pig. In the Scout Law it does say 'A Scout is Clean,' and you are the reverse of that, but I break the Scout Laws too, sometimes, and nobody ever kicked me out."

Mouse quickly followed up his advantage, "OK, so Pig and I will clean up the tent and try to do better. OK?"

Paxton looked puzzled. "What's with you, Mouse? Are you all right? You don't sound like yourself."

"Yeah, I'm OK. It's just I got mad about what you said to Pig."

"You should get mad more often," said Pig, helpfully.

Paxton snorted, said, "Clean up the tent," and left. Mouse was trembling. He had never let loose like that before, and the adrenaline surge made him weak. One thing was sure; no way would Paxton put him in the Eagle Patrol for the contests. Instead of sadness, Mouse felt nothing but relief.

It turned out just that way too, but there was a twist that came as a big surprise. As the troop walked to the site of the balloon rescue stunt, Brian Paxton fell back and handed him a piece of paper. All Paxton said, and he said it with a grin, was, "Let's see how easy you think leadership is after you've tried it once yourself."

The handwritten piece of paper read:

Troop 51 Patrol List for Camporee
Patrol #5
    Patrol Name: Eagles
    Patrol Leader: Brian Paxton
    Asst. Patrol Leader: Ace Friedling
    Scouts: Lee Hamlin, John Grubber
            Andy Weston, Chuck Wing
Patrol #6
    Patrol Name: Mouse's Mice
    Patrol Leader: Mouse Monroe
    Asst. Patrol Leader: Pig Hammerman
    Scouts: Bobby Carfield, Beaner Sikes
            Jim Zimmer, Pee Wee Barnstaple

Mouse gulped as he read the list. Paxton had put him in charge of the first and second year Scouts and made Pig his assistant. Had he done it to make a point? Was it punishment or maybe some kind of joke? Mouse was surprised to find he viewed it almost as an honor. He would not have been happy being around Chuck and Paxton all day anyway, and this was sort of exciting. He wished he could change the name Paxton had picked though. Mouse's Mice sounded like he was an expert of some sort. Maybe that was what he got for telling Paxton his job. Mouse's Mice — that really put the pressure on.

Mouse handed Pig the list. A few seconds later his friend burst out laughing, "Mouse's Mice! That's a good one! You'll show 'em, Mouse."

Mouse wasn't so sure. At least he could try.

5

Mouse and his new patrol walked up a trace that followed along the top of Bear Run ravine. The path ran through a section of hardwood and everywhere the colors of fall delighted their eyes. Before and behind came the other seven patrols that would take part in the competitions. The rules said that only six-man patrols could compete, so all the teams were the same if you just counted heads. Mouse could not help but notice, though, that his Mice were more varied in size than the Scouts in the other patrols.

Pig was the biggest of them. He was close to 6 feet tall, stocky and strong, but not very quick on his feet. Mouse himself was next in size, just a shade shorter than Pig but thin as a wire.

The other four Mice were 11- and 12-years-olds and much smaller than their leaders.

Bobby Carfield was the tallest of them. A head shorter than Mouse, he was pudgy and unathletic. Bobby was a favorite target for Chuck's practical jokes, and Mouse knew that some guys at school liked to pick on him, too. Bobby's problem, as far as these boys were concerned, was that he was too smart with his head and way too smart with his mouth. His attackers felt this was reason enough to make trouble for him, especially since Bobby might cry, but he would never fight back or tell on the bullies who harassed him. Mouse thought maybe Bobby's brains would come in handy, but worried he was more talker than doer.

Next in size were Beaner Sikes and Jim Zimmer, who were a bit shorter than Bobby and inseparable pals. They played baseball and soccer together and were full of zip and energy. Mouse figured that would come in handy, if he could just keep them focused on the job at hand.

The last and the least of the Mouse's Mice Patrol was Pee Wee Barnstaple. Guys who didn't know him took one look and thought Pee Wee must be a Cub Scout somehow come to the wrong place. Once they got to know him though, no one ever had any doubt he was Boy Scout clear to the bone. His real name was Pete Barnstaple, but after his first campout, the older guys had taken to calling him Pee Wee after Pee Wee Harris, the legendary Scout in the cartoon section of *Boy's Life*. Pete took that as a compliment and now everyone called him that. Just like Pee Wee Harris, Pee Wee Barnstaple was full of strange ideas and grand plans. He understood the theory of every Scouting activity, but was sometimes a little faulty in his execution. Mouse had always found Pee Wee to be interesting and amusing, but wasn't too sure how effective a team member he would be. Pee Wee might just turn out to be a distraction, with his constant wacky chattering.

As they marched along, Mouse considered the pros and cons of each of his Scouts and tried to think how best to make a patrol of them. He wanted his Mice to do well at these competitions, even though they had little chance of winning anything — the other patrols just had too many experienced hands. Rolling ideas around in his head, he finally concluded that his job was to see that the patrol did well, but more importantly, he had to make sure each of the guys had fun and felt a part of the group. Just how he was going to do that remained a mystery, but it felt good to have a plan, even if it was a loose one.

The long caterpillar of Scouts wriggled out of the woods five minutes later and clumped up in a clearing about half the size of a football field. A gusting breeze from the west flicked the tops of the surrounding trees and caused a constant slow rain of banana-yellow leaves to tumble and bump to the ground all around them. The sky was mostly blue, but occasional puffs of cloud could be seen racing off to the east. Word had it that thunder showers were to be expected in a couple of hours.

At the center of the clearing, a large campfire burned bright and clear, evidently built by a pro. Next to it stood Mr. MacFarlan, looking like a round, red apple in his brightly colored patch shirt. Mouse was not at all surprised when MacFarlan once again explained the rules. Funny thing though, now that he was a leader, Mouse found himself listening intently to what the man had to say.

"Good morning, Scouts!"

"Good morning, sir," came the almost sullen reply. The boys had had enough of that particular game.

"You guys sound half asleep," said MacFarlan. "You had better wake up if you expect to win this one.

"Around you, on the edges of the clearing, you will see numbers on some of the trees. When I blow the whistle, each patrol will go to their particular tree, where one member will climb up and get the ball of ropes that has been hidden in each."

Mouse and the others craned their necks to spot tree number 6, their patrol number. It was Pee Wee who spotted it first. He pointed and let out a cry, "There!"

"Settle down," said Mr. MacFarlan. "Once you have got your ropes you will separate them and tie them into one long line with square knots. You should also tie a bowline at each end. When you have done that, proceed to the edge of the ravine, over there, and a judge will check your knots. Once he says it's OK, you can go on to the next step."

Mouse looked in the direction of the ravine — seemed simple enough so far.

"Next, you will go down into the ravine using your rope and get your patrol's water balloons. Each Scout in the patrol has to bring up one balloon. I think that you will find this to be the tricky part, but let me assure you that every patrol has the necessary equipment to perform this task. You just need to use your noodles!"

Mouse didn't understand. They could just send one or two guys down at a time and the others could pull them back up. As long as either he or Pig was at the top, it wouldn't be that hard.

"Each of the filled water balloons will be about the size of a grapefruit and as Scouts get back to the top with their balloons they will run to the fire here and throw them in. When his balloon breaks, each Scout is to call out his patrol name and the number of balloons broken so far. When the last balloon for a patrol is broken, the Scout who threw it should shout his patrol name and then the word, 'Done!'

"Do you all understand?" finished MacFarlan.

"Yes, sir," came the subdued response. There was mumbling in the ranks. What was that about a tricky part? Why was he talking about grapefruits?

"OK then, here we go," and with that MacFarlan put whistle to mouth and blew a long, shrill blast. By the time the sound echoed back, his audience had vanished in eight directions. Smiling hugely, he bounced off in the direction of the ravine.

Mouse and most of his crew were at tree number 6 almost before the whistle stopped bleating. Pig and Bobby were just a few steps behind. High in the branches of the yellow-clad maple they saw what might have passed for a hornet's nest in more normal times. That must be the ball of ropes.

"Let me go up! Let me go up!" cried three eager voices. Mouse looked at them — Beaner, Jim and Pee Wee. Beaner had a tree house in his back yard; he would be good at climbing trees.

"Beaner, you're the man. Pig, give him a boost to the first limb."

Mouse was pleased that no one argued. He was going to like this leadership stuff. It was just a matter of picking the right man for the right job, and then everyone would see that the right choice had been made and go along without argument.

Pig hunkered down against the tree, and Beaner scrambled onto his back to stand on his shoulders. Then, as Pig slowly stood up, Beaner walked up the trunk with his hands. In short order, he had hold of a low limb and scrambled like a monkey up through the dark branches. In no time at all, he was up to the nest of ropes. It was not tied down in any way, so Beaner just picked it up and tossed it down. It bounced off a few limbs, setting loose a flurry of leaves, then fell free and landed with a thump on the ground.

Eager hands tore at the great complication of ropes. Someone had taken trouble to really tangle them up and the unsnarling proved difficult. Unexpectedly, there was a bag hidden at the center of the rope ball. Mouse plucked this out expecting further instructions, but when he opened it, he found only six large balloons. His heart raced. This was the trick, then. They had to somehow fill these balloons to the size of grapefruits with water from the stream at the bottom of the ravine. He was puzzled. How could they do that?

Ten minutes later, the last two lines came apart and these were quickly knotted to the other four. The patrol now had its long rope and they ran with it to the ravine. A Scout leader standing by a place marked with the number 6 quickly checked the knots and gave them the thumbs up. Mouse was glad the rope passed inspection, but was not surprised. What Scout can't tie a square knot, and most of the Mice could fashion a bowline as well.

Now came the tricky part, just like the man had said. Mouse didn't have a clue how they could fill water balloons without a faucet or a hose. Maybe when they got down there they might find something like that, but he doubted it.

Briskly, Mouse said, "Pig, I think the best plan is for most of us to go down and figure out how to fill the balloons. Will you stay here to haul us back up? Once we're done you can go down and fill your balloon."

"Sounds good to me," said Pig. "How are you going to fill them?"

"I don't know yet. Maybe there is an old spring down there we can use, or maybe we can hold them under a waterfall, or sloosh them through the water real fast. Do any of you guys have any ideas? No? Well, think about it as we go down. There has to be a way. The man said there was."

Mouse threw the loop of a bowline around his neck and shoulder. Pig did the same with the other end of the rope. Then they stretched the rope taut and Mouse walked backward off the cliff while Pig edged forward, maintaining the tension. Mouse was pleased to see the smaller Scouts grab on to the line to help, though Pig could have managed alone.

Mouse liked the backward walk down into the cool of the ravine. Suddenly the stream at the bottom was very loud, and the sun was very far away. The slope he descended was not vertical, and at first, he didn't really think he needed the rope. Some places he stepped turned out to be slippery, though, and in the end, he was glad he had it. Anyway, that was the rule — use the rope — so that's the way they would do it.

At the bottom, he threw the loop off and shouted, "OK."

Like a long twisting snake, the rope crawled rapidly back up the slope. He didn't wait to see it disappear into the daylight 40 feet above. Instead, he turned to explore the area for a spring or a faucet that could be used to fill the balloons. In seconds, he had confirmed what he had already suspected. There was nothing down here, nothing but the rushing creek, cascading noisily over small waterfalls.

By the time a winded and shaken Bobby Carfield arrived three minutes later, Mouse was in the stream trying out various ideas for filling his balloon. Bobby sat on a handy rock and watched as Mouse held the stretched neck of his balloon under one of the waterfalls. No good. The water pressure just wasn't strong enough to inflate it.

Five minutes later, five of them were down. Mouse could hear the noise of other patrols shouting back and forth up and down the small stream as everyone grappled with the same problem. He was frustrated. Do what he might, Bear Run could not be coerced into filling his balloon with water. The other guys had tried the same things, but they had no better luck. Beaner and Jim just gave up and began splashing each other. Bobby just sat there and watched, evidently seeing no reason to move. "A lot of good he's doing," thought Mouse, "but at least he is not hurting our efforts." Beaner and Jim were now beginning to expand their splashing to include the others, and Mouse realized that he had to get them settled down or the patrol would never crack the problem.

"Beaner! Jim! Go to the center of the stream and dig a deep hole."

"Do you have an idea?" asked Beaner, hopefully.

"Maybe. Do it fast as you can."

"How deep?" asked Jim.

"I'll tell you when to stop."

"OK!" and they went at it.

Mouse nodded, satisfied. The hole was important only because it would occupy Beaner and Jim until a solution to the problem was found.

Looking around, Mouse noticed Pee Wee had fastened his balloon over the top of his squeeze-bottle canteen. He had upended the canteen and was now squeezing away for all he was worth, trying to force water from the bottle into the balloon. That might work! MacFarlan had said that each patrol had the needed equipment. Each patrol definitely had canteens. That must be it! He hurried over to Pee Wee and together they worked to improve the technique. Mouse would fill the canteen while Pee Wee held the neck of the balloon. Then they would reattach the balloon and Mouse would squeeze as hard as he could. It was slow work, but in five minutes, they did manage to fill the balloon to the size of a very small grapefruit.

"Got it!" It was Bobby, still sitting on his rock, but now there was a knowing smile on his face.

"Got what?" said Mouse a little peevishly to the lazy Scout.

"I know how to fill the balloons. It's simple! Fill the canteen, inflate the balloon with air, attach the balloon to the neck of the canteen and then just dump the water in. It will work!"

Mouse and Pee Wee were instant converts to the new scheme.

Mouse shouted over to where Beaner and Jim were now up to their knees in water, "Beaner, Jim, forget that. Come over here and watch." Then he and Pee Wee followed Bobby's instructions.

Pee Wee filled the water bottle while Mouse puffed his cheeks out round and inflated the balloon.

"More," came a suggestion from Bobby, so Mouse blew the balloon up to its full size. Then he understood. They needed to allow some extra space for air leakage during the attaching part of the procedure. Soon they had a balloon full of air and a bottle full of water. It was pretty easy to slip the opening of the balloon over the neck of the canteen, and then it was just a matter of turning the rig upside-down. Mouse held his breath and watched as the water went glug, glug, glug down into the balloon. They added another bottle of water to be on the safe side, and then Mouse bled off the excess air. The balloon was a bit too large, so he let a little water squirt out as well, then tied it off. One down, five to go.

"OK, that's got it. Can you all do that?" he asked. He looked up. Bobby was on his feet and Pee Wee was rushing over to help him. Beaner and Jim were already hard at work.

"Good plan, Bobby!" said Mouse — maybe sometimes thought and observation were better than hasty action.

"You guys gave me the idea," said Bobby modestly.

Mouse turned to the others, "OK, fill four more. I'll go up and let Pig down. Bobby, would you stay down here to help him?"

"Sure," said Bobby.

"Once you get the last balloon filled, you come up, then Pig. He is the heaviest and we may need you to help haul him out."

"Got it," said Bobby, then he went red-faced as he strained to blow air into a balloon.

Mouse didn't dawdle. He slipped the rope around his shoulder and then, holding his balloon in one hand and the rope in his other, he yelled up to Pig, "Hoist away!"

The walk up was more like a run. Pig was really pulling hard and Mouse could barely keep his feet moving fast enough. The pressure didn't ease when he reached the top, either, and he went stumbling forward. He knew he was going to fall. "Not on the balloon! Not on the balloon!" he screamed silently as he fell, turning just in time to land on a shoulder. His balloon scooted away to bobble and undulate for 5 feet through the grass before coming to rest. Mouse scrambled to his feet and quickly picked it up, treating it like a delicate treasure.

He placed it gently on a clump of grass, then switched ends with Pig. It was a strain, but by digging in his heels, he was able to control the larger boy's decent into the shadow world of the ravine. Mouse had just slipped out of the loop and was about to run to the fire when, from below, came the shout, "Hoist away!" OK, so they would all go to the fire together. That was better anyhow.

Five minutes later, five boys strained on the line to hoist Pig up out of the ditch. They brought him up slow, and he stepped over the cliff's edge as though he was climbing stairs. The Scouts scattered to grab their balloons and then went racing toward the distant fire where a crowd was already gathered. Mouse, Beaner and Jim were the first to arrive.

"Mice Patrol, number 1," screamed Mouse as he flung his balloon into the smoky flames. It popped and seemed to emit a puff of steam as the water hit the glowing coals.

"Mouse's Mice two, Mouse's Mice three," shouted Beaner and Jim as two more white puffs rolled skyward.

Pig was only a few steps behind and slammed his balloon into the center of the flames as if he meant to extinguish the blaze all together. Water splashed everywhere. "Mouse's Mice four!"

Bobby was next. Mouse looked beyond. What had happened to Pee Wee? He saw two other kids coming fast and yells from the crowd told him they were the last of their team to arrive. Where was Pee Wee? Then he saw him. Pee Wee had fallen and was now scrambling around in the grass to get his balloon. He had it! The two other guys were ahead, but not by much.

Meanwhile, Bobby had arrived. He threw his balloon rather limply into the fire and started to shout, but then stopped. His balloon must have hit a wet spot, because it bounced out the other side of the fire pit without breaking. As it rolled away, Bobby moved fast, a different boy from the one who had sat lazily by the stream. He ran right through the dying fire, scooped up the errant balloon and turned to slam it fiercely into the center of the fire pit. The fire could have been stone cold out, and that balloon would have broken! "Mouse's Mice, uh," then he saw Mouse holding up five fingers, and yelled "Mouse's Mice five!"

Now they all turned to watch Pee Wee's progress. He was running as fast as his short legs would carry him. His water bottle bounced at his hip, a compass flopped at his neck. One arm pumped up and down as he tried to pass the two Scouts in front. Mouse could see he wasn't going to succeed, he turned to do a quick count of the Scouts cheering by the fire and then looked at Pee Wee again. No way was Pee Wee going to catch those two. The first of the boys raced right over the fire, spiking the balloon into the pit as he passed, "Moose Patrol Five."

The next kid was ten feet away, Pee Wee a step behind. Mouse made up his mind, "Throw it, Pee Wee!"

Pee Wee understood right away. He cocked his arm and let fly. The round, yellow balloon passed just over the head of the leading Scout, fell and hit the ground — three feet short. The other Mice groaned but the balloon didn't care. It bobbled and

65

bounced onward, rolling more and more slowly, then entered the fire pit to settle on one of the last remaining hot coals. Silently it popped, letting loose a meager puff of steam. Pee Wee roared out, "Mouse's Mice six — Done!!!"

The leading kid had ducked when the balloon came winging by, paused just a little to watch as it rolled to its death. Now he slammed his balloon viciously into the pit and shouted, "Moose Patrol six — Done."

There might have been arguments, but the Moose Patrol, along with everyone else, appreciated the gamble Mouse had taken and Pee Wee had pulled off. Pee Wee got most of the pats and congratulations. That was fine with Mouse. Good for him!

"Good work, Mouse." It was Brian Paxton.

"Thanks, Brian." Somehow, that was all the praise Mouse needed.

"What made you take the gamble?" asked Paxton. "He could have missed and the balloon would have broken outside of the fire."

"Yeah, I know, but I looked at the Scouts standing around. There were at least thirty of them, so I figured we wouldn't place anyway. Why not gamble? If it worked, Pee Wee would be a hero. If it didn't, we wouldn't lose any points for trying."

"That makes sense. One thing is for sure; you just made Pee Wee famous."

Mouse smiled, "He'll like that. Did you guys win?"

"We got third place. The Rattlesnakes came in first and the Mule Deer placed second."

"How did the Mice do?" asked Mouse.

"That little stunt of yours got you fourth. Not bad. Not bad at all. Now let's see how well your guys can chop wood."

6

The patrols snaked out of the clearing, and Mouse could easily see Mr. MacFarlan's bouncing form leading the way at the head of the column as they pushed eastward. The Eagle Patrol was just in front of the Mice, and after a while, Chuck Wing fell back to where Mouse and Pig walked side-by-side.

"Here is where we eat your lunch, animal boys," he sneered.

Mouse ignored the comment, but Pig responded, "Just try to eat my lunch and see where it lands you."

"It's an expression," said Chuck, irritated, "it means we're going to beat you guys bad at the log chopping."

"An expression, huh," said Pig. "Here's one for you — don't count your chickens before they hatch."

Chuck laughed. "You guys are about as strong as chickens. You guys don't have a chance."

Mouse was getting irritated himself now, but the habits of a lifetime kept his mouth clamped shut. A few minutes ago, he had been talking to Paxton without any problem, now here he was clamming up again. Why was that?

It was Pig who replied, "Actions speak louder than words."

Chuck glared at him. "Some of your guys are barely big enough to pick up an ax."

"Good things come in small packages," replied Pig.

"I can't believe you wimps think you have a chance. Wait until the other guys hear this."

"Absence makes the heart grow fonder," said Pig with a smile.

"You're crazy," muttered Chuck, then hurried forward to rejoin his own patrol.

Bobby Carfield came running up. "I figured out a better way!"

"A better way?" said Mouse.

"A better way to fill the water balloons."

Mouse laughed. "Its over, Bobby. You should think of a better way to chop a log in two."

"But, it just came to me. Want to know what it is? You don't even need a canteen."

"OK. Let's hear it," said Mouse.

"Well, what you do is fill up your mouth with water and then blow it into the balloon, then you pinch the balloon's neck until you can drink more water and repeat the process. It's just like blowing air into the balloon except you use water. I'm sure it will work."

"Hmm, I bet it would, too. The only problem is that you would have to drink water from the creek. I wouldn't want to do that."

"Especially with a bunch of other Scouts just upstream muddying the water," added Pig.

Bobby chewed on that for a second, "Yeah, you're right. Still if you had a clean water supply and no canteen, then my new way would be better."

"Start thinking about log chopping," said Mouse patiently. "That's what we have to worry about now."

"OK," said Bobby and he marched along beside them, his forehead wrinkled, his lips pursed.

From behind came the sounds of Beaner and Jim horsing around and arguing the fine points of the Steelers game the previous Sunday. Mouse glanced back to check that Pee Wee was still there. He was back there all right, canteen banging against his hip, compass bouncing at his neck. He had even added a new piece of gear to his outfit. Wrapped around his chest, bandoleer-fashion, was the rope from the previous event. "You just never know when a rope might come in handy," he had said. One end of it had gotten loose and trailed behind, snagging roots and branches, delaying the small Scout's progress. There was a smile on his face, though. No doubt, he was reliving his moment of glory back there at the fire pit, as they all marched along under the kaleidoscope trees toward the next contest.

Shortly, the column came to another clearing. It was not far from their encampment, as they could see the shine of cars through the trees to the south. In seconds, the patrols spotted the numbered logs and moved quickly to examine them. Ten feet behind each log stood a referee holding an ax. Mouse saw right away that these were Scout axes, not full sized ones. That cheered him up considerably. The smaller boys could handle an ax of that size, and the bigger Scouts would be slowed down a bit by the smaller blades. Maybe they had a chance after all.

Five minutes later, he was in doubt again. Beaner and Jim were riding the middle of log number 6 like a horse. Pee Wee and Bobby were sitting on one end of it eating snacks. And, Pig had wandered off into the woods and was now returning with a short, thick stick in his hand. Mouse shook his head. This wasn't right. They should be plotting strategy, not fooling around like this. Their referee, a very healthy looking young man of about twenty, all spit and polish in his Class A uniform, looked at Beaner and Jim with obvious displeasure. Uh oh.

Mouse walked over to them, "Hey you two, get off of there."

"OK. We were just playing," said Beaner, contritely.

"Yeah, you do that too much. This isn't playtime, you know. In a minute, you're going to be chopping that log in half. Do you know how to do that?"

"Sure," said Jim and proceeded to stand in front of the log and take mighty strokes with an imaginary ax. "How's that?" he said with pride.

"Not so good," said Mouse. "You want your legs further apart in case you miss the log. That way the ax head will hit the ground instead of one of your feet."

Jim changed stance and swung his invisible ax again. "Like this?"

"Yeah, that's better, except your right hand should slide down the handle as you swing. That accelerates the ax and allows you to strike harder."

Jim adjusted his swing. "How about that?"

"Yeah, that's good. You need to slant your strokes to chop out the wood in a 'V.' The 'V' should be about as wide at its top as the log is thick. Let's see you do that now."

When Mouse was finally satisfied, he said, "Good, Jim. Now will you make sure that Bobby, Pee Wee and Beaner know this stuff, too?"

"OK!" said Jim, happy to be in charge. Turning around he called out, "Bobby! Pee Wee! Get up! Come over here!"

Mouse watched the little guys for a few seconds and saw that play time and the rest break seemed to be over. Now for Pig. What in the world was he up to?

About two-thirds of the way down its 12-foot length, the log swelled out to form a bump about two feet long. The rest of the log was about 14 inches thick, but at this bump, it was closer to 18 inches. Pig was busily tapping around the bump with his stout stick. He turned as Mouse approached and said, "Listen."

Tap. Tap. Tap. Thud.

"What's that mean?" asked Mouse.

"Means it's rotten inside, where the trunk swells right here."

"Doesn't look rotten to me," said Mouse. "The bark looks strange, but just sort of stretched and lumpy, not rotten."

"Yeah, trees get this way sometimes. It happens when one gets damaged, maybe because another one falls against it. The bark grows and spreads to cover the injury. Sometimes though, the tree can't cover the opening fast enough, and disease or bugs get inside before it closes. The outside of the tree ends up looking

OK, but inside it's damaged. This log is rotten under that bump. You can tell by the sound of it."

"You sure about that?" asked Mouse.

"Pretty sure."

Mouse heard confidence in Pig's voice. Maybe this was the edge they needed. It all depended on if they were supposed to chop the log in half, or chop the log in two. He slid over to the referee and spoke quietly to him for a minute.

MacFarlan's whistle sounded from the center of the clearing. He was waving his arm in a circular, gathering motion and the Scouts moved over to hear what he had to say.

"Good morning, Scouts!" shouted the round man, yet again.

"Good morning, sir," came the halfhearted reply.

"You sound weak, Scouts. You will need to be strong for this one. Strong and quick and smart, but most of all safe — or it's going to cost you."

He paused a second to let that sink in, then continued.

"I see you have all found your logs. Once you have cut them in two, we'll use them for tonight's campfire.

"These logs were culled from the forest around you. Naturally, we felled the weakest and sickest trees. None of them are good for much of anything but firewood, but don't worry, you won't catch any tree diseases from being around them."

He paused, hoping for a laugh, but when none came, he continued more seriously.

"OK, then. Safety. First thing is, everybody must stay behind the lines you will find in front of your logs. Only one Scout with an ax can be near a log at any time. The rest of the patrol has to be behind the line. When I blow the whistle, the contest will begin. Your first man will then run to the referee and get your ax. Carrying this in a safe manner, he will approach the log and make ten cuts. The referee will insure that this is done in a safe manner, and if not, will instruct the Scout on proper technique.

"After taking ten blows, the Scout will carry the ax to the next man in line. That Scout will then go to the log and take *his* ten swings. Understand?

"This process will continue until the log breaks in two. When that happens, the last chopper will return the ax to the referee. Then, and only then, the whole patrol will rush forward, attach ropes to the two parts, and drag them to where we are now standing. When both parts have arrived, the patrol leader will yell your patrol name and the word 'done!'

"If you chop unsafely, the ref will delay you only long enough to correct your technique, but if you travel unsafely with your ax, you will be required to sit down for 30 seconds to think over your sins, then you will be allowed to proceed.

"Do you all understand that?" he asked.

"Yes, sir," came the faint response. Evidently, some understood better than others.

One Scout raised his hand. Mr. MacFarlan pointed, "Yes?"

"It's about the ropes, sir. Where are the ropes we are supposed to pull the logs with?"

"Oh, thank you. Glad you mentioned that. You will use the same ropes as in the last event. Just tie them into two lines instead of one. Use square knots for that, and timber hitches to connect them to the logs. You might want a bowline at the other end to make the pulling easier."

"But, sir, we didn't bring our ropes along."

"That's OK," replied MacFarlan. "Just send one of your guys back to get them while the others start chopping. We aren't going to wait for you though, so whoever goes had better hurry.

"No more questions? OK, get ready."

Five Scouts went racing off toward the site of the previous competition, but the rest lined up behind the marks on the ground and awaited the starting whistle.

Mouse smiled at Pee Wee and said, "You were right about the rope being a handy thing to have," then he led Pee Wee to the head of the line. They would chop in order from smallest to largest — Pee Wee to Pig. Mouse explained about the rotten log. Pee Wee had trouble believing it.

"You want me to chop through the center of that thick part to the right of center?"

"Yes," said Mouse urgently. "It's our only chance."

"But, we'll have to chop an extra four inches," Pee Wee said doubtfully. Then the whistle blew and the race was on.

Pee Wee sprinted away toward the ref with Mouse's final words ringing in his ears, "Just do it!"

Pee Wee elected to jump the log rather than going around. Somehow, he miscalculated, hooked a toe and went rolling forward to land in a heap at the ref's feet. Hoots of derision came from Chuck at the next log down. In a second though, Pee Wee had popped back to his feet and was accepting the Scout ax with care and dignity from the grinning ref.

He quickly walked back toward the log, holding the ax head out a little and flat to his body in best Scout fashion. He squared his feet, shifted the tool and swung a mighty blow. The ax bit into solid wood, right at the thickest part of the log. Mouse was relieved. Not only was Pee Wee following instructions, but he was obviously more deft at chopping logs than jumping them. He wasn't particularly strong, but his technique was flawless.

The ax rose and fell nine more times, and Pee Wee had removed a wedge of wood about three inches deep. The Eagles next door had done about the same, but that patrol was chopping through the thinnest part of their log. Mouse was worried. Pee Wee had found only good wood, not the rotten center that Pig had predicted. Next door, Chuck pointed in their direction and laughed loudly.

Pee Wee carried the ax to the line, where Jim gingerly took it and walked back toward the log. Mouse looked around. The other logs he could see were showing some signs of wear, about the same as theirs, except for the patrol two down. They seemed to be a third of the way through their log already. Turning his attention back to Jim, he watched as that Scout made three strokes that had very little effect. Jim was not nearly as good as Pee Wee.

"Slant the blade. Alternate your strokes," Mouse shouted.

Jim heard and adjusted his swing. On his sixth stroke the head of the ax disappeared inside the log and Mouse let out a cheer. Jim had broken through. The center *was* rotten. Pig looked pleased and gave a little bow in Mouse's direction. Jim had problems though. The ax blade was wedged tight and he wasted precious seconds freeing it. Finally, he wiggled it out and then quickly finished his remaining strokes.

Beaner and Bobby came next. Mouse whispered to them to not chop at the center of the log, but down along the near and far sides. The rotten center would take care of itself when the time came. They did their best to follow instructions and Beaner did quite well. Bobby, on the other hand, made a mess of his turn, but at least, he played it smart. When he saw he was no good at this game, he finished his turn with six very quick, sharp strokes and walked the ax back to the line.

Mouse came next. He calmly carried the ax to the ref and then returned to roll the log over. This cost him a few seconds, but meant that he and Pig would be chopping on the clean side of the log. There would be no more tricks, though. It was now up to him to sever the log, or at least put a large notch in it so Pig could finish the job. Mouse hit a perfect blow with the small ax, but the results were disappointing. It was like the wood was tougher on this side. He struck the opposite blow with similar results. After ten strokes, he was only three inches down, and a thicker four inches remained before the stick could realistically be expected to part. He glanced over at the Eagle's log as he walked back to the line. Lee Hamlin had just finished his strokes. Their log looked like it should have parted already.

Handing the ax over, Mouse said, "Sorry, Pig. It's tougher on this side. I left you pretty much to do."

74

Pig looked determined. "We'll see. Nobody's eating *my* lunch."

He walked toward the log. Nearby, Chuck was now the ax man for the Eagles. Seeing Pig was a few steps ahead, Chuck moved fast to catch up, as if he was in some kind of a foot race. He moved too fast, though, and held the ax all wrong. There was a shout from the Eagle's ref, and Chuck quickly found himself sitting on the ground, watching as Pig, fifteen feet away, stepped up to his log. Pig paused to glance at Chuck, and then went to work. He handled the small ax without thought. His swing was smooth as a well-oiled machine. The head of the ax rose high and then descended with massive violence to sink hilt deep in the tough wood. Pig's second stroke came from the other side and sent a great wedge of white wood flying away toward Chuck. It hit short and bounced to nudge Chuck's left foot. He jerked back as if stung, then slithered further away from Pig's flashing blade. Before that quick motion was even complete, Pig had struck twice more, and another chunk of wood hit, rolled and bounded to fall at Chuck's feet. Chuck moved again, no doubt beginning to feel persecuted. He could have saved himself the effort — Pig raised his booted foot and slammed it into the cut. There was the sharp crack of breaking wood and the log parted. The Mice went wild.

Pig handed the ax to the ref and the Mice came pouring across the line, trailing two already prepared ropes behind. Pee Wee and Bobby rigged a timber hitch around the smaller part while Mouse and Pig worked on the larger. To left and right came shouts of success from other patrols.

Pig looped the bowline over his shoulder and began dragging the large log toward the center of the clearing. Mouse and Bobby quickly grabbed the line to help with the hauling. The log was heavy and tended to fishtail, but they quickly got it up to speed. Mouse threw his heart into it, but his head was wondering how well things were going with the small end of the log. Suddenly, though, Pee Wee, Beaner and Jim came racing by with their half bouncing wildly behind. Now, Mouse only had to worry that they would crash and burn before they got to the center of the clearing. Up ahead he heard the cry of, "Wolf Patrol, Done!" but suddenly they were all there, too, and he was able to shout, "Mouse's Mice, Done!"

They had placed second!

7

The Eagles placed fifth in the log chopping, and so it was with very different feelings that the two patrols returned to camp for the midday meal. The Eagles had placed third in the balloon rescue, Mouse's Mice were second in the log chopping. That meant that the Mice led in the overall rankings, but the day was only half over.

Somehow the morning's competitions had brought all of the Scouts closer together, and there was much back and forth as the older boys congratulated the younger ones on their unexpectedly good showing. Pee Wee's balloon toss was relived in memory, the business of the rotten log was earnestly discussed. Mouse was happy. Even if they didn't manage to beat the Eagles that afternoon, the Mice had shown they had pluck and energy.

Hoagies were on the menu for lunch, and Paxton insisted that the Eagles prepare the food for both patrols, as a sort of recognition of the morning's result. He was senior patrol leader of the troop, as well as patrol leader of the Eagles, and so the older guys went along with the idea, smiling at the irony and treating the young Scouts like royalty — "Would you like some additional tomatoes on that, young Master Pee Wee? Would you care to try more of this vintage bug juice, Lord Hammerman?"

There was one Scout, however, who refused to play along. He stated loudly and repeatedly that he thought the Mice had cheated by going through the rotten part of the log. His friends pointed out that the referees had not agreed when he had raised the issue back at the clearing, and that perhaps he should just let the matter drop. Chuck, however, would have none of that. His mood darkened even further after chow, when Pig said loudly and for all to hear, "Thanks, Brian. It was a pleasure to eat the Eagle's lunch."

Mouse winced; he knew Chuck would not forget.

About the time lunch ended, it started to rain. It wasn't just a shower, either. Water pounded down like someone up there had a giant garden hose and meant to wash all of the pretty leaves from the trees. Some thought the afternoon's events would be rained out, but Pig peeked up from under the dining tarp where they were all huddled, and said, "A big shower is soon over." The old proverb proved true and by 1:30 the sky was blue once more.

Shortly after that, they heard a far off whistle and headed back to the clearing where the log chopping had taken place. They arrived soaked to the knees, but were pleased to see that some wise man had thought to cover the heap of logs with a tarp. With that much dry wood, the evening campfire would be a scorcher.

Inevitably, Mr. MacFarlan stood beside the heap of logs.

"Good afternoon, Scouts!"

"Good afternoon, sir," came the soggy reply.

"Scouts, you sound tired. You better wake up for this one, though, or you will end up in the next county.

"I have here *eight* pieces of paper that contain *eight* different routes past *eight* checkpoints scattered throughout the woods. When I blow my whistle, the *eight* patrol leaders of the *eight* patrols will come forward and get one. Then it will be your job to find the *eight* checkpoints in the order listed. Once you do that each of the *eight* patrols will come back here. First patrol back wins.

"Go fast, but go safe. Watch out for snakes and porcupines. Don't get *ate* by a bear!"

A couple of the Mice groaned at the lame joke, but MacFarlan's whistle interrupted that. Mouse shouldered forward to grab a list, then he and Bobby peered at it and talked about the best strategy to use in completing the circuit of checkpoints.

Pee Wee had his compass in hand and turned to align its scale with the red end of the needle. Then, the three of them stood close, and Mouse read out the first set of directions.

"Checkpoint D: 260 degrees, 400 feet."

Pee Wee looked hard at his compass scale and then pointed. Bobby had a quick glance at the instrument, then agreed, "That looks right."

Mouse noted a distant tree that was along the line indicated by Pee Wee's pointing finger, and the patrol raced off toward it, as straight as the terrain would allow. As they ran, each counted steps, so they could gauge the distance traveled. When they got to the tree, Mouse had counted to 60. He figured that at 3 feet per stride, they had come about 180 feet along the line to the first checkpoint. They had a little more than that same distance still to go. Looking forward, he saw a man standing in the woods about the correct distance away. That must be the place.

They raced onward, and Mouse soon realized the man was Grandpa Mike. He was standing right beside the oil well Mouse and Pig had found that morning. A tag pinned to his hat had a large, red letter "D" printed on it. Good enough!

Mike quickly initialed their sheet, and then Mouse read out the second set of instructions.

"Checkpoint E: 150 degrees, 650 feet."

Pee Wee did his stuff with the compass, Bobby checked the direction of his point, and they went racing through the woods again. They crossed the road and dove into the forest on the other side. It seemed to Mouse that this line would take them down below their campsite, and sure enough, they soon came down onto the bench that ran below camp. It was halfway down Toby hill and they soon saw a man with a large letter "E" prominently displayed on his cap.

Mouse was getting the route sheet initialed, and Pee Wee was busily orienting his compass, when the Eagle Patrol came roaring in from the west. Paxton was in the lead, and the rest of his Scouts were bunched up just behind. They could all easily see Pee Wee standing there with his head bent over his needle, but nonetheless, the last boy in line crashed into the small Scout and sent him and his compass flying. Chuck had run right over Pee Wee.

"Sorry there, little fellow. I didn't see you," said Chuck, but somehow he didn't sound all that sincere.

Pee Wee bounced to his feet, and said, "Yeah, sure," as he looked around desperately for his compass. The other Mice gathered round to help with the search, but slowly it dawned on them that the instrument was lost in the litter of leaves and sticks that covered the ground. As the Eagles sped away toward their next checkpoint, Chuck turned and looked back. Mouse happened to glance up and saw the satisfied smile on his cousin's face. That crash had been no accident.

Mouse knew they were in trouble. Every minute they spent looking for the compass put them further behind. "Did anybody else bring a compass?"

Everyone shook their head glumly, except Pee Wee who said, "Well… We could use my backup compass."

Mouse smiled. Trust Pee Wee to be prepared. "OK, get it out. We'll come back and find your other one later."

As Pee Wee dug through his pockets, the other boys made a pile of sticks and stones to mark the place to start looking later.

Finally, Pee Wee announced, "Found it!"

He sounded doubtful, and when Mouse saw the backup compass, he understood why. The thing looked like it had come from a box of Cracker Jacks. It was about half an inch across, and only the primary compass points were marked. He snorted, but said, "OK, I guess it will have to do."

Quickly he read the next instruction.

"Checkpoint F: 270 degrees, 500 feet."

Pee Wee seemed confused as he attempted to read the tiny compass, and it was Bobby who did the pointing.

Mouse knew they were losing time. They had to get moving.

"Come on," he said, and they raced away on the new tack.

Before they had gone 200 feet, there was Bear Run ravine right in front of them. They were just at the top of the old dump Mouse and Pig had found that morning. If they continued on their present course, it would take them right down through mounds of rusting bedsprings and battered baby carriages, ironing boards and washing machines.

"This can't be right," said Mouse. "Spread out along the line of the ravine and look for a man with a letter 'F' on his hat."

Mouse took his own advice and swung right, walking quickly along the edge of the ravine until he came to the downed tree he had noticed that morning. He went on past it and gazed down into the noisy cut in the earth. There was no one down there.

Then he had an idea. If he got out on the trunk of the downed tree, he would be able to see all up and down the ravine without all this running around. If there was a man anywhere down there, he would see him for sure.

Quickly, he slid down the dozen feet to where the root ball of the tree lay tipped to the sky. Scrambling up over this, he walked out on the wide horizontal trunk of the massive hickory until he was halfway across the ravine. He had a great view, all right, as long as he didn't slip. Still, there was no sign of life along the course of the white, tumbling run. Nothing. There was nothing down there but rocks and moss, whitewater and noise. He turned and went back along the trunk. Up above, Pig's head appeared.

"Mouse, we figured it out. Bobby read the compass wrong. We went in the opposite direction from the way we should have gone!"

Mouse yelled up, "OK, get the patrol back to the last checkpoint and try again! I'll catch up."

Pig's head disappeared, and Mouse climbed the upended roots of the tree. As he came over the top, he looked down and suddenly knew why the tree had fallen — where the roots had pulled free from the earth there was a hole. Not some little woodchuck or rabbit hole, but a monster of a hole. It was nearly four feet wide, and an ancient, squared beam ran across its top. The hole was two feet high and looked to be very deep. Cool!

After scrambling back up the hillside, Mouse raced to catch up with his fellow Mice. He arrived panting, just as they were starting out again, this time in the opposite direction. As they raced along, Pee Wee held something up for Mouse to see, "The checkpoint guy found it!" It was his good compass!

Mouse smiled. Maybe they still had a chance.

Six checkpoints later they arrived back at the clearing. As they ran in, Chuck very loudly said, "Ah, the lost patrol returns at last."

Mouse thought of ten cutting replies, but wouldn't think of saying any of these to his cousin. Sure, Chuck had contributed to their problems, he had made them lose the compass; but it was Mouse who had not double checked when they started using the cheap one. The problem had been with its needle. One end was painted black to indicate north, but Bobby thought the other, silver end, meant north, and that was why they had gone the wrong way. Anybody could have made that mistake.

MacFarlan announced that the Eagles had won the orienteering contest and a cheer went up from that patrol. The poor Mice had placed last. That, and the Eagle's success, dampened their spirits greatly. The last contest was the string burn, and they would have to win it to even have a chance of beating out the Eagles now.

Fat chance that would happen.

8

Eight fire pits stood in a long line across one end of the clearing. It was the same opening in the woods where the balloon rescue had taken place that morning. To the Mice, that glorious event now seemed but a remote memory. The poor result in the orienteering was fresh in their minds and had stolen away their confidence.

They moved listlessly to stand next to fire pit number 6, and glumly waited for the string burn to begin. Pig scanned the nearby pinewoods for potential sources of fuel on this very wet afternoon, but he was the only one that seemed the least bit interested in the coming contest. Beaner and Jim halfheartedly tried to spit over the strings that crossed their fire pit. Bobby stood alone, looking very sad, and Pee Wee spent his time kicking the ground and muttering quietly about cheap compasses. Mouse knew these last Scouts blamed themselves for the patrol's recent poor showing; he would have too. Still, it wasn't their fault. It was his fault.

He was frustrated. They had to shake off the blues if they were to have any chance at all. He had a trick up his sleeve, but it would do them no good unless the patrol pulled together and wanted to win. How could he light a fire under these guys?

The Eagles were at the next fire pit over, and Chuck was all smiles. His patrol now led the competition, and he was having a grand time shouting insults over at the Mice, rubbing it in.

"You guys got lucky this morning with your sneaky little trick, but it's over now. It sure looks like we might win the big prize, and even if we don't, we'll beat you clowns."

Some of the other Eagles frowned at that. Everyone knew Chuck was at least partly responsible for the downfall of the Mice. It didn't seem fair or honest for him to be trying to make them feel worse than they already did. It wasn't Scout-like to kick a man when he was down.

Chuck didn't see the frowns, or just didn't care. "Eagles eat mice for dinner!" he cheered.

Mouse was getting steamed. He didn't need Chuck's taunts on top of his other worries. He swung around sharply to fire a remark back at his cousin, but Pig spoke first, "Be careful there, Chucky. You don't want to bite off more than you can chew."

"I can chew you up, anyway, Pig Man," said Chuck, as he started forward. The other Mice were suddenly beside their leaders, and for a couple seconds it looked like Chuck would end up fighting the whole patrol.

Paxton was there quickly though, pushing Chuck back toward the Eagles, and giving Mouse a look and a nod that seemed to say, "I'll take care of Chuck. You take care of your patrol."

Mouse nodded back, a grim smile on his face. He was pleased. Paxton still trusted him to run the patrol. Suddenly, Mouse knew he couldn't let him down. Amazing! He had been screaming mad at Brian only that morning. Maybe that was what leadership was — the ability to inspire loyalty and confidence in your followers.

"Come on, you guys. Come over here and listen. I know how we can beat Chuck at this next little contest."

Chuck's mocking words and threatening actions had not gone down well with any of them. As they hunkered down to listen, the Mice still looked grim, but they also looked ready for anything, if they could only stick it to the obnoxious Chuck.

"OK, you guys, this is the last contest. We've done all right so far. Sure, we screwed up on the orienteering, but think about the other two contests. Bobby and Pee Wee, you got us through the water balloon contest, and we all did pretty well on the chopping. So, cheer up! I have a way we can win this last contest. Won't that just drive Chuck crazy?"

"How are we going to beat all these older guys at lighting a fire?" asked Beaner. "Some of them must have done string burns a dozen times."

"Yeah," replied Mouse, "but we have Pig's knack with a fire, and I have another little trick that will give us an edge."

That made them smile. Pig's little trick with the log had worked out very well indeed.

"What's the trick?" asked Pig. "I *really* want to beat Chuck at this one."

Heads came together, and Mouse explained.

"Is that legal?" asked Bobby in amazement.

"I think so," said Mouse. "Listen closely to MacFarlan when he gives the instructions. As wet as it is, they may even be expecting someone to try this dodge."

Pee Wee chimed in, "Yeah, you're right. I didn't think we had much of a chance of getting a fire going at all, let alone winning, but doing it your way, it's a cinch."

Mouse cautioned, "Don't get cocky. Maybe MacFarlan will say its illegal, or maybe everybody will think of it."

Then, he split the patrol in two. Pig, Bobby and Pee Wee would supply the wood. Mouse, Beaner and Jim would supply the magic.

MacFarlan's whistle blew, "Good afternoon, Scouts!"

"Good afternoon, sir," came the murmured reply.

"You sound tired, Scouts — ready for a nap. You had better be wide-awake if you expect to win this one.

"For our last contest, we will be playing the game called 'The Venerable String Burn.' That word 'venerable' just means that Scouts have been playing this one for fifty years. It will be very challenging today, though, because of that little shower we had earlier. Some of you have done this before, but let me just quickly review how things are going to work.

"Each patrol has a fire pit. On either side of this are stakes that hold two strings stretched across its center. The lower string is 12 inches above the ground and the upper one is 6 inches higher.

"When I blow my whistle, the game begins. First, you must gather sticks, weeds and other natural materials. You will use these to construct a teepee, or a tower, or any shape fire lay you want. Whatever shape you choose, the lay cannot be higher than the lower string across your pit. Referees will stand by to check your work.

"When your referee is satisfied, he will hand you two matches. Using just those two, you must light your fire. Once you get it going, you cannot touch or adjust your materials in any way. You can, however, blow on the fire to encourage the flames. Your fire will hopefully grow in size and burn through both strings.

"When the upper string parts, your referee will raise his hand, and you should yell out your patrol name and the word 'Done.'

"Does everyone understand the rules?"

There was much shaking of heads up and down. Yes, they understood very well indeed. This was old stuff to most of them. Mouse has heard "natural materials" and was encouraged. Now if MacFarlan just didn't say anything to ruin it.

The round man continued, "OK, I see you are all experts. Just remember this, though, you cannot use any man-made materials or any stuff you brought from home to get your fire going. Your fuel must be all natural."

The Mice were exchanging smiling glances now. What they planned was certainly natural enough. Mouse was a little concerned; the idea suddenly seemed so obvious.

MacFarlan raised the silver whistle and gave a shrill blast. Forty-eight Scouts charged in as many directions, intent on finding dry tinder, twigs and sticks. Pig, Bobby and Pee Wee headed straight into the pines, where they hoped to find dead, brittle branches deep under the bigger trees. They had lots of company. The trick would be to get the bigger stuff started. Other Scouts were attacking that problem by looking for thatch that had escaped the rain. Some were looking for dry pinecones and dusty moss.

Mouse ran rapidly through the woods, back to the clearing where the log chopping had taken place. Beaner and Jim ran behind, dodging branches, jumping downed limbs and doing their best to keep up. At the center of the clearing, the tarp still protected the pile of logs, and under this the trio found handfuls of only slightly dampened thatch. That might had been enough by itself, but Mouse had other plans.

In seconds, they were running again, still headed directly away from the contest. Mouse looked back. No one followed. He felt a rush of joy. Now if they could only move fast enough.

In another minute, they arrived at the old oil well. Mouse was amazed. How come no one else had thought of this? It seemed impossible. They wadded up their thatch to make primitive scrub pads, and then went to work on the well. They dabbed at the joints of the pipes, they scoured the old beams and they mopped up every bit of oily residue in sight. The flaxen pads turned black with the stuff, their hands as well. Mouse liked the smell. It was sweetish and reminded him of old cars, steam locomotives and vintage motorcycles.

"That's good enough," he announced and they tore off back the way they had come.

When they burst into the clearing where the contest was going on, Mouse was relieved to see not a single column of smoke. The dampness of the afternoon had proven too much for even the best of conventional efforts, and nearly all the teams were just sitting around, their two matches wasted on watery lays. Some few teams weren't done yet, though. When these saw the Mice come rushing by, hands black with oil, they understood immediately. A dozen Scouts raced off toward the old well. Mouse smiled. Too late. They were just too late, if the next step went according to plan.

Pig grinned with relief as they pounded up. "Great! Let's get this puppy fired up!"

The lay was shaped like a four-sided tower, its top scraping the lower string. Mouse, Beaner and Jim took turns gingerly shoving their oil-soaked pads into a hole in the bottom of the lay, and then upwards into its center. Mouse looked over at the ref, "We are ready, sir."

The smiling referee handed Mouse two matches. Mouse's confidence in the oily gambit soared. The man understood and seemed to approve of their scheme.

Mouse held out one of the matches to Bobby, who jumped away as if burned. No way did he want to mess this up.

"Give it a try, Bobby," said Mouse. "Don't worry; if it goes out we'll let Pig use the other one."

Bobby still looked hesitant.

"Bobby, you can do it," said Mouse gently, as he placed the match in the boy's hand. Mouse was rooting for the pudgy Scout. The talker was about to become a doer.

Bobby knelt down near the hole at the base of the pyramid of sticks. He gulped, bent to strike the match on his belt buckle, and then moved his hand forward. Just as it was about to enter the hole, the match died to nothing, and Mouse watched with dismay. The doer would never be a doer again if he failed at this. Suddenly, Pig was leaning in close, blowing gently on the match in Bobby's trembling hand. Nothing happened for a second, then slowly it crept back to life.

Mouse was astounded, "How did you do that!"

"Wasn't out," replied Pig, casually. "Just looked out."

Bobby, still trembling and now moving very slowly, inserted his hand into the hole and upwards, so the flaming match could feel at the bottom of the oily mat of thatch. Slowly, slowly a black tendril of smoke made its way up through the sticks. Bobby withdrew his empty hand. Pig immediately started blowing softly into the hole, providing air to the infant blaze.

In seconds, the column of smoke thickened and Pig rolled back onto his knees. "OK, everybody, blow on the base of the fire. Take it slow until you see flames, then give it everything you've got!"

The Mice needed no encouragement, and the fire needed little more. Now that the oil was alight, it wanted to burn. Scouts all around saw the greasy smoke and rushed over to be present at the destruction of the strings. The lower one fell apart before flames even appeared, but it was a sudden pillar of fire from the center of the lay that pushed up and killed the upper one.

"Mouse's Mice, Done!" screamed Mouse, happy, happy, happy.

The Mice did a little dance as their blaze really took hold, throwing heat and oily smoke in all directions.

The referee summed it all up for them when he remarked, "Well, I sure wouldn't cook over it, but it's a great little string burner."

9

The evening campfire was a real barn-burner. Flames from the great pile of logs ripped up thirty feet into the air and sent sparks flying up a hundred feet more, to slowly dim and die in the twilight sky. Forty-eight Scouts sat on ponchos and tarps, enjoying the songs and skits, and eagerly awaiting the awards ceremony.

Finally, about 10 o'clock, Mr. MacFarlan stepped forward.

"Good evening, Scouts!"

"Good evening, sir!" they roared back, and in a few seconds the hills around echoed their greeting.

"You sound happy, Scouts. That's good. We have had a great day today, and now it is time to announce the winners of the competitions. I could just say that the Rattlesnakes won the balloon rescue, the Wolves won the log chopping, the Eagles won the orienteering and Mouse's Mice won the string burn. I could say that, and it would be *true*, but it is just as true to say that we *all* won.

"On Monday, you will be back at school, and your friends will talk about what they did on this glorious Saturday. Listen to them, and compare what they have to say to the genuine adventures that you had out here today. Five years from now, your friends will have forgotten how they spent today, but I bet in *fifty* years, you will still remember this Saturday spent in the woods."

There were cheers at this. Everyone knew it was true.

"Now, Scouts, it is time to announce the overall rankings. Will the patrols I announce please come down to receive their ribbons and then stand with me by the fire.

"Third place in the Clarion County Camporee goes to Mouse's Mice of Troop 51, Clarion!"

Mouse and the Mice scurried down to the campfire, where Mouse accepted the white third-place ribbon with trembling hands. The patrol bunched up around him to have a look, and they were all smiles. The crowd hooted, whistled and cheered — Mouse didn't know whether to bow, shake clenched hands in the air, or what. He finally settled for a wave and a big smile, and that went down just fine. Then Mouse's Mice stood in a line, with their backs to the roaring blaze, and watched as the other winners were announced.

The Wolf Patrol of Troop 84 had placed second, and the Rattlesnakes of Troop 171 took first place. There were more noisy congratulations as these patrols came forward to accept their ribbons. Mouse cheered along with the rest. It was good being down here in front, even if his backside was slowly being fried by the enormous fire. He could stand the heat, it would all be over in another minute. They would finish with *Scout Vespers*, just like they always did, and then everyone would trail off to their campsites through the dark, starry night.

Mr. MacFarlan surprised him. When the cheering had died down a bit, he said, "Take a look at these three patrols, Scouts. The Rattlesnakes and the Wolves are mostly in their final years of Scouting, and you can tell that they have not only won today's contest, but are Scouts through-and-through, and will go on to win at the other games in their lives.

"Now look at Mouse's Mice. These are much younger Scouts. How did these young men come to stand before you tonight?

How did they win out over patrols who were older and stronger? I will tell you how. These young Scouts looked beyond winning contests by sheer strength and size. They listened to the rules, and then used brains instead of muscle to stay in the running. This was especially true during the Soggy String Burn."

There were a few groans at this. Some boys still thought it had to be cheating to start a fire with oil.

Mr. MacFarlan smiled. "What would you say if I told you that when we planned the string burn, we expected that most of you would use oil from the old well to start your fires? We knew it was going to rain, and so we prepared for it. Think back. Remember the orienteering course? We laid that out so that each patrol would get a good look at the well. It was then up to you to figure out that in this particular place, sitting as it does on the old oil fields of Pennsylvania, crude oil is as natural as the air you breathe or the water you drink.

"The young Scouts of Mouse's Mice are to be congratulated for being observant, and for having the courage to follow through on what they believed to be true. Good work, Scouts!"

Since only patrols that had used the crude oil trick had finished the string burn, there were many in the crowd very ready to agree with MacFarlan's statements, and the Mice got another round of applause. Still, there were mutterings among a few.

Mr. MacFarlan waited a few seconds and then continued, "Good night, Scouts. We will finish up with *Scout Vespers*, and then would you please return quietly to your campsites. See you again next year."

The Scouts stood quietly and then, as the fire crackled and the stars overhead looked down, they all sang the old, old song to the tune of *Oh Christmas Tree* — something even the oldest man standing there had learned to do when he was but a lowly Tenderfoot Scout,

BUCK'S LOOT

Softly falls the light of day,
While our campfire fades away.
Silently each Scout should ask
Have I done my daily task?

Have I kept my honor bright?
Can I guiltless sleep tonight?
Have I done and have I dared
Everything to be prepared?

* * *

Back at camp, Paxton saw to it that the troop fire was stoked up, and soon everyone was making camp pies and recounting the doings of the day. They talked of Pee Wee's championship balloon toss, of Pig's having bombarded Chuck with his wood chopping, and of the great oil fire that had finally won the Mice third place. The older Scouts eventually drifted off to Paxton's tent to play euchre, leaving the campfire to Mouse and his crew. Everyone was stuffed with pies except Pig, who continued to wolf them down as quickly as the pie irons came out of the fire.

Just before eleven p.m., Grandpa Mike wandered up to join them. He was still in Class A's, and as he approached, the yellow light of the fire gleamed off of the coin at his neck, making it appear more gold than silver.

"Good job out there today, boys," he said to the group of small Scouts.

"Thanks, Grandpa," replied Mouse.

"Thanks, Mike," chorused the others.

"Would you like a camp pie?" asked Pig.

"Thanks anyway, but I guess I had better be heading back to Clarion. Tomorrow is a big day, you know."

"Are you helping at the Autorama?" asked Bobby.

"Yes," Mike replied with a chuckle, "and with just about every other blessed event all week long. Tonight the firemen will be

93

cooking all night, so we can feed the volunteers who are coming in to help with traffic control and security. Then I'll work the fire company food stand every day, and drive a fire truck on Wednesday. I expect I'll be pretty worn down before the week is out."

"Cool," said Beaner, "I wish I could do stuff like that."

"Well, you're a little young for a fireman, yet," said Mike with a smile. "Maybe in a couple of years. Anyway, I better get moving." And, he turned and walked off into the inky dark, headed for the car park.

Pee Wee said, "I wish I had one of those."

"A grandfather?" asked Mouse.

"A fire truck?" asked Beaner.

"A food stand?" asked Pig. "Me too!"

"No, you guys. I mean one of those coin neckerchief slides like Mike has. Remember that dump we saw this afternoon? I bet that's where he found his coin."

"Hey, I bet you're right!" said Mouse.

"Let's go look for more," said Jim, and the proposition quickly gained support.

Mouse stuck his head into Paxton's tent, interrupting the card game just long enough to tell his senior patrol leader where they would be.

"Make sure you bring them all back," was Paxton's only reply, and Mouse was pleased, once again, at the confidence the older Scout now placed in his leadership abilities. It felt good to be respected.

The expedition was quickly mounted. Flashlights swayed this way and that, as they walked the short distance to the top of the dump. Then beams of light scoured the bottom of the ravine, revealing only creaming water, spongy green moss and dark trees below the mounds of rusting metal. After a minute, Pig led the patrol down the path that skirted the upstream side of the dump. As they descended, the temperature dropped 20 degrees, and the sky above was blotted by dark, motionless treetops. The boys clumped together a little — an almost unconscious defense against the suddenly dark and mysterious night.

When they reached the stream, they turned right and walked 50 feet farther.

"This must be about where Mike found his coin," said Pig.

To their left, the noisy stream tumbled on down the dark valley. On their right, old refrigerators, stoves and washboards climbed steeply up the face of the ravine.

"Now what?" said Jim, a little in awe of the spooky place.

"Now we hunt," said a confident Pee Wee, as he started kicking at the leaf litter, moss and weeds that covered the path. His search was quickly rewarded. "Hey," he screamed, "I found one!"

Reaching down, he plucked something from the disturbed clutter at his feet, buffed it with a thumb and held it up for all to see. Six flashlight beams bounced from its dull surface. He had indeed found one. It was a silver dollar with the head of an old-fashioned lady stamped on it. Below her was a date — 1878.

The lights did not linger on the trophy. Suddenly everyone wanted one, and for the next ten minutes commotion reigned as feet flew and boys screamed as they found more coins. Then the mother lode petered out. They kept looking for a while, eventually clearing a stretch of path about 15 feet long down to bedrock and hard-packed dirt. Finally, though, they gave it up, gathered in a circle and compared their finds. Five hands held five identical coins. All had the same woman pictured on one side; all had the same date. The Scouts were buzzing loudly about their plans for the coins, and commiserating with Pig, who had not found one, when suddenly someone came out of the darkness.

"What have you got there, small fry?" It was Chuck.

"Look at the coin I found," bragged Jim, holding it up for inspection. "We found five of them!"

"Pretty nice. Can I see it?" and Chuck plucked the coin from his hand.

"Hey," said Jim, indignantly.

"Hold on, hold on. I just want to look at it."

"Well, I want it back!"

"OK, OK. What will you take for it?" asked Chuck.

"I don't want to trade," replied Jim.

"I'll give you a pocket knife for it."

"I don't want a pocket knife. I want my *coin* back."

Mouse saw he would have to step in. He didn't care if it was Chuck; he wasn't letting anybody rob Jim of his newfound treasure.

Just then, though, Pig announced, "Someone's coming down the hill on the other side."

"A bear?" asked Bobby.

"Not unless they carry flashlights in these parts."

The light bobbed and weaved down the hill, and in less than a minute, its owner crossed over and came up to the Scouts.

"Don't shine those lights in my eyes," said a stern voice. The inquisitive beams immediately dropped down past the man's dark blue jacket and denim jeans, to shine on black boots crusted with dried mud. This was no Boy Scout leader.

"What are you boys doing down here, raising a racket at this time of night. Don't you know there are some people who are trying to sleep?"

Mouse was quick to reply. "We're sorry, sir. We just found a bunch of old coins, and I didn't know anyone lived anywhere around here."

The man's light came to rest on Mouse's face.

"You didn't know I lived around here? Aren't you the mouse I chased out of my field this morning?"

"Uh, oh," thought Mouse. He started to speak; "I...," and then he didn't know what to say. That old familiar frozen tongue feeling returned. It would take forever to explain that the man, Mr. Grit, looked different without his big straw hat and bib overalls, and then what? Then Mouse would look like a fool. Finally he just said, "I forgot," and felt like an idiot. An idiot and

96

a fool, that's what Grit had called him that morning. Was it true? The day had gone so well…

"Who's in charge here?" said Mr. Simon Grit.

Mouse knew he was, but his mouth was dry, his tongue felt huge and seemed to fill his whole mouth. No one spoke.

The man quickly tired of waiting and turned to face Chuck. "You there, you're the biggest. Are you in charge?"

"No, sir. I just came down here because they were making so much noise," said Chuck.

"Then you're the only one here with any sense. Let's see that coin you've got."

Chuck quickly handed over Jim's coin. The man rubbed at it almost lovingly, peering closely at each side. He said nothing, but Mouse, looking at the man's pale face and moving hands, somehow came to believe that he was shocked, or surprised or maybe amazed by the object now in his hands.

"How many did you find?" asked the man.

"Five," said Chuck.

The man was silent. Mouse held his breath. What would Grit do? Mouse saw his eyes narrow. A strange, thin-lipped smile appeared, then the man shifted a step to one side and pointed his flashlight up the hill. What was he doing? There was nothing up there, was there?

The beam of light scanned back and forth among the trees near the top of the ravine, and then it stopped, centered on a small yellow marker.

"See that sign up there?" the man said, somehow sounding satisfied. "That marks the beginning of State Game Land number 72. My name is Simon Grit, and I am the deputy conservation officer for this section."

He paused a second to let that sink in. Mouse didn't know what was coming next, but he knew he wouldn't like it.

The man continued, "I'm sorry, but you can't keep the coins. All archeological treasure found on State Game Lands is the property of the Commonwealth of Pennsylvania. As an officer of the state, it is my duty to confiscate such items. Please give me the coins." Then, he held out a large hand and waited.

The Scouts were stunned. They looked at each other, undecided just what to do. They looked at Mouse. Mouse stewed. He felt powerless, almost paralyzed. They had found the coins fair and square. It didn't seem right that a stranger could take them away. He knew that Grit was what he said he was. Pig had said the same thing that very morning, but still, it didn't seem right.

Grit lost patience. "NOW," he said sharply.

Mouse's hand moved to comply, even as his head spun, trying to think of some way to delay. He had to think of something. He had to do something.

Three other hands followed his lead. The coins dropped into Grit's hand. The clink of them as they fell into a heap was just audible over the mocking hiss of the stream.

"That's better. Is this all of them?" said Grit.

"Yes, sir," the boys said quietly. Mouse spoke not at all.

"OK. Here is what we're going to do. You are going to go back to your campsite, and you are not going to say a word to anyone about finding these coins. I don't want fifty Boy Scouts down here breaking the law. Do you understand?"

"Yes, sir," said Chuck.

"OK. Good. What I will do is turn the coins over to my boss and tell him where they were found. There is some chance that he will let you have them back, but don't get your hopes up. I'll also tell him that you never actually took the money off the game lands, so either way you won't get into any trouble with the law."

"Thank you, sir," said Chuck.

Mouse didn't feel like there was much to be thankful for. Grit was stealing their treasure, and using the law to do it. Sure, Chuck would agree. He had found none of them. Mouse had to do something. This wasn't right...

"That's OK," said Grit, "Now get up the hill!" And, with that parting remark, he swung on his heel and strode off into the night.

Mouse watched him go and was suddenly overwhelmed with sadness. He had failed.

It was a subdued bunch that marched up the path back to camp. Mouse walked alone at the back, thinking of things he should have said, wondering if Grit's actions were legal. They should have gone and gotten Mr. Ellsworth. It was his fault the coins had been lost. He should have stood up to Grit and argued for some compromise. He had not, though. Instead, he had frozen like spit on a winter morning. Some leader he had turned out to be.

As he reached the top of the slope, Mouse saw Chuck waiting.

"You had me wondering earlier today," said Chuck with an amused tone.

Mouse didn't know what he was talking about. He kept his mouth shut.

"I thought you might be getting too big for your britches, with your sneaky little patrol. Now I see you are the same old Mouse."

Mouse just looked at his feet, glad Chuck couldn't see his face. His eyes felt watery, his throat thick with emotion. He knew if he spoke, it would come out a sob. He would not give Chuck the satisfaction.

"Winning a few silly games in the woods doesn't mean much does it, little Mouse? It's the real world that counts and you will always be what you have always been — a quiet guy who knows his place. I've always liked that about you."

Chuck gave a satisfied smirk and swaggered away, leaving Mouse to stand under the lonely night sky. He was close to tears. It had all gone wrong. He was what he was and forever would be — a mouse among men. Something deep inside still rebelled at that, but in this place, at this time, all Mouse felt was hopelessness, misery, and despair.

99

Then Pig appeared at his side, quiet as magic. He looked at the crumpled Mouse, stared off at Chuck's retreating back, got a furious look on his face, and muttered, "I *really* don't like that guy."

10

Mouse woke with a start. It was dawn. The long restless night had finally ended. Pig was already gone. That didn't really matter much now, but Mouse thought he might as well get up and take a little walk of his own. He might bump into his friend. Even if he didn't, anything beat lying here to endlessly replay the dark thoughts that had stolen most of the night. Misery in motion beat misery in bed. He knew sleep would not come again; he was surprised it had come at all.

Slowly, he wiggled from his bag, then put on his jeans, flannel shirt, sweater and jacket. Stepping over Pig's clutter, he made for the door, where he slid into his boots and stepped out into the new day. The sky was blue, the air nippy — cold enough that he could see his breath. Winter wasn't far off, but for another day at least, it was autumn — the best of seasons. He was glad to be up and moving. All was quiet around him as he walked through the forlorn looking campsite.

He saw that the flap of the food tent was open, and a faint smile pulled at his lips. Pig was around somewhere, eating his early breakfast. Mouse wasn't hungry and so walked on out of camp. He stood in the middle of the dirt road, peering up it in the direction of home, and then down the other way, to where it disappeared into a bank of rolling fog. There was no sign of life anywhere. No Pig. No nothin'. He didn't really mind.

He slouched along another 20 feet to the top of the dump and scanned the ravine below. Memories came flooding back — flashlights in the woods, angry voices… failure. Maybe he would just stand here and think about things until the camp woke up. Then, maybe, the company of others would help him to forget.

He gazed idly about, then the flowing water in the run below caught his eye. He watched as it charged one little waterfall after another. His course in life somehow seemed just as set as the course of that small stream. He could no more change the way he was than the water below could suddenly climb up out of its ravine. Down, down and down it went until… until a downed tree blocked his view. For minutes, he stared at it with unseeing eyes, his thoughts in another place, but something about the tree nagged. He remembered that tree. It seemed a lifetime ago it had happened, back when the world was a happier place, and the Mice were scrambling to win the orienteering contest. He had been out on that tree looking…. looking for a checkpoint… the cave! It was like a shout in his mind. All his worries were forgotten. The cave was still there waiting. Mouse smiled. This would be good.

He hurriedly returned to the tent and grabbed his flashlight. Minutes later, he was perched among the roots of the great, stricken hickory tree, sending a beam of revealing light down into the black, almost rectangular, hole in the ground. He couldn't see much except some splintered beams and a dark flat floor, but that was enough. This was the stuff of adventure, and his heart beat faster. He knew he should tell someone. He knew he should have a buddy. He knew what he was about to do was irresponsible. He didn't care. He was a mouse all right, but somehow this cave seemed a test that would show if he would always remain one. If he was up to this lone challenge, he might be up to others in the future.

Strangely, he wasn't at all scared as he lay down on his back and wiggled feet-first down into the ground. It was easy going. The old cave smelled of earth and mold, and other unknown odors long trapped underground. His downward progress stopped when came to the flat floor of the place. He stood up cautiously, but found there was plenty of headroom. He moved his light rapidly up and down, right and left. This was no cave. This was a mine!

The place *seemed* safe enough. Its walls were rough, and in places, large rocks jutted out into the passage. There were cracks and crevasses here and there, but they looked old. The rock walls and roof of the place looked strong. There seemed to be no sign of the miners who had dug deep into the hillside. There were no picks or shovels, no buckets or wheelbarrows, just the mineshaft itself stretching out beyond the reach of his light.

Mouse started forward. He pictured himself passing under the road above and heading straight for the troop's campsite. It was funny to think that they had been sleeping right over this long lost mine for the whole weekend.

Then his light picked up a gleam of silver. He knew right away what it would be, but nonetheless, he held his breath as he approached it. Then he was sure. There at his feet was a scattering of about a dozen silver dollars. He stooped to pick one up, and the blood rushed to his head. He felt a little dizzy. He examined the coin under his light. Yup, same as the others, 1878 — except this one didn't look nearly as worn as the ones they had found down by the stream.

He pocketed it, and then considered the coins still on the floor. It was almost as though they had leaked from a hole in the ceiling. He ran his light up the wall and saw a bit of strap hanging down from a ledge high above. The strap looked to be of leather and ran back up over the natural shelf. Mouse reached up and pulled on it, then pulled harder. It tightened and took the strain, and then he could feel something begin to slide. A couple more coins dribbled down. Mouse kept pulling, his heart pounding. The edge of a larger leather object appeared, then it seemed to stick. The light in his one hand illuminated the scene, as he jerked at the strap with his other. For the first time, Mouse wished he had some help — someone to reach out and catch the thing as it came free of its perch. Suddenly, it was too late. He saw it as it fell; it was some sort of leather bag and coins were tumbling out of it. Then it knocked the flashlight from his sweating hand. Bag and flashlight hit the floor together, and the place went dark.

Mouse felt around on the floor and found the light, but it was broken. He searched for the bag, then hefted it and felt inside. The thing was nearly full of coins. Even in the dark, Mouse knew exactly what they were — silver dollars. There must be hundreds of them.

Five minutes later, he was still on his knees, feeling around on the rocky floor for coins and shoving them into the top of the bag, when he heard a muffled shout.

"Hey, Mouse!"

Mouse jerked his head around to look toward the entrance. Was it Grit? No. It was the voice of a boy. It must be Pig. Great! He could use a little help getting his treasure out of the mine.

Mouse stood and lifted the heavy bag — the thing must have weighed close to 30 pounds. Hugging it to his chest, he shuffled toward the faint light at the end of the tunnel. There, he peered up into the daylight and saw the shape of his friend, backlit by a blue sky crisscrossed with the dark shapes of tree limbs.

"Here, grab this," he said, and shoved the bag before him up the slope into the light. Hands reached down to grab it and Mouse smelled a faint, rank odor.

Scrambling up the slope toward daylight, the smell grew stronger.

"Gees. You smell like you've been wrestling with a skunk," he said.

"Don't you worry about that, little Mouse. It looks like we've got enough money here for me to buy myself a brand new set of clothes." It wasn't Pig's voice — it was Chuck's!

Mouse scrambled up out of the hole. He found Chuck on his knees, looking into the bulging bag. A broad grin was on his face.

Suddenly, Mouse was very mad, "That's not *our* money. That's *my* money."

"Well, I guess I helped take it out of the ground, didn't I? That makes it part mine."

Chuck's grin grew colder. He leaned forward to look down at Mouse and his voice went tough as he added, "Unless you'd like to argue about it."

Mouse heard the threat. Chuck could beat him to a pulp, but suddenly, he didn't care. Let him. No way was Chuck getting a piece of this discovery. It was Mouse who discovered the cave. It was Mouse who explored it. It was Mouse who found the bag. It was Mouse's treasure and that was all there was to it. What he needed was a witness. Now he was sorry he hadn't had Pig or one of the Mice explore the cave with him. He'd have been happy to share the glory with any of them. Not with Chuck though!

Mouse looked all around for signs of another Scout to witness the beating he was surely about to receive. It had been years since Chuck had actually hit him, but Mouse never doubted the larger boy was still capable of using physical violence to enforce his opinions.

Mouse's eyes caught movement on the hillside opposite, and suddenly he had a more immediate problem than his cousin. There, coming downhill toward the stream, was the one man in the world who he least wanted to see at this particular moment — Simon Grit.

"Shh," he said, so forcefully that Chuck's eyes blinked wide.

"Duck down," ordered Mouse, as he set the example by crouching low behind the immense ball of hickory roots. Then he grabbed at Chuck's shirt to bring him down, too.

Chuck lost his balance and fell, then roughly batted Mouse's hand away. He started to go for Mouse, but then paused long enough to follow the line of his cousin's pointing finger. Now he understood.

"Good work," he whispered hoarsely, "We sure don't want him in on this."

The boys peeked through the tangle of roots to watch the progress of Simon Grit down the opposite hillside. He was certainly not out for a random stroll, for he hopped the stream and went straight to where the Mice had found their coins the night before. He started pushing stuff about with his feet. There was no question what he was looking for.

Mouse and Chuck exchanged glances and kept very still. Grit was not 60 feet away, and they were trapped behind the root ball for as long as his investigation lasted.

Ten minutes passed. It seemed like ten hours. Mouse cautiously moved to the other side of the upturned mat of roots to see if there was, perhaps, some escape on that side. The hill fell away steeply, and he could see the path continuing down toward Toby Creek. They could get down that way, but Grit might see them... or he might not. If he did see them, and if they were carrying the coins, no amount of explanation would satisfy the man.

Mouse brought his mouth close to Chuck's ear — the skunk smell was horrible, made his eyes water.

"Chuck, we've got to hide the bag and sneak off down the ravine. He could stay down there for hours."

Chuck evidently had had enough of waiting too. He shook his head in agreement. So, with cupped hands, they dug at the disturbed earth under the roots, where the massive tree had pulled loose from the hillside. In five minutes, they had managed to dig a hole big enough to hold the bag. Chuck shoved it firmly into place and then they mounded small stones and clods of earth over it until it was deeply buried. By the time they were done, no trace remained of their hidey-hole.

No one who wasn't in on the secret could possibly find the bag or the treasure that it contained.

Now they crept from the root pit, as quietly as they could, though some noise was unavoidable. The rushing stream helped to mask the sound of their movements, and in another five minutes, they were down the trail, round a bend and safe from discovery.

They walked along single file. Mouse was in front, staying ahead of the smell. Where had Chuck found a skunk at this time of day? More importantly, what should they do about the bag?

Chuck spoke. He must have been thinking about that, too.

"We can't go back for the bag today. If anybody at the camp saw it, Grit would be sure to find out."

Mouse had to agree. Minutes after that bag showed up in camp there would be a ring of Scouts around it. Minutes after that there would be 30 Scouts down in the ravine, where Grit would be all too interested in what had brought them to such a place before breakfast on a Sunday morning.

"Yeah, you're right. We should go tell Mr. Ellsworth about it and see what he thinks we should do."

"No," said Chuck, fiercely. "I don't like Ellsworth and I don't trust him, either. Once he hears about the coins you guys found last night, and what happened to them, he'll make us give Grit these, too."

Mouse liked Mr. Ellsworth, and knew his Scoutmaster was an honorable man. The fact that Chuck didn't like him mattered not at all. What would Mr. Ellsworth do, though? He might just give the coins to Grit, and Mouse would hate for that to happen. If he had to give the treasure up, he wanted to give it to someone with more authority than a part-time game warden.

Chuck didn't like Mouse's silence. He stopped and stared hard at his younger cousin. "Listen, Mouse. We're not going to tell anyone anything until we get back to town. Then, we'll talk to Grandpa Mike. He'll know what to do."

Mouse considered that idea, and decided he liked it. Grandpa would listen to Mouse's version of events, and once they returned to the mine, Mouse could show him that only his footprints led inside. His broken flashlight was still down there, too, and that would be further proof. Once Grandpa was convinced of where the bag had been found, and who had done the finding, Mouse was sure that he would do the right thing. Yeah, they would wait and talk to Grandpa Mike. That suited him just fine.

"OK. That sounds like a good plan," said Mouse with a smile.

The two walked on and shortly came to where the path dipped and curved down to ford Toby Creek. The scene was alive with the sight and sound of crashing water. The blue sky above reflected off the meandering creek and made it seem a world away from the dark ravine with its treasure and the searching man who would steal it. They left the trail there and turned south to follow the west side of the creek. A few hundred feet downstream, they came to a narrow game trail that snaked up over the hill. They followed that up and up, out of Toby valley — Mouse climbing hard and fast so as to keep ahead of his smelly cousin. Why did Chuck smell of skunk?

They soon huffed up to the top, coming to the bench below camp. Suddenly, Pig was beside them.

"Where have *you* been?" asked Chuck, suspiciously.

Pig was all innocence, "I was downstream there, about 100 yards, watching the turkeys." Pig was so matter-of-fact, it sounded as though these were tame turkeys in a farmyard, and that it was the most natural thing in the world for him to go visit them.

Then Pig smiled an evil smile and asked, "Where have *you* been, Chuck? Playing with skunks?"

Chuck just scowled and strode on ahead, leaving a putrid scent trail behind. Mouse and Pig took a slightly different route to avoid the odor, and hurried to arrive at camp ahead of Chuck.

As they entered, Mouse could smell fried eggs and bacon. Then, he saw Pee Wee and Bobby on their knees, scrubbing at a frying pan with sand to clean off some black goop that looked like burnt egg.

Pig said sadly, "Look's like we got back a little too late for breakfast."

Mouse gave him a nudge and pointed. Paxton was over by Chuck's tent, motioning for them to join him. When they got close, Mouse and Pig swung away to stand up wind. It didn't seem possible, but Chuck's tent smelt even worse than the boy himself. They watched as Chuck approached, and were not at all surprised at Paxton's first words.

"Gees, stop there Chuck!" he said. "You smell just like your tent. Where have you been? Mr. Ellsworth says you should take that thing down and put it, and any clothes the skunk sprayed, into a garbage bag. I've been looking all over for you. Why'd you run away?"

"I didn't run away," said Chuck huffily. "I was just waiting for the skunk to leave. Anyway, I found these two while I was out there. Pig here seems to think that looking at turkeys is more important than showing up for breakfast. You ought to make him pack up the tent."

Paxton wasn't buying that. "Mr. Ellsworth said you were to do it. Stowing the tent won't make you smell any worse than you already do. Maybe Pig and Mouse would like to help, though."

"No way!" they exclaimed together.

"Well then, you two go help with the cleanup and Chuck, you get on with striking your tent. What did you do to the skunk to make him squirt you, anyway?"

"I don't know!" Chuck whined. "I woke up and there he was. I kept perfectly still, but he already had his tail up. When he squirted, I just grabbed my boots and got out fast. I saw Mouse going over the hill and I went after him. I can't figure it out. I'm sure I zipped the flap last night, but somehow he got in anyway."

Mouse and Pig left then. They had been given their assignment and found it far preferable to what Chuck would be doing for the next half-hour. They found Beaner and Jim staring at a large, soot-blackened pot. It was half full of dubious looking scrambled eggs.

Mouse asked, "Just how many eggs did you guys make?"

Beaner looked up, "Only two-dozen, but this batch didn't turn out so well and nobody wanted them. We were just wondering if we should bury them or try to force them into the garbage bag — it's already kind of full."

Pig grabbed up the pot. "Don't worry about it, Beaner, my boy. We'll take it from here."

The two small Scouts disappeared like fog on a sunny morning. Pig reached into the garbage bag and came up with two plastic forks and a used napkin. He used a corner of the napkin to buff the forks semi-clean, then handed one to Mouse and said, "Breakfast is served," and dug in. The mound of eggs was dingy yellow, with here and there a fleck of black or white. Mouse could hear the crunch as Pig chewed. Ah, that's what the white bits were — some inexpert egg-cracker had not succeeded in keeping the shells out of the pan. He considered for just a second, and then dug in himself. He was hungry.

After they had surrounded the contents of the pot, Pig gave his review of breakfast. "You know, the eggs weren't half bad. The burnt bits added a gritty, charcoal flavor. And, the eggshells gave an interesting texture and crunch. I've had worse."

Mouse chuckled, "They weren't the best, but they were more than cousin Chuck will get. Now let's clean up the rest of the pans like Paxton said to do."

"Sure," said Pig.

As they worked together, head-to-head, at scrubbing the pot clean, Mouse said, "I wonder how come that skunk picked on Chuck? How did it manage to even get into his tent?"

Pig looked up smiling, eyes wide with innocence. Then, his smile turned wicked. He gave Mouse a broad wink and whispered, "Birds of a feather flock together."

Two hours later, Troop 51 departed Bear Run for their homes in Clarion and its surroundings. Some would forget the Clarion County Camporee; some would remember only a smell, a sight, or a sound. Others would hold onto fond memories of heroic deeds witnessed or performed. A few, though, would be changed forever by the events of this weekend in the woods.

Pig's dad showed up just before the main contingent was about to depart. He drove a battered, old Ford pickup with *Hammerman Timber* stenciled on its side. Pig paused for a second near Mouse and said, "Thanks for bunking with me, Mouse. It was nice to have company, even if you do sleep with your eyes wide open."

Then he smiled and added, "We did all right yesterday, didn't we?" and walked away to join his waiting father.

Minutes later, Mouse sat in an overcrowded van and watched as his cousin got into the back seat of Mr. Ellsworth's car. Chuck sat on a clear plastic tarp, and his only company back there was a large garbage bag full of his tent and most of his belongings. He was wrapped in a blanket and in a savage mood. Mouse tried unsuccessfully to feel sorry for him. The younger Scouts ducked down so they could not be seen, and giggled quietly at the plight of the older boy — he who, so often, had tried to spoil their fun. In the same mysterious way these things always happen, Chuck had been awarded a nickname, and this, along with the famous victory of Mouse's Mice over the Eagles, was surely destined to become a part of the lore of the troop.

As the van bumped out of the field and onto the road for Clarion, a filthy, hungry, sleepy Mouse thought about nicknames. He was still Mouse, just as he had been when he arrived on Friday night. All his plans for changing that had come to nothing. Still, the name no longer held much sting. His name might be Mouse, but he had at least shown that sometimes he was more than the name implied. Yes, he still mysteriously froze up at times, still became tongue-tied and confused. But, most of the daylight hours yesterday had been wonderful. He had led his patrol to victory, and had made friends of Scouts who, at the start of the weekend, had just been guys he knew. Sure, Grit and Chuck had caused him problems, made him miserable, but maybe, just maybe, he would get better at dealing with such people if he just kept trying.

Yes, and there were names lots worse than Mouse Monroe.

He heard it whispered again, heard the giggle that followed. It wasn't nice, and Mouse would never use it. Nevertheless, it was, as such things often were, perfect in its way. His large and troublesome cousin, Chuck Wing, now had a nickname all his own. Mouse smiled just a little; *Stinky Wing* would be a tough one to live down.

BUCK'S LOOT

11

Shortly after the 11 o'clock service started, Simon Grit's thoughts began to wander. Immaculate Conception Church was crowded with worshipers. At the altar, Father Hahnfeld proceeded smoothly through the Mass, even though amplified announcements and vague crowd noises occasionally filtered in from the sunny excitement of the day outside. Simon heard neither the priest nor the noises from outdoors. Beside him, sandwiched between himself and his wife, Susan, sat their ten-year-olds, George and Peter. Simon didn't notice as the boys fidgeted and frequently turned to peer toward the large windows at the front of the church. He didn't hear Susan's fierce whispers to the errant boys or see her signals for help. Simon could have silenced the twins with a single hard look, but Simon was elsewhere, and the look on Susan's face changed to one of concern as the Mass progressed.

Simon move sluggishly to kneel or stand as appropriate, his eyes pointed in the direction of the altar, but what he was seeing was much, much farther away. He never leaned forward to check on the three girls seated beyond Susan. Six-year-old Terry and eight-year-old Nancy were pretty in their print dresses and paying close attention, but Simon never saw. Abby, his 15-year-old, was the last in this long line of Grits, acting as a sort of bookend on the left, as Simon was supposed to act as a bookend at the right, but for once Simon took no interest in the service or in the behavior of his brood. He didn't see the priest or smell the incense. He didn't hear the reading from the Book, or feel the sanctity of the holy place.

Simon saw the dump and the coins. He heard Papa, his grandfather. He smelled the dusty, green ferns and the rot of the ravine. His mind skittered about in time and place, seeking to solve the old, old puzzle that had been so much a part of his boyhood. He heard Papa's voice tell the story once again. He felt the crunch of the leaves under his small feet as the two of them walked ancient byways in search of clues. He once again felt the sadness of his grandfather's passing, the event that had marked the end of the marvelous adventure.

Those boys last night had found more than they realized. It was as if their lights and their noisy excitement were a signal of some sort, meant to draw his attention, meant to rekindle his desire for the sweetest dream of his early years. He now knew where the treasure lay hidden. It was no wonder he and Papa had never found it. It was buried under the dump, the dump that was once a much smaller and newer thing, but had grown to cover the whole hillside by the time their search had even begun. He knew he would find the treasure now — their treasure, his and Papa's.

Simon snapped back. People were rising and the service was ended. He smiled, eager for the moment of discovery that had eluded them all those years ago. He could hardly wait to begin.

The boys burst from the church like housedogs let out of doors. Simon held a small hand in each of his, and the boys pulled and strained to drag him toward the excitement on Main Street. He glanced back and saw that the girls followed, and so, let the boys move him along, steering them down the sidewalk to the corner of Eighth and Main. There they turned and half-crossed

Main Street, when he applied the brakes and brought them to a stop beside a fireman. As they stood waiting for the girls to catch up, the boys gawked at the fireman's uniform, but Simon looked on up the street and smiled. The treasure would have to wait for another day.

This was the first Sunday of Clarion's annual Autumn Leaf Festival, or ALF as most called it, and Main Street had been transformed into a huge antique car show that went by the very fifties-sounding name of the *Autorama*. The name made Simon think of a bowl-o-rama or rama-lama-ding-dong, like in an old rock song. Autorama seemed to fit the event so well, even if now the full name was the *S & T Bank Autorama*, which somehow made it sound more like a used car sale.

Rising up on his toes, Simon could just see over the crowd. Three rows of the old cars ran for blocks down past the courthouse and the carnival. Two of these were in the normal year-round parking places that lined Main Street, the third sat right on the center line of the road. This left two wide aisles where the crowds could stroll and gape at the old iron. The day was as sunny as heaven, and the temperature was just as perfect. People had come out in force for this, the inaugural event of the ALF. Simon had never seen so many. It was more like the crowd leaving a football game than what one would expect at an old car show.

The family started down the right-hand aisle. It was slow going, but there were a hundred smiles from strangers, and dozens of hellos from townspeople that he and his wife knew. The kids kept bumping into classmates, and best of all, there were the cars. The boys loved the cars, and Simon was proud of them for it. He pointed out mag wheels, explained the many steps in applying Candy Apple paint jobs, did imitations of Hollywood pipes and was having a grand old time. They passed through the Corvette section, and he again felt the sweet envy of those so lucky as to own so impractical and beautiful a car. Then he realized, with a start, that the treasure would make such a thing possible. He pictured Susan and himself tooling through the legendary turns on the County Home Road in a banana yellow '63 Corvette. The top was down; sunglasses protected their eyes; the sun was an hour from setting, and the car cornered beautifully as he zipped through hard curves and floored the gas on the short straights. It would be great!

Suddenly, Susan was at his side. "This is what you have been dreaming about all day, isn't it," she said with good humor.

How could she know? He gave her a puzzled look.

"Come on," she laughed. "I know you too well. You were thinking of the old Chevy back in church. Now here it is and you're off in dreamland, again."

Simon looked ahead, and sure enough, there it was — a deep cool red, its chrome gleaming in the sunlight, the curve of its rear fenders beautiful and distinctive. He was so happy to see the old girl again, on this of all days.

He grabbed Susan close and walked her over toward the old car. "She looks great doesn't she?"

The ruins of a handsome man sat in a lawn chair next to the car. He was big, blonde and balding. His arms were still massive but now had a soft look about them, and his beer belly was immense. Simon was a little taken aback at the changes, but then the man smiled that same old roguish smile, hauled himself up and reached out a brawny hand.

"Simon Grit, you old son of a bitch. How the hell are ya!"

Simon could feel Susan stiffen. Though he had been a famous ladies man, Odell Pinkus had never been *her* type. Simon spoke quickly, before his old friend could further antagonize his wife.

"Howdy, Odell. The old bus looks great. Did you paint her again? Say, can Susan show the kids around the inside?"

Odell considered. Simon knew he was asking a lot. Old cars were meant to be seen and admired at the Autorama, not pawed or prowled by the passersby.

"Come on, Odell," he wheedled, "I owned her for twenty years. The judging's over and Susan will make sure they don't rip off any of the chrome."

"Well, seein' as it's you," Odell paused, still reluctant, then reached a decision. "What the hell, go ahead. Just be damn careful."

Susan wasted no time in herding the little birds into the old red car, and away from Odell and his colorful mouth.

"Couldn't hardly say no, could I?" Odell grinned. "Seein' as how you two spent so many hot nights in her."

"What does he mean, Daddy?" asked Abby from behind. Only then did Simon realize she had not gone with the others to investigate the interior of the car.

At the sound of her voice, Simon's face had shaded to red. He glared with menace at Odell and could see by the widening of the man's eyes that the message had been received loud and clear. Simon stepped to the side to reveal his daughter.

"Odell, this is Abby, my oldest. Abby, this is Odell Pinkus, an old friend of mine from high school."

"Howdy, Abby," said Odell, with a smile that had won many a fair heart. "You look just as pretty as your mom did at your age."

Abby looked a bit confused by his direct gaze and the reference to her looks, but managed to say, "Thank you, Mr. Pinkus."

Simon thought, yeah, she does look like her mom did back then. Soon she would have guys like Pinkus here chasing her. Now that was a scary thought! Simon pointed at the car. It would be better to talk about the car.

"Abby, this is my old 1958 Chevy Impala. I sold it to Odell just before you were born."

"I thought he was gonna keep the sucker forever," said Odell, "but I guess he needed a truck more'n he did a car once he went back to farmin.'"

"Yeah, that's about right," replied Simon, "but boy did I have some good times in this old ride."

Odell laughed, "Abby, you shoulda seen the first time Si drove into the old Gulf. Must have been about 1968. We're sitting around talking girls and cars, and in pulls this farm boy driving an old Chevy.

We'd seen him around at school, of course, so about six of us went over an' had a look at his car. Gawd, it was a mess."

Simon smiled, "It had been sitting in the barn since my grandmother died. My grandfather never drove it after that. My father had never approved of it, so he didn't drive it either. He always said it was no farmer's car."

"How did you end up with it?" asked Abby.

"Well, when my grandfather died he left everything to my dad, everything except the car. The old Chevy he gave to me. It was the best present I ever got. It saved me from being a farmer."

"Ain't you a farmer now?" laughed Odell.

"Yeah, but I'm not the kind of farmer my old man was," said Simon, a little irritated. "I'm a farmer that has been some places, done some things. I'm a farmer by choice, and it's all on account of that car."

"We put some miles on her, didn't we?" said Odell. "Remember those times we drove up to Watkin's Glen for the races and the beer? Gawd, I miss those days."

Simon thought that those were perhaps not the best car stories to regale Abby with.

"Yeah," he said, "and then I got the scholarship at Penn State and drove her back and forth to State College for four years, until I graduated. After that, I cruised timber for Hammerman's and took her down nearly every blacktop, dirt road and cow path in the county. It was about then I started dating your mother and together we sure put a lot of miles on this old bus. On our honeymoon, we drove up through Niagara Falls and into Canada, then out to Michigan where we canoed the Ausable River. There are a lot of memories in this old girl. It's been six shades of red over the years, but it never looked as good as it does today."

"Thanks," said Odell, pleased. "I got over fifteen thousand bucks in her and I figure I could sell her for twenty-five. Come on and look at the new mill. I finally found a 348 for her last spring and spent the summer doin' the conversion."

The two men moved to the front of the car, where the hood stood open to show a large and gleaming engine. They talked about four-barrel carbs, the new transmission and changes to the suspension. Simon knew Abby couldn't understand most of it, but she hung around anyway, either because she liked to hear the men talk or because she couldn't figure out how to extricate herself from the conversation gracefully.

As they talked, the crowd flowed slowly past. For most, a glance at the engine was enough, but occasionally, someone would ask a question, and then Odell or Simon would smilingly respond. Simon was enjoying himself immensely.

Two boys, about 11 or 12, came up and looked at the engine, then at Simon. They wore Steelers T-shirts and jeans, and had a lank, athletic look about them. No beer-bellies here, Simon thought wryly.

"Hello," he said. "That's some engine isn't it? It's got a displacement of 348 cubic inches and was originally designed to be used in trucks. Chevrolet made it available as an option for the Impala in 1958, and it really makes her go. From a dead start this car can go to sixty miles an hour in ten and a half seconds."

Simon grinned broadly, expecting the boys would be impressed by the numbers – he certainly was. But, they looked at him and seemed embarrassed for some reason. He could see the taller of the two was struggling to find a reply. When it came, it was completely unexpected.

"We were talking to Mr. Ellsworth, our Scoutmaster, when we got back to the clubhouse," the words rushed out of the boy, "and Pee Wee told him about the coins, and Mr. Ellsworth said we should have told him right away, and he said we should find out who you are going to give them to and what will happen to them. Will they end up in a museum or what? If they do, will it say we found them? Is there a reward do you think?"

Simon considered his reply – so, so many embarrassing questions. Gone were all thoughts of the car and his smiling spirits with them. He saw the boys pull back a little at his change of expression, but still they waited for his reply. Could he just say he didn't know what they were talking about? No, there were too many boys who knew exactly what had been said and done. OK then, he would delay; give them a politician's answer. First, he sat down on his heels, so he could talk more quietly.

"I told you not to tell anyone about the coins, remember?" he asked, reasonably. Anger wasn't what was needed just now. "That was so the woods didn't get torn up by treasure hunters. Now what will happen?"

"It was just us and Mr. Ellsworth and Pee Wee who were there," said the second boy a little defensively. "It was Pee Wee who told, not us."

"Did Pee Wee tell him what I told you about not telling?"

"Yes. Mr. Ellsworth said he understood and would keep the secret," said the taller boy.

"That's good. It's the weekend still and I haven't done anything about what you found, yet. I will though, you just need to be patient. When you deal with the State Game Commission, nothing happens very quickly."

The boys seemed encouraged by this reply, and Simon figured he had a few days to make good on his promise to turn the coins over to Swagman, his boss at the game commission. Then he had another thought, dug out his notebook from his jacket pocket, scrounged for a stub of pencil and asked, "Can you tell me the names of the five boys who found the coins?"

The two were smiling now, sure that they would soon be heroes. "I am Beaner Sikes and this is Jim Zimmer. We found two of them."

Jim piped up, "Pee Wee Barnstaple, Bobby Carfield and Mouse Monroe found the other three."

"OK," said Simon, "give me your phone numbers and I will call you when I find out something."

A shadow of doubt crossed Jim's face. Simon smiled, he could read the kid's mind, and so added, "Don't worry. I'm not a stranger. You know my name is Simon Grit and you probably go to school with my sons."

"George and Peter Grit?"

"Yeah, you got it. They're inside the car there."

Jim smiled, "I know them. They're in fifth grade."

Simon wrote down the happily-offered numbers. He could handle these two. They would believe whatever he said, and were unlikely to challenge an officer of the Pennsylvania Game Commission.

The rest of his family had finally tired of pretend-driving the Impala, and suddenly Simon was surrounded by happy children who had had enough car show and were now ready to visit the carnival. Beaner and Jim waved hello to the boys then disappeared down the street in the other direction. Simon breathed a sigh of relief. Time to go. He rose to face Odell.

"So long," he said. "It was great to see you again."

"Hang in there," countered Odell and then he went to examine the interior of his mint condition Chevy.

Simon hoped it wasn't too bad. There was sure to be small fingerprints on all the chrome, but hopefully, that would be the extent of the damage. Turning to his wife he said, "Nobody threw up in there, did they?"

Susan laughed, "Wouldn't that just ruin Odell's day."

"Yeah, I'd never hear the end of it for the next twenty years."

Susan reassured him, "Not to worry. We didn't take it off of the main highway, didn't scratch a fender and no one got carsick."

Smiling at the thought, he walked beside her as they herded their clan up the street toward the carnival. Then he had another thought. Boy, it was a good thing Susan had not been around when he was talking to the two boys. She knew the whole sad history of his treasure hunting days. If she were to find out about the boy's coins that could mean real trouble. Then he began calculating how best to play the whole situation. The more people who knew about it, the more restricted were his options. How much of the conversation with the boys had Abby overheard? Would she mention it to Susan? If she did, then what?

They came to the corner of Fifth and Main, where a cop stood on a short wooden stand and surveyed the crowd for trouble. Silly, thought Simon. There was never any trouble at ALF, only a few quarrelsome drunks and noisy fraternity parties at night. The thing in New York sure had people spooked. What was going to happen, anyway? Were they expecting terrorists to show up and attack the old cars? He didn't think so.

A strange, small boy came out of the crowd toward Simon. He was dressed in jeans and a T-Shirt that read "Camp Mountain Run." A Boy Scout, thought Simon. For some reason the kid was wearing a canteen. On a hike? No, this kid was about to ask about the coins. This had to be Pee Wee what's-his-name. The magic word was "coin." He couldn't let Susan hear the kid say anything about finding coins.

"You're Pee Wee, right?" said Simon quickly.

"Yes, mister. Pee Wee Barnstaple. I just wanted to ask you about..."

"I already talked to Beaner and Jim," Simon cut in. "They are down the street about a block looking at the Corvettes. I'm taking my kids to the carnival now, so why don't you just talk to them?'

Pee Wee wasn't so easily disposed of, "I just wanted to tell you that I told Mr. Ellsworth about..."

"It's OK," said Simon hastily. "I'm not mad. Beaner told me."

Pee Wee looked embarrassed, "It's just that a Scout is trustworthy and I told you I wouldn't tell, and then it just sort of came out and then..."

"It's OK, Pee Wee. Just go talk to your friends, OK?" pleaded Simon.

"OK. Thanks," and the small fellow trotted off to the east, a boy on a mission. Simon couldn't help but smile. What a character.

"What was that all about?" asked Susan.

"Not to worry. Just a little business left over from the Boy Scout campout down at Bear Run yesterday. How many tickets do you think we should get?"

Happily, she took the bait and said no more about Pee Wee, their talk turning to which rides to ride, how many tickets to buy and other carnival-going topics.

For the next two hours, they were part of the happy crowd. Simon rode the ferris wheel, the merry-go-round and the dodge-em cars, but there he drew the line. No way was he riding the Tilt-A-Whirl or Gravitron or any other such mechanism designed to thrill. He'd be dizzy for hours afterward.

He was standing at the railing watching the rest of the family spin on the Tilt-A-Whirl and eying with distaste the young carney who ran the thing, when a deep, self-important voice beside him said, "No stomach for it, Grit?"

It was Clyde Swagman, his boss on the game commission.

"You got that right. The last time I rode one of those I was with a girl in high school. I got off it and could hardly stand up. The carney who ran the thing came over and laughed at me. He was a lanky, good-looking kid — wore jeans and a white T-shirt with a pack of cigarettes rolled up in the sleeve. You know the type?"

Swagman snorted, "Yeah, you don't see them much any more. Black leather jacket; engineer's boots; long, long chrome chain connected to a wallet or a set of keys. Real outlaw types. That's what I wanted to be when I was a kid. They drove the girls wild."

Simon laughed aloud, picturing the plump, pompous Swagman as a carnival outlaw.

"You got it. Well, this carney put the moves on my girl and I nearly had to fight him, dizzy or not."

"Did she go with him?" asked Swagman.

"I could tell she was tempted, but no. She rode home with me. She was mighty quiet though and never went out with me again after that night. I guess she was after someone a little scarier than me."

Swagman chuckled a bit at that, then turned serious, "Speakin' of scary, did the Boy Scouts manage to leave my forest intact out your way? I heard they had one hell of a campfire last night."

"It was big all right, but I had a look from up on the hill, and they did it right. Some of those guys are pretty good, you know."

"They better be," growled Swagman. "Did you check out the campground after they left? Any fires left smoking?"

"I did. They poured water all over everything, left the place clean as a whistle — no food, no new trash in the dump."

"Good thing too, or they would have heard from me," said Swagman importantly. "Were they down at the fall on Bear Run at all? You know it's like a magnet for druggies and boozers."

Simon laughed, "This bunch wasn't druggies or boozers, Clyde. This was the Boy Scouts. I did find a bunch of them down that way around 11 o'clock last night, but I just chased them back up the hill, and there was no harm done."

"What were they up to?"

"Just watchin' the waterfalls by flashlight, I suppose," said Simon smoothly.

"Well, OK, I guess. If you say so."

"Yeah, it was all right," said Simon.

"OK. Well, I gotta go. I hear there are some campers up at Hemlock Island, and I figure they are just about set up by now, so maybe it's time I paid them a little visit and told them they got to move along." He seemed pleased at the prospect of exercising his authority. "See you in a couple weeks, when hunting season opens." He gave a stiff nod, and was gone.

Simon stood thinking. Now he had done it, or rather not done it. He should have told Swagman about the coins. If he had, though, his publicity-seeking boss would have broadcast the news far and wide. Swagman made a very big deal about everything that happened on State Game Lands. If he thought the boys had broken the law, he would prosecute. Whatever happened, he would make sure that the *Clarion News* had all the details of the discovery of antique coins at Bear Run, and of Clyde Swagman's investigation into the matter.

Susan and the kids returned and then they hit the food stands for dinner, but Simon's heart wasn't in it. His thoughts were of Papa and the treasure, of five boys who expected him to report their discovery and of the repercussions if Swagman ever found out about either the boy's discovery or what Simon would do tomorrow. He would be at the dump early and he would find that treasure. He just wished he was going to be digging on his own property; things would be so much less complicated.

12

The binging of his digital alarm clock woke Mouse at precisely 6:30 a.m. on Monday morning. He reached over to tap the thing silent, and then just lay there for a minute, reveling at the crisp, clean feel of the sheets. Ten minutes later, he finished brushing his teeth, and then watched as water poured magically from the faucet, scrubbed his toothbrush clean and ran off out of sight down the drain. There was a note from his Mom on the kitchen table, wishing him a happy day, and as he waited for the Pop-Tarts to jump out of the toaster, Mouse thought what a wonderful day it had been so far.

For starters, he had slept alone in his own neat and clean room, rather than in a cluttered, dirty tent with noisy old Pig. Then there was the bathroom. It was like a sultan's dream when compared to what he had used on the weekend. A canteen for a faucet and the woods for a toilet didn't begin to compare. And now there was breakfast — breakfast was the best part yet. All he had to do was dream, and the toaster would serve his breakfast cooked to perfection. The was no messing about starting fires, no unsatisfactory toasting over an open flame, and no messy cleanup operations afterwards. There was just no place like home, but you never realized that until you spent a couple of days living in a tent. Sure, there were no magnificent sunrises, no magical rambles in the woods, but then, there were no skunks either. He smiled and wondered how long it had taken Chuck to get rid of the smell.

When he had finished with the Pop-Tarts and drained his glass of Gatorade, he smiled again, gave his dishes a quick scrub, and put them in the rack to dry — so simple, so elegant!

It was now about 7 a.m. and time to get moving, time to leave the empty house and head on down to school. He threw on his jacket and ventured out into the morning, feeling happy, but also just a bit lonely. His dad was in Japan until the end of the month, but that wasn't so bad — Dad was often away selling electronics to exotic people in far away places, so Mouse was used to that. It was his mom he missed. She was always around, morning and night — someone to talk to, someone to go to for advice, someone who loved him, someone who was just always *there*. Not this week though. This week she was teaching her normal round of classes at the university, same as always, but she was also managing a vegetarian food stand on Main Street for the church. She had talked to him about it, explained she would be working early and late for the whole week of ALF. She had asked if he thought he could manage pretty much on his own for a week.

"Sure, Mom," he had said with outraged voice, but now he was missing her already. Ah, well. It was only for a week.

Mouse walked down Liberty toward the high school. The sky was clear and cold. Dew sparkled everywhere and made the autumn leaves look like stained glass in a church window. He was a little ahead of schedule and so swung up Sixth to Main, to pass by the food booths and the carnival rides. The cleanup crews had already been and gone, and Mouse liked the sharp lines and neatness of the still sleeping festival attractions. The place looked sort of like an oil painting — all the picture needed to make it perfect was a few more people. Yeah, there were people, lots of people, but they were all in the cars and trucks that rushed by, safe from the day behind walls of metal and glass. Mouse felt alone. What in the world was wrong with him? He had gotten up and got ready for school by himself dozens of times without all this fretting. Did he really miss his *mommy* that much? "What a wimp," he thought disgustedly.

As he passed the entrance to the deserted carnival midway, Mouse was surprised to see Pee Wee, walking jauntily toward him between the closed-sided booths. Mouse changed course so they would meet.

Pee Wee was wearing school clothes, but the canteen and the compass looped around his neck, along with the small Scout's habit of looking all about as he traveled, gave him the air of a wary woodsman on the lookout for big game.

Mouse smiled, "Ho, Pee Wee. What are you tracking?"

Pee Wee looked a little puzzled. "I'm just walking to school, same as I always do," he replied.

"So what's with the canteen and compass?"

"I might get thirsty and a compass is *always* a good thing to have along," then he smiled. "I remember a time when I had *two* compasses and *still* got lost!"

"Yeah, you're right about that," laughed Mouse. "We sure had a great time on Saturday, didn't we?"

"You bet!" said Pee Wee, most definitely. "I wish there was a real Mouse's Mice Patrol. I had the best time ever with you guys. You are a great leader, Mouse."

"Thanks," said Mouse, shy of such unreserved, undeserved praise. "I had a lot of fun, too, except for the part where we lost the coins."

Pee Wee's face clouded. "Yesterday, I was at the Autorama, and I saw that man who took the coins. When I tried to ask about them, he just sent me down the street to see Beaner and Jim. I couldn't find those guys, and I think maybe the man was just trying to get rid of me. What do you think? Could he be trying to steal the coins for himself?"

Mouse considered, then said, "I don't know. He said he would turn the coins in to the game commission. Today is the first day he could do that. Maybe he did talk to Beaner and Jim. Won't you see them at school?"

"Yeah, sure," said Pee Wee. "We're in the same room."

"Well, you could talk to them and find out if what Mr. Grit said was true."

"OK. I'll talk to them at recess," replied Pee Wee. "What should I do if Mr. Grit was lying?"

"If he was, we'll tell Mr. Ellsworth about the whole thing and see what he says." Mouse considered, then added, "Are you going to the fire truck rides on Wednesday?"

"You bet!" replied Pee Wee, enthusiastically.

"OK," said Mouse, "I'll see all you guys there, and we'll talk it over then. Mr. Ellsworth and Grandpa Mike are sure to be there. If we need advice, we can ask one of them."

"Great!" said Pee Wee, then he looked at a big watch strapped to his small wrist, did a comic double take, and gasped, "I'm late. I'm late!" and clanked away toward the grade school at high speed, leaving Mouse to shake his head as he walked in exactly the opposite direction, on toward the high school.

Mouse walked into his homeroom just as the bell rang. He spent the morning in geometry, chemistry, and in study hall boning up for a Spanish quiz later in the day. His earlier loneliness was now forgotten, but from time to time he did think about the new information supplied by Pee Wee. If Grit was denying having the coins, then he had a reason. Mouse remembered the way he had been digging around down by the dump. There was something funny about the persistence with which he had gone about it, almost like he knew there were more coins to be found. How could he know that? No answer came to mind, unless Grit somehow knew that the Scouts' coins were part of a larger treasure, the treasure Mouse himself had found. But how could he know that? Wouldn't everybody know about such a thing? Wouldn't Grandpa Mike have said something when he was telling his coin story? The whole thing was very puzzling. Where had the coins come from?

For the first time ever, Mouse sat with Pig at lunch. The weekend had created a bond between the two, and as they sat at the side of the room eating pizza, they talked over old times and reviewed Grit's behavior down in the ravine on Saturday night and discussed Pee Wee's news. They were just finishing up, when Chuck came across the cafeteria toward them. Mouse noticed people turning to look as Chuck passed. Had word of his weekend adventure with the skunk gotten around that quickly? Then Chuck was standing in front of him, and Mouse understood. It was very, very faint — very, very subtle, but about his cousin there still lingered a trace of something, a vague wispy odor of skunk.

"Howdy, Mouse. Howdy, Pig Boy."

"Hi, Chuck," said Mouse without enthusiasm. Pig remained silent.

"Hey, Piggy, could you disappear? I have something important to talk over with Mouse."

Pig slowly got up and said, "A donkey carrying gold is still a donkey."

Chuck didn't quite understand, but he knew he didn't like what he had just heard. "You better watch your mouth, Hammerman."

Pig moved to stand close to Chuck; he suddenly looked none too friendly. Mouse was surprised. Pig was actually taller than Chuck, and looked a good bit stronger besides. Pig was just fifteen, same as himself. What would his buddy be like when he was Chuck's age?

Chuck didn't exactly cringe at Pig's close approach, but he didn't venture any more sharp remarks, either.

Pig gave a sniff, a small smile, and then said, "Great braggers are little doers, Stinky," and walked away in the direction of the serving line.

"That kid is weird," said Chuck, angry and confused.

"Well, he is different anyway," agreed Mouse, repressing a chuckle. "One thing is for sure though, he's mighty handy in the woods."

"Yeah," said Chuck, unimpressed. "Too bad life isn't a camping trip."

Mouse didn't want to argue. "What did you want, Chuck?"

"I just wanted to tell you that I was talking to Grandpa Mike last night, so you won't have to," replied Chuck.

"You talked to Mike? We were supposed to talk to Mike together! I tried to call him three times to set up a meeting, even left messages, but he never called back."

"Yeah, he told me you were trying to reach him, when I talked to him," said Chuck, smiling now. "You better not call any more this week, little Mouse. He's busy as hell."

"Look, Chuck. If you think that I am just going to be a quiet little mouse while you steal my treasure, you have got some more thinking to do!"

"Keep it down, Mouse," Chuck said with alarm. Heads were turning. "We didn't talk very long. He was just leaving, said I could talk to him at the fire truck rides. I just told him I needed to ask him about something I'd found on the weekend."

Blood rushed to Mouse's face, "*You* found! What do you mean *you* found? *I* found, not *you* found."

Chuck winced. Mouse was way, way too loud. Pig, clear over at the lunch counter, turned to look in their direction. "OK, OK! Keep it down, Mouse. *We* found. *We* found. OK?"

Mouse just stared stonily up at his cousin and Chuck continued, "Anyway, like I said, I didn't tell him anything. He didn't want to hear it. He just said he'd talk to me at the fire truck rides on Wednesday. He'll be driving one of the trucks and afterwards he'll talk to me, uh, us."

"And why didn't he call me, do you suppose?" asked Mouse, still very irritated.

"He asked if I knew why you had called. I told him I would take care of it. He would tell you the same thing he had just told me, so I figured I would save him the trouble."

"Why didn't you call me last night, then?"

Chuck smiled; no, it was more like a sneer. "I figured it was way past your bed time, little Mouse. Anyway, I've told you now."

13

Early in the afternoon, Simon Grit noticed the air was suddenly cooler. Looking up through branches heavy with dark-green needles, he saw that low misty clouds, gray with moisture, now scraped the treetops. A very light rain was falling up there, but the needles of the pines and the colorful nodding leaves of the hardwoods seemed to act as blotting paper to keep the moisture out of the ravine. Simon enjoyed the new coolness of the day, and the sensation of working under a huge umbrella that protected him from the mist that would quickly soak more exposed places. He figured the horses would be under trees or sheltering in the barn, and the chickens would be keeping under cover too, as they pursued their endless search for seeds and small bugs. He was alone, but somehow felt the presence of his grandfather, watching as he heaved and strained to clear a path up through the dump toward the top of the ravine.

Simon's amazement at the size of the mound of cast off junk had grown as the hours had passed. What he had always taken to be a thin covering of rusted metal on a remote hillside was turning out to be much more. To his dismay, the dump had real depth, and his progress after the first hour had been slow.

That morning, after Susan and the kids left for school, he had quickly tended to the few absolutely necessary chores, and then prepared himself for the real business of the day. He scooped up a flashlight from the pantry and found a rusty, beat up old crow bar leaning against the ancient tractor in the barn. He grabbed a pair of thick leather gloves, and headed across the lower field and down into the ravine. The day had been sunny, and he had had every confidence he would succeed in the first hour. The sunlight pierced the canopy of the trees and dappled the noisy ravine with patches of lemon that danced and seemed to urge him on.

At first, he whistled merrily as he shifted bent up refrigerators, rusting stoves and mounds of smaller appliances — looking eagerly under each for more coins. He found none, but that didn't matter much. What he was really looking for was an old mine. It had been 30 years since he had last heard the story, but back before that, he had heard it often, and no detail had slipped from memory in the intervening years. The big thing to look for, the big thing to find was the mine. What was important was to clear a path through the debris down to rock or earth, starting from where the boys had found the coins, straight up to the top of the slope. If luck was with him, that would turn up the entrance. He smiled, remembering all the odd nooks and crannies he and Papa had poked into during their long, fruitless search decades earlier. He was confident, though, that this time the first likely hole he found would lead into a long lost world bedecked with silver.

Simon had made good progress that first hour, but slowly he became aware that the dump was not only wide, but also deep. By the time he was halfway up the slope, he had dug a trench that was five feet deep, its sides like some historical record of the evolution of household appliances, farm machinery, and oil field equipment. The top layer contained the newer, more easily moved stuff, but below this was a jigsaw of old frayed drilling cables, barbwire, mysterious iron castings and rusted pipe. And, spotted about in this more compact mass, like cherries in a fruitcake, were wringers, car engines, toasters and sinks, with here and there a radio full of broken tubes, or an ancient round-eyed TV presenting ragged, glassy edges that were best avoided. It was an interesting puzzle, digging the trench, but gradually Simon became aware of the passage of time and of the arrival of heavier rain, and still he had discovered nothing — no coins, no mines. So far, at least, the dump lay on hard, stratified rock or densely compacted earth that showed no sign of having ever been disturbed.

He pulled off a glove and shoved back a sleeve to check the time, and was surprised to see that it was 2:30 already. He had not stopped for lunch, nor taken any kind of break from the heavy, increasingly dangerous, work for over 6 hours. Now his determination to move the next pipe, shift the next stove, roll away the next heavy hunk of nameless rusting metal, faded away. He was halfway to the top, but looking down the way he had come, he suddenly realized that this scheme of his was not practical. He couldn't shift all the junk on this hillside in a month of trying, and the entrance to the mine could be anywhere — under any of the rusting mounds that stretched out left and right.

Suddenly Simon had had enough. He teetered up to sit on the edge of his rusty, crumpled trench and considered other possibilities. OK, so it would take a hell of a lot of work to shift all the junk. Was there another way? He was looking for a mine, probably an ore mine, as there would be no coal cropping this far down the ravine. So, iron ore, then. Yeah, iron ore for the old furnace. That made sense. A mine like that would not be near the top of the ravine, or they would have just dug down and stripped out the ore — so the entrance to the mine would probably not be higher than the height of the trench he had already dug. The question was, how could he quickly find a large hole under the rolling mounds of trash? If he could find more coins they might point him in the right direction, but he had found none. A metal detector? Yeah, he smiled at that lame idea. A detector would go crazy around this much metal. How else…

He cocked his head. What was that? He listened hard, trying to ignore the white noise of the waters below, and the pat-pat of drips from the now saturated trees. Then he heard it again and moved slowly up over the slick surface of the dump toward the top. A car was approaching Bear Run Camp. Who would be visiting Bear Run on a dismal Monday afternoon? Only one name came to mind. Swagman.

Simon inched the last couple of feet on his belly, and then settled behind a squashed metal garbage can and waited. He heard the thunk of a car door closing, and fervently hoped it was not Swagman doing the closing — Swagman come to nose around, Swagman looking for some way to make trouble.

Simon eased slowly to the right and peered between the blades of an old reel-type push mower to search out the intruder. Then he saw the stranger's head appear on the skyline, and was vastly relieved. It was the head of a boy. As more of the kid came into view, Simon saw he was wearing an orange and black letterman's jacket — a Clarion Area athlete, then. Suddenly the build of the boy, the shape of his head, snapped into place. It was that older Scout who had been there when the other ones had found the coins. So he'd come back, huh? Had he driven all the way out here after school to look for more coins? Or… maybe there was more to it than that.

Simon would soon get the truth out of the intruder!

He lunged to his feet and was surprised at how insecure his footing was. The kid took one look at the weaving, dirty, dangerous-looking apparition risen from the trash heap, and fled.

Simon yelled, "Hey, stop!" but of course the kid didn't.

Suddenly, his left foot skidded away on the slick porcelain of an old round-cornered refrigerator, and he toppled over backwards, down toward the trench below. His left leg hit first and something tore at it as it took the force of the fall. He felt the denim of his pants rip, and then a sharp stabbing pain. The whole upper wall of the trench gave way under his weight, and slowly crumpled down to fill in his day's work. Simon was nearly buried by the trash avalanche, but somehow managed to stay ahead of the slow-moving collapse. A minute later, he lay bruised and cut by the stream, very thankful that he had not been buried where no man would ever find him. Unsteadily, he got to his feet and began the uphill trudge home, hand pressed to bloody thigh.

An hour later, Simon was sitting on the front porch watching the clouds roll away when Susan and the kids returned from school. The bloody pants were hidden in the engine compartment of the old tractor, and he had tended, as best he could, to the long, jagged gash in his thigh. It had been appallingly deep, and dirty with rust and greasy crud. He had some doubts that the bottle of peroxide he had poured into it would be antidote enough against infection. If the pain of that operation counted for anything at all though, he would get by. He hoped the gauze he had wrapped round and round his upper leg would keep the smiling wound closed, and as he smiled at his returning brood, he most of all hoped to keep his injury a secret.

"Hi, Susan," he said casually. "How was your day among the barbarians?"

"It was better," she sighed. "I've got the rowdies pegged now and have them spread to the four corners of the room. How was farm life?"

"The rain put a damper on things, but we should be set for Friday, if we can just get a start on the picking this evening. The sky is clearing nicely."

Susan nodded in agreement. "Well, I'll get dinner started and you can work with George and Pete on their reading. Abby can look after herself and see that the little girls tend to their homework."

"That sounds fine," said Simon, "It will make a nice change from the rest of my wasted day."

139

"Was it that bad, then?" asked Susan.

"It was OK, I guess," then he turned and shouted toward the sound of the TV, "Abby, turn off the TV. George, Pete, get your books and come out here."

For the next couple of hours, he was happy to just sit and read with the boys, to eat his dinner, and to let the conversation swirl around him. If he had less to say then usual, no one seemed to notice. After dinner, all seven of them got gloves and baskets, and walked up to the top field to pick gourds and Indian corn until dark. The clouds of midday could still be seen far to the west as bands of orange, glowing like neon across the face of the huge, fiery-red sun.

They made good progress. As he worked, Simon thought some more about how to find the mine. What he needed was a long stout pole to probe down through the trash. He would have to pick the places he probed carefully, but the idea seemed worth a try. Certainly, it was a safer occupation than digging, especially now that his leg was injured.

They walked back toward the old white farmhouse, now painted reddish-orange by the last rays of the dying sun. His thoughts were other places, and his body felt old and sore. Quite a day — it had been quite a day.

"Simon, you're limping," said Susan with concern.

Simon winced; he had forgotten to get behind her so she wouldn't notice. "Yeah, I had a little fall today and hurt my leg."

"Are you all right?"

"Yeah, I'm fine. Nothing's wrong that a good night's sleep won't mend."

So that was it, he thought sadly — the first lie to Susan. He just couldn't tell her. She would worry at the extent of his injury, and wonder how he had gotten it. That would lead to more lies, because the one thing he could not tell her was what he had been up to down at the dump when it happened. She had never known Papa, but Simon's father had told her about the obsessive, crazy treasure hunting of his son and father. If she knew he was hunting that treasure again, the questions would really start.

He felt bad about lying to her. He and Susan were a team, and honesty had been a linchpin of their life together for many, many years. The treasure would make everything right, though. All he had to do was find his treasure of gleaming, silver coins, and all their hopes and dreams would come instantly true!

14

Tuesday, just after lunch, Mouse walked into art class. The room was a clutter of easels where chattering girls worked away at their latest projects. The few boys in the class kept to themselves back in a corner by the windows, and as Mouse walked past the female artists on the way back there, he passed quite close to Abby Grit. He turned as he passed and had a quick look over her shoulder — her pastel of a field full of sunflowers was very pretty.

She turned and gave him a smile, something that had never happened before in all their schooldays together. Mouse waited a second, sure he would freeze at this unexpected attention, but no, he felt fine. "Hi, Abby. I like your picture. Is that field of flowers out at your farm?"

Abby replied, a little shyly, "Yes. It's down the hill from where I saw you last Saturday." Then her expression clouded. Looking a bit nervous, she added, "Mouse, I'm sorry my dad shot at you that day. I know you were trying to do the right thing."

Mouse didn't really want to talk about it, but he was thankful that she wasn't laughing anymore. "Thanks, Abby. I guess I sort of deserved what I got. At least he missed." Mouse added a wry smile and then continued on his way, threading past the girls toward his own easel at the back of the room. He glanced at other half-finished creations as he went and decided that Abby's was better that any of them.

Mouse sat down next to Pig, who was already hard at work on his giant picture of a turkey's head. He was working from memory, and Mouse was amazed at how well it was coming out. The bird stared directly out of the canvas, the reflection in its eye showing a hunter, dressed in red, with a shotgun on his shoulder. The hunter was looking away and seemed completely unaware of the old turkey staring at him. Mouse's own effort was much more commonplace. He was copying a picture by Norman Rockwell called *The Scoutmaster*. It looked OK, he guessed, but Pig's picture made his seem pretty plain. The turkey seemed to have some deeper meaning, and it was interesting to look at again and again.

"Hi, Pig. Your turkey looks good enough to eat."

"If you could catch the old fella'," said Pig with a smile. "I looked for him again after school yesterday, but never did find him." Then he looked over at Mouse and whispered, "I saw something else, though."

"What was that?" asked Mouse, picking up a 1B pencil and returning to the task of copying the next grid square from the picture to his rough sketch.

Pig's eyes returned to his artwork, where he resumed adding tiny gray feathers around the turkey's left eye. "When I got home from school, I followed the trail behind our barn down through the woods toward Toby. I saw three turkey buzzards floating on the thermals above the creek, then I found some raccoon tracks, and I heard a couple of squirrels arguing with each other up in some beech trees, but there was no sign of any turkeys. So I decided to check out the other side of the creek. I hopped across on the rocks and worked my way up Bear Run. I was moving real slow and quiet up the hill, on the side away from that old dump, when I saw them."

143

"You saw the turkeys?"

"No. I saw Simon Grit crawling on the dump."

Mouse had a sinking feeling. He stopped drawing. "What was he doing? Why was he crawling?"

"That confused me, too," said Pig. "There was a big ditch right up the middle of the dump, and he was climbing above that, up towards the top of the ravine."

"A ditch?"

"Yeah, it was weird, like he had moved all the stuff out of the way to make a path or something."

"Yeah, weird," said Mouse with as much conviction as he could muster. He knew what Grit was after — at best more silver dollars, at worst a treasure in coins.

"Yeah, and that's not all," Pig continued. "Chuck was out there too."

"Chuck!" said Mouse loudly. "What was Chuck doing out there?"

Pig laughed quietly, "I don't exactly know what he was *going* to do — he never got the chance. Grit stood up and shouted at him, and Chuck ran back to his car and got out of there fast. When Grit rose up out of that dump and started yelling, old Chucky must have been scared half to death."

Mouse didn't answer. He might not be sure what Grit was up to, but he knew exactly why his slimy cousin had been out there. Chuck had gone to retrieve the treasure.

Pig continued with his tale, unaware of Mouse's tense expression. "Then, Grit lost his balance and fell into the ditch, but he seemed to bounce and ended up down by the stream. The last I saw of him, he was limping up the hill toward his house holding his leg."

Mouse had only been half listening, but realized that he had to say something. "Was he hurt?"

"I just said he was. Not too bad though, and I was glad of that. Mr. Grit wouldn't have been pleased to see me, even if I was there to help him."

"Yeah, you're probably right. He'd think you were back to look for more coins," said Mouse.

"I wasn't, though," replied Pig, firmly. "I was looking for that old turkey. I never did find it, so I gave up after a while and just headed on home. Pretty good adventure, though, don't you think?"

"Yeah. Mystery and violence, too. All you need is some sex and you could sell your story to Hollywood for millions."

Pig smiled at that and then concentrated on his picture. Mouse did the same, mechanically copying the lines of the Scoutmaster picture to his own bigger version, but his thoughts were raging elsewhere.

After school Mouse headed for home, but then remembered the house would be empty, and so decided to swing up through the carnival. It had seemed like it would be fun to have the house to himself for ALF week, but after two days of it, he was finding the place lonely and depressing. He was used to his mom's company at the end of the day. He really enjoyed talking things over with her. He wasn't sure he wanted to tell her about the treasure or his problems with Chuck, but just having her around would have been comforting. As it was, he felt more and more like it was just him against the world.

Mouse dawdled at the carnival. The place was going full-tilt, and he saw many kids he knew from school enjoying the rides, playing the games of chance, and munching on food stand fare — elephant ears, cotton candy, funnel cakes, candy apples. He was so tempted by the apples that he scrounged his pockets for some money, and then sat on the courthouse steps to eat his sticky, red treat on a stick. Across the way, he saw a group of older guys heading for the baseball-pitching booth, and realized Chuck was among them. That started the whole miserable chain of thought going again.

He was sick of it, but powerless to stop it once it got started. Chuck knew everything Mouse did about the treasure, and he was not to be trusted. If Chuck had actually driven out there yesterday, then he meant to retrieve the sack of coins and bring it home. Once he had it, his cousin could say anything at all about how he found it, and Mouse would just sound like a spoilsport or a villain if he dared to disagree. Possession was nine-tenths of the law, like everybody always said. Chuck *might* have good intentions about sharing the cash or the glory, but years of experience with his cousin argued otherwise. Luckily, Chuck had not gotten the treasure yet. Grit had put a stop to that yesterday, and today he was here at the carnival. Mouse could still do something to stop him. But what?

And, what did Grit know? It seemed as though Chuck had almost led him to the hiding place where the treasure lay buried. Maybe Grit had figured out where Chuck was headed. But, no. Pig said that after Grit shouted at him, Chuck had gone away. If Grit had had any real idea what Chuck was up to, nothing would have stopped him from investigating further. So, that was good. But, Grit would probably be more determined than ever to scrounge that dump, now that he had seen Chuck there again. That was bad. If Grit found the treasure, would he keep it for himself, claiming perhaps that he had found it somewhere on his farm? Or, would he abide by the law and turn it in to the state?

Too many questions! They buzzed in his brain — made him dizzy. What should he do? What could he do? He didn't have a driver's license, let alone a car, and so could not retrieve the coins himself. It seemed like Grandpa Mike was his best hope for sound advice, and Grandpa Mike could take him out there to get the treasure, too, but Grandpa Mike wasn't the least bit interested. If his grandfather was talking to anybody, he was talking to Chuck. The night before Mouse had briefly gotten hold of his grandfather on the phone, but as soon as Mike had realized who it was, he had curtly told Mouse to stop with the calls; that he was too busy this week for boyish nonsense.

146

More and more, Mouse was coming to believe his grandfather would take Chuck's side in any dispute. The two of them were so very alike in many ways. Grandpa was an ex-football player and often bragged about his athletic grandson. The two lived across the street from each another, over by the glass plant, and Mouse knew the families were close. Mouse's mom was Mike's daughter, and Mouse supposed Mike loved her, but there was no denying his grandfather viewed her job at the university with suspicion and a certain amount of disdain. Mike had worked with his hands all his life, and had a distrust of money made in any other way. Mouse's dad and Grandpa Mike steered clear of one another for exactly the same reason. Mike thought that trotting the globe to sell technology was a crazy way to make a living.

No. The more Mouse thought about it, the less he liked his grandfather as the referee in any disagreement between himself and Chuck. But who else was there? Who could he trust to be fair and impartial?

Mouse had come to the end of the candy apple — only a browning core and a sticky stick remained. He had also come to the end of another agonizing round of consideration. What should he do about the coins? He was sick of the question, and suddenly he just wished the whole problem would go away. But, *no way* was he going to submit meekly to Chuck's taking credit for the discovery. Mouse would turn the money over to…. to who? The money was on State Game Lands, so that meant Mr. Grit — or did it? Ahh. Now there was a thought. Grit worked for the state. Grit would have a boss. Mouse could just skip over Grit and go to that man. Just let Chuck or even Grandpa try to argue with the State of Pennsylvania!

The courthouse bells rang 4 o'clock. They were directly overhead and very loud. Mouse peered up the violently foreshortened courthouse tower to double-check the time. Yup, 4 p.m. His eyes tracked down 100 feet of rusty, red brick, past the windows of the upper floors, and came to rest on huge double doors leading into the interior of the ancient building. The doors seemed to summon him. OK. It was time to do something about this whole sorry mess. Time to show a little initiative, time to show some backbone.

He climbed the white limestone steps and pulled with all his might at a massive door. It didn't move. Was it past closing time already? Then the door swung ponderously outward — not locked after all, just huge and very heavy. Inside, a second set of doors opened more easily, and he stood in the main hall of the building, gazing around in awe. The floor was covered with a pleasing pattern of earth tone and patterned tiles, and the ceiling was huge and very high. Tall black doors led off to various departments left and right. The place seemed made for giants.

He examined the curious labels that marked the function of each office that let off of the lobby — Tax Claim, Voter Registration, Prothonatary, Register and Recorder, Commissioners, Assessors. None of them seemed right. Prothonatary was the most confusing — it sounded like the name of an ogre. Who was Prothonatary?

What Mouse wanted was the State Game Lands department. What would that be called? He walked back and forth, peering shyly into the various offices, but could not see that one was any better than another for his purpose. On his third circuit he made up his mind to just start asking somewhere, though the prospect made him very nervous. He was no good at talking to people in positions of authority, and the courthouse must be full to the roof with such people. The place gave him the willies. He half-expected that, at any moment, a guard would appear and haul him off to face the vicious Prothonatary.

Mouse flicked with his tongue at dry lips and walked shakily into the last office on the right. He picked that one because it was farther from the front door than any of the others. Maybe they didn't get many visitors. Maybe they wouldn't bite his head off if he asked a few questions. The sign above the door said

"Assessors." He only had a vague notion of what that meant — something to do with taxes. Maybe.

Inside the door, a high L-shaped counter kept customers at bay. Beyond this were various desks, tables and mysterious cases. More cases stretched down the side of the room toward the back of the office. The walls were plastered with maps of Clarion County. The ceiling of the big room had originally been as high as the one in the lobby, but at some time in the past, someone had subdivided the room vertically to create a balcony of a different style that overhung most of the office. Mouse liked it. It gave the place more human proportions and was curious to see. That and the maps. Mouse was fascinated by the maps.

At the back of the room, a woman with very red hair, wearing a bright green dress, pounded away at a computer keyboard. She reminded Mouse a bit of his mom, though she looked preoccupied and unhappy. Mouse nerved himself to speak to her, but she was so far away, he would have to almost shout. He just couldn't bring himself to do something that extravagant. It would be like shouting in church.

The other occupant of the room was a whole lot closer, just the other side of the counter, in fact, seated at a desk by the windows, surrounded by stacks of maps. He was a middle-aged man, with a stocky build that was carrying a lot of meat — he was not quite fat, though. The man had thinning gray hair, wore very thick glasses and was remarkably sloppy. His clothes had an unpressed look, his hair was mussed and he had perhaps ten pencils shoved at various angles into his shirt pocket. All around him were scraps of paper covered with what looked to be numbers. Dozens of these had fallen to the floor, where they lay, looking like little square leaves fallen from some very strange tree. The sloppy man's attention was totally focused on creating more of these notes, and he seemed completely unaware of Mouse's presence. Mouse looked hard at the man and decided he liked it that way. There seemed something almost sinister about the man's total lack of interest in anything except his maps and his note taking.

Mouse stood quietly at the counter for half a minute, hoping the harassed woman would take notice of him. Soon he became a little embarrassed about being ignored, and so started examining the county map on the wall near the door.

After a couple of long minutes, Mouse sighed. It seemed he had somehow been rendered invisible inside this strange building of giants and foreign sounding names. Maybe he would just leave and look up the information he needed in a telephone book. He took a step out the door, and the red-haired woman's voice rang out, sharp and unpleasant.

"Bert, wake up. You have a customer!"

She sounded exasperated, as if this was far from the first time Bert had needed a nudge. Her duty done, the clatter of her hands on the keyboard resumed, and Mouse turned to see the rumpled man rise and move heavily toward the counter. He did not look angry in the least, just dazed and confused — as if waking from a dream.

"Hello, young man. What can we do for you?" And, he even managed a small smile, almost as if he really was interested in Mouse and his mission. Mouse felt himself warming to the man.

"Uh, I wanted to find out who runs the State Game Lands."

The man smiled winningly, "I can help you with that. Which of the State Game Lands did you want to check on?"

Mouse was confused. Check on? Had he said check on? What did the man mean? Mouse had to say something; he had to respond to the question somehow. He didn't know what State Game Lands and so blurted out, "Bear Run Campground?" and blushed furiously.

Amazingly, the man seemed to take that as a reasonable response. "Yes. I know where that is. Wait a minute and I'll get the map for you."

He walked to a nearby rack of hanging maps and shortly returned bearing a sheaf marked Paint Township. He opened it seemingly at random, chuckled and muttered to himself as he examined a map. Then he looked at another, then another. Mouse was confused. What was the man doing? Mouse wanted to run away, but couldn't. It was as if his feet were glued to the floor. His head spun. What was the man, Bert, looking for? What would be the next strange question? How much of a fool was he about to make of himself?

Finally, Bert stabbed a finger to paper and said, "Aha! Bear Run Campgrounds. That's right here! It looks like you were wrong about its being on State Game Lands, though. See how the property line follows this old road down to Toby Creek? North of that line *is* State Game Lands, but to the south it's private property."

Mouse looked where the finger rested on the map, and suddenly felt better. He could understand this map if he tried, but it was a funny thing — not like any map he had ever seen before. There were few topographic features marked, and it was drawn on a huge scale. Straight lines crisscrossed and divided its surface, and it was peppered with numbers and strange alphabetic notations. After a second though, the part where the finger rested suddenly made sense. Right. There was the road. There was Bear Run. So... there was where the mine was. Oh! Now that was interesting.

Mouse's fear and confusion were gone in an instant.

"I understand," he said. "The State Game Lands end at the road. What do these numbers mean?"

Bert smiled proudly, like this was something he had himself invented. "That's the plat number. We can use it to look up who owns a particular piece of property. Wait a second, I'll tell you."

Once again, Mouse was baffled. Tell me what? As the man puttered about among stacks of large books, Mouse again looked at the map. The mine did start on State Game Lands, but he was sure he had walked into it a good thirty feet. That would have carried him clear under the road. Suddenly, he remembered thinking at the time that he was under the campsite. So, the treasure had not been on State Game Lands after all. Who owned…

Bert returned holding a big book. He reversed it and laid it on the map so Mouse could see, and said, "Bear Run Campground is owned by Theopholis Sweet." He looked up at Mouse and added, "That would be Judge Sweet. His office is upstairs."

A long-suffering voice came from the back of the room, "Judge Sweet retired five years ago, Bert. Anyway, the young man wants to know how to get in touch with the State Game Commission, not the boundary lines or owner of some campground in the middle of the woods. Why don't you listen to what people ask?"

"Uh, sorry, I guess I was thinking about something else. Thanks, Edna," replied Bert. Those were the words, but Mouse heard the despair. For how many years had Edna been correcting Bert, picking away at his self-confidence? Mouse bet it was more than a few. It didn't seem fair for Edna to peck at Bert like that. Not everyone could be perfect.

Mouse said, "Don't be sorry. You answered the question I should have asked. This changes everything. Thank you very much, sir." He said it loudly, so Edna would understand the statement was meant for her as well as for Bert.

Bert's smile returned. There seemed to be a twinkle in his eye as well. Finally he had scored on Edna. "You're quite welcome. Is there anything else I can do for you?"

"Yes. Is this address here where I would find Judge Sweet?"

"Yes, indeed. That's where we send the tax bills, so that's where you would find him. 501H Main Street. That's the Hahne Building. You can see it from our windows."

"The Hahne Building?"

"Yes, it's across the street. It's that big old yellow building on the corner of Fifth and Main. The one with Bob's Sub in it. That's the Hahne Building. Judge Sweet's office would be upstairs, I believe, isn't that right, Edna?"

"Yes," was her curt reply. Mouse glanced over. Edna did not look happy. Good.

Mouse remembered now. They had *said* Judge Sweet owned the land at the opening ceremony. That's the man he needed to talk to.

"Thank you very much, sir. That is all I needed to know."

"Certainly, young man. Come back any time," said Bert with much satisfaction.

As Mouse pushed at the giant doors to escape the courthouse, he was still smiling — at Bert's small victory over Edna, and because he now knew something Chuck and Grit did not. Judge Sweet was the man to see.

Mouse found an inconspicuous door, marked Dancer's Studio, at the side of the great square yellow-brick building. Just inside was another door leading to the right. The smell alone told him it was a back way into Bob's Subs. Straight ahead was a steep and long set of stairs leading upwards. He climbed. They turned at a landing and led him higher still. As he went, his elation of a few minutes before vanished. He knew what Judge Sweet looked like, but was suddenly very worried about how the man would receive news that treasure on his land had been removed and hidden away. This wasn't Bert he would be dealing with this time. This man was a judge or, at least, had been a judge. This man had more authority than anyone Mouse had ever spoken to in his entire life. He felt trembly and weak, but forced himself up the stairs.

Mouse timidly pushed open the door at the top; half expecting the judge would command the entire floor, that busy secretaries would be rushing to and fro, that telephones would be ringing frantically for attention. Strangely, though, all was quiet. He stood in a large lobby covered with well-worn wall-to-wall carpet. The place did not have a prosperous air. He started looking for the judge's office and found some dancing practice rooms, and the offices of the Clarion Arts Council, but no Judge Sweet. Mouse was very relieved. He couldn't help it if Judge Sweet wasn't up here. At least he had tried.

Then he noticed the dark hallway. Surely, a judge wouldn't be back in there. He felt compelled to check, though, and as he walked down the dim passage, past long-ago sealed and painted-over doors, into the deeper gloom at the end of the hall, he became aware of the smell. Cigar smoke. Mouse's heart began to race. He didn't like this. He hated talking to strangers, especially men. He wanted to turn and leave before it was too late, but his feet carried him on toward the last door on the right. Old gilt letters on opaque glass announced:

Theopholis Sweet
Attorney at Law

Mouse's mouth went dry. He swallowed, trying to think of how he would start this conversation. He wanted to walk quickly and quietly away. And, it came to him — quick and quiet, just like a mouse. Nerving himself, he raised his right hand and knocked three times.

A single loud word knifed back at him through the door, "Come!"

Mouse turned the knob, pushed the door open and entered a different world. Currents of cigar smoke floated in sunlight that entered the large room through four immense double-hung windows with arched tops. The smell was horrible. Mouse's eyes started to water; his nose began to itch. He sneezed, and the smoke swirled away momentarily. The ceiling of the office must have been 15 feet high, and bookcases full of hundreds of what he took to be legal volumes lined the walls. Here and there, a picture was set on one of the shelves, and these seemed to be mostly of horses. The floor was covered by a well-worn red oriental rug. At the center of the large room sat a massive desk made of dark wood, much of its surface covered with neatly placed books and stacks of papers. At the very center of the desk, the offensive cigar lay in a cut-glass ashtray, sending an expanding column of gray smoke upwards into the cloud that filled the upper air of the office.

Behind the huge desk sat Judge Sweet. He wore a dark, striped business suit, white shirt, and a thin red and black tie. It was the same man all right — the old gentleman from the camporee. This was no Boy Scout leader, though. This man looked every inch a judge, and Mouse was petrified. What did he dare tell this man? That he had stolen a treasure from his land? No! That would take far too much explaining. What crazy notion had brought him up here without a plan?

Mouse felt Judge Sweet eyes examining him closely. He was waiting for Mouse to speak, but Mouse didn't have the faintest idea what to say, or even how to begin. He had to say something, though. Anything!

Finally, the old man cracked a small, resigned smile and said, "Well, what are you selling, young man?"

15

Theo Sweet examined the young man. The boy's eyes had gone wide at his question, so evidently he wasn't selling anything. Nonetheless, Theo had a feeling the boy had not shown up at his door purely by accident. The kid was mighty slow at responding, but that was all right — gave him time to look him over. Let's see, he was five foot nine and weighed about 130 pounds. He had a slight build and was dressed for school in khaki pants, dark polo shirt and lightweight blue jacket. The clothes looked to be of good quality. He had dark brown hair, an honest enough face and looked vaguely familiar. White sneakers and one of those monstrous backpacks that kids hauled around these days completed his outfit. He seemed a presentable young person, but was obviously terrified, uncomfortable or just tongue-tied. Theo wondered which it was. He thought of himself as a kindly man — was good with children, gave to his church, and so on. So what was it about him that made people get nervous and sweaty?

Ah, the silent one was about to speak.

"You are Judge Sweet?" The voice was thin and a trifle high pitched, lacked confidence, but there was no doubting the tone. The boy knew full well to whom he was speaking.

Theo smiled to put the boy at ease. "Yes. And your name is?"

"My name is Albert Monroe," more confidence now.

"Albert is a pretty awful name," said Theo by way of getting the conversational ball rolling. "What do your friends call you, 'Al'?"

"No sir, everybody calls me Mouse."

"Mouse is an unusual name, isn't it? I never heard it before last weekend, and now here you are, another one! It seems as if all of a sudden the world is overrun with mice."

The boy seemed stunned by this bit of humor, and so Theo continued, "That other Mouse took a bunch of misfits and small fry, and just about won the Clarion County Camporee. You should have seen those Boy Scouts go!"

The lad smiled for the first time, and Theo thought, that's better. "Ah, so you are *that* Mouse — the famous one. You should be pleased. You ran your patrol pretty well. I especially liked the trick with the crude that won you the string burn. That was nicely thought out. You have got a head on your shoulders."

Theo Sweet paused then added, "What brings you here today, Mouse?"

The boy was the slightest bit more relaxed now, and answered after only a short hesitation, "When we were out at Bear Run we found something, and since it was on your land, I thought I should talk to you about it."

Theo smiled. Now he understood. "That's OK. You can keep it. People find them all the time. I have a jar full around here somewhere. Kurt Snelling up at the university once told me they are between 5 and 10 thousand years old."

The kid got that frozen look again. Theo wondered what it was he had said, but plowed ahead anyway.

"Do you have it with you?" he asked.

"Have it with me?" stammered the boy.

"Do you have the arrowhead you found with you?"

The boy's look of confusion held for another moment and then disappeared as though he had just remembered something.

157

He jammed hand in pocket and after some hunting, came up with half an arrowhead. Theo took the chipped piece of stone and examined it closely.

"Yes, that's part of one, anyway. Keep it. Years from now, you'll stumble across it among your junk and remember the campout where you found it.

"When I was Scoutmaster of the troop the boys found them all the time. That and other things, too. One time one of my Scouts even found an old silver dollar down along Bear Run. He wanted to sell it, and I had to practically order him to keep it. I even made it into a neckerchief slide for him. He still wears it today. Maybe that's what you ought to do with your arrowhead."

"Was that Mike Wing who found the coin?" asked the boy.

"Yes, it was. I guess you must know him. He is still an assistant Scoutmaster with the troop, I believe."

"Yes, sir. He is also my grandfather."

"Oh! Well then, you and I are related. Mike Wing is my second cousin. Here, sit down, cousin Mouse. Call me judge. Most everyone does, even though now I am just an old retired judge. OK?"

Mouse hesitated, then said, "OK... judge."

Theo smiled and reached out to shake hands. No wonder Mouse had looked familiar. There was still some of the old Sweet blood in there somewhere. Mouse was looking happier now, and Theo, too, was pleased at their connection.

Mouse said, "About that coin. Why do you think that coin was down along the run? Who would throw something like that away?"

Theo knew the answer to that one. "There used to be an Indian trail that led across the old farm and then on down the hill to Empire Furnace. Did you see the ruins of the furnace down by Toby while you were out there, Mouse? No? Well, it's still down there, unless it evaporated. Anyway, I figure that one of the men coming or going along that trail just dropped the coin, and there it lay for years on end, until Mike stumbled onto it."

158

Mouse didn't look convinced and asked, "When was the furnace last used?"

"Well, it was an iron furnace. There were about 30 of them in the county at one time or another. They made a kind of rough product called pig iron that was floated down to Pittsburgh for further refining. If I remember correctly, the last of them went out of business about 1870, but Empire Furnace was blown out way before that. Say about 1845. I know because that is when my great-great-grandfather came into possession of the land. He was your ancestor too, but you better add a few more 'greats' if you want to brag about him." Theo smiled. He enjoyed talking about the old days, especially with family.

Mouse took the information in stride and stuck to the point he wanted to make, "The coin that Grandpa Mike wears has a date of 1878."

Theo frowned wryly, "Oh, well then forget the furnace theory. By 1878, the furnace was gone, the farm was gone and nobody at all lived out that way. They did discover oil about 1885, up at that well you saw, but probably that bunch would never have walked the Indian trail. They were hard workers, hard boozers — not interested in anything except the next well and the next bottle of Monongahela Bitters. Did you see that awful dump? Well, I think it was the oil crew that got *that* started, but I don't figure any of them were throwing silver dollars down into it."

"Would the people who run the historical museum know about something like that?" asked Mouse.

Theo heard the courthouse clock strike 5 o'clock. Interesting though it was, he had better wrap this up. Maggie would be expecting him home soon to get ready for the pop concert down at Immaculate Conception Church. He stood up, saying, "They might, but I doubt it. Probably your best bet on something like that would be for Mike to take the coin to Gus Comstock over at Comstock's Coins. Gus is a bit strange, but if anyone could tell him more about the history of his coin and how it came to be out

159

in the woods, it would be Gus." Then, Theo held out his hand for a second time. "Well, Mouse, it's been a pleasure to meet you. I have got to go now, but do come up again. I can tell you lots of interesting things about your ancestors. Maybe you would like to bring one of your friends, and we could go out and have a look at the old furnace some time."

Mouse's hand was not man-sized, but his handshake was firm enough. The boy turned to leave and Theo added, "Hang on; I'll walk down with you."

They walked across the sad carpet, pounded limp by thousands of tiny dancers' feet, and down the long steep stairs. The boy was pretty quiet. Theo could tell there was still something on his mind, but didn't have the faintest idea how to pry it out of him. The direct approach didn't somehow seem appropriate, so he just talked to Mouse about this and that. One of the things he learned was that Mouse lived in the old Biltstetter mansion, just a block short of his own, more modest, Victorian on Liberty Street. The kid's family must have some money if they could afford to heat that old monster.

They walked down the alley and soon came to a brightly colored crowd of costumed children and fretting parents gathered at the municipal parking lot.

"That will be the Kiddies Parade getting organized," said Theo. "Are you in that?"

Mouse snorted, "Not since I was little."

Then, Theo saw the sign and started expounding on one of his pet gripes, "See the name on that banner? The *Kentucky Fried Chicken Kiddies Parade*? What kind of a name it that? It almost sounds like 'Chicken Kidneys'. And the festival! What was wrong with *Autumn Leaf* as a name? Now all the signs call it *The National City Autumn Leaf Festival*. Why can't these organizations just give a contribution and be done with it? Why do they have to plaster their names all over everything? Where will it all end?"

Mouse thought briefly, then smiled and said, "*The Clarion Beverages Pop Concert*?"

"Ha, very good," chuckled Theo. "How about *Sam's Wrecking Airplane Rides*?"

Mouse grinned, "*The Clarion Chiropractic Dodge-em Cars.*"

Theo smiled. The kid was quick.

Theo looked at the crowd getting ready to march, and was pleased to see a face he knew. "Good afternoon, Mr. Grit. I see that you are contributing a large contingent to the parade."

The man turned from straightening a little girl's princess costume. He started to smile, then his eyes darted to the side and the smile faded a good deal.

"Good afternoon, judge," Grit replied, but there was no joy in it, and Mr. Grit was suddenly very busy adjusting his girl's costume.

Theo and Mouse walked on, Theo thinking something was funny about Grit's reaction. Something to do with Mouse, it seemed. Theo swiveled his eyes to glance at Mouse's face — same thing there. Mouse looked distracted, confused, like he was trying to sort something out.

The two continued their walk, but each was now wrapped in his own thoughts as they reached Liberty and strolled past fine old homes, and maples ablaze with color. Shortly, they came to the old relic where Mouse lived and said their good-byes.

Theo continued on down the street, still thinking about the mysterious boy. For some reason, he had come away with the distinct impression that Mouse Monroe was in some sort of trouble. He tried to fit the bits and pieces together into some sort of hypothesis, but nothing popped out, and as he turned onto his own walk, he shrugged — more facts were needed. The only thing he was absolutely sure of was that Mouse Monroe had not come knocking on his office door to talk about a broken arrowhead.

161

16

Wednesday afternoon at 3:15, Abby Grit stepped lightly down from the school bus and followed her smaller brothers and sisters as they scampered ahead toward the house. This was one of those days when her mom had school business at the end of the day, and so Abby was once again in charge of the house and the little kids. She didn't look forward to it with much enthusiasm, but at least her dad would be around somewhere if the small fry got out of control. The girls never gave any trouble. It was the boys who were a pain. Luckily, a threat to "go get dad" was almost always enough to keep them in line.

The TV was already on by the time she walked in the front door, and she quickly settled the dispute over what they would watch by putting *The Lion King* in the VCR. They had seen it a hundred times, but seemed content to watch it yet again. She didn't begin to understand why, but was happy to have a little time to herself.

Abby took her things up to her room and changed into her grubbies, then went to report their safe arrival home, after yet another harrowing day at school. She had not seen her father in any of the fields as they walked up the lane, and that usually meant he could be found in the barn, so she went out there first. The place was noisy with agitated chickens and the mooing of cows. She fed a little hay to Flying Top, her favorite filly, then visited the loft, but saw no sign of her father. That puzzled her. She stepped back outside and circled the barn, searching the fields with restless eyes. All was green and quiet. Her dad's truck was where it should be; he must be around somewhere. She wasn't worried, well maybe just the slightest bit — he had been acting strangely the past couple of days.

As Abby walked out toward the high cornfield, she thought more about her father. Lately he seemed distracted. The strangest things startled him. First off, there were those boys at the Autorama. He seemed to know them, but had acted funny with them. It was almost like he was trying to soothe and quiet them. That was not at all the way *her* father dealt with children. Then, on Monday, he had gotten that mysterious gash that he tried to keep secret. Abby was still unclear about how the accident happened. They had not even known it was anything other than a scratch until Tuesday morning. Her mother had found blood on the sheets of their bed, and then there had been some uproar! Abby never got to see the wound, but based on the sharpness of her mother's voice, and the hurried departure of her father for the emergency room, it must have been pretty bad. Later in the day, she found out the gash in her father's thigh was eight inches long. That sure sounded huge.

Finally, there was the incident last night. The whole family had gone to the Kiddies Parade. Nancy and Terry wore princess outfits with veils and conical hats, and looked very pretty. George and Peter, dressed as woodsmen, looked just like the ruffians they were. It should have been a good time, but Abby could tell her father's heart wasn't in it. It was as if his thoughts were a million miles away. Then, while they were making final adjustments to the girl's costumes, Mouse Monroe and a neatly dressed older man had walked by. Her father had gotten very agitated after he saw them; his mood changing from distraction to depression. Why? Who would be scared of Mouse Monroe? — certainly not the man who had called him an idiot and chased him off the farm just last Saturday.

After Mouse and the old gentleman had gone, her father turned to her and asked, "Wasn't that the same kid I chased away?"

"Yes," Abby replied, "That's Mouse Monroe. He's in my grade at school."

Her dad glowered, "That boy is trouble."

That hardly seemed fair, but she let it pass, and asked, "Was that his grandfather he was with?"

Her father's eyes widened, "I don't think so. That was Judge Sweet. I have testified before him a couple of times on poaching cases. He's retired now, but still has an office uptown somewhere." He tried to speak casually, but Abby heard a tenseness in his voice that seemed odd. Something about seeing the pair together had badly upset her father.

Abby reached the top of the hill and could now see pretty much the whole farm. Her father was nowhere in sight. Why was he acting so strangely? It had begun last weekend, when Mouse had scared the deer, or maybe just after that — maybe it had something to do with the Boy Scouts being camped out at Bear Run. It was only 100 yards down the hill to where the path to the campground began at the corner of the field. It would be odd to find him down there, but she was out of ideas and becoming very concerned. If her dad was down in the ravine, she would likely be able to spot him from the hill above. If he wasn't, well she would just go back to the house and wait for him or Mom to return. What was happening to her dad?

Abby followed the trail in under the maples at the edge of the field. It was nice in there. The autumn leaves reminded her of colorful lace, and the chuckle of the stream below sounded friendly and welcoming. It was pleasant and cool, and just fifty feet along, she spotted her father's red shirt. He was downstream a hundred yards, up in the old dump. She was relieved and suddenly very curious. What in the world was he up to down there?

Abby didn't *try* to sneak up on him, but the chatter of the water masked the slight sounds of her approach, and his back was to her. For some reason, he was poking down through the rubble with a long stick. What was he doing?

She spoke loud enough for her voice to carry up to him.

"Hello, Daddy. We're home."

He jerked around and nearly lost his balance, but after teetering for a second, he was suddenly all right. He worked his way down through the rubble, greatly favoring his wounded leg, and soon joined her on the trail that ran below the dump.

"Hi, Sweet Pea. I guess I lost track of the time. What are the kids doing?" He sounded too cheerful. Abby thought he was trying to distract her from asking what he had been doing. What was going on down here? This was really getting to be too much!

"The kid's are watching *The Lion King*, and I have been looking everywhere for you," she said accusingly. "Why were you poking in the dump with that stick? Are you looking for something?"

Her dad laughed bitterly. He didn't sound quite right.

"That'd be a waste of time. Who could find anything in this mess? All I've found are a few worthless curiosities. Want to see?"

He showed her a small pile of artifacts salvaged from the rolling mountain of junk. There was an old-fashioned eggbeater, a radio that had the word "Emerson" on it, some tarnished spoons and some rusty tools. A few of the items looked all right and that puzzled her.

"How come this stuff isn't rusted or broken like everything else?" she asked.

"Most of it was under something bigger that protected it from the weather."

"I really like the eggbeater. Could you fix it?" she asked.

He considered the bent-up object. "Yes, I suppose I could, but who would want an old thing like that?"

Abby, wasn't sure either, but found she was fascinated by the things he had selected. She looked around and found something for herself. "Look! A salt shaker!"

He smiled a nice normal smile and motioned with a finger for her to add it to his stack of stuff. That started her going. She walked down the path, examining the heaps of trash, peering under things, sometimes moving small items aside with a stick. It was fun — sort of like shopping, sort of like hunting treasure, even if it was all worthless old junk. Then, she had a worrying thought and paused, "Are there snakes in here?"

"Haven't seen any, yet. Look! A toaster!" and he held up his find, grinning. This was more like the dad she knew and loved. They continued poking around for another five minutes, and she was surprised at how quickly the pile of interesting things grew. As she continued hunting, she realized he had not been looking for this kind of stuff when she first arrived. If he had, the pile would have been much bigger.

Abby rolled a heap of cans to one side and saw something good. She picked it up and held it high, "Look! An old coin!"

Well, that sure brought him running. He took it, buffed it clean on his shirt and held it out so they both could examine it. The head of a woman with old-fashioned hair stared off to the left. This was surrounded by a circle of stars. Above the woman, there were some letters that Abby could not make out, but she could read the date below well enough — 1878.

"Beginner's luck," said her father, sounding bitter again.

"What do you mean?" she asked.

"Well, it just seems like everybody can find these coins but me. First it was those Scouts, and now you come waltzing in, and in minutes, you find what I couldn't find in days."

Abby was confused but pleased too. Now she was getting somewhere. "Why do you want to find coins? Are they worth a lot of money? Er, I mean they are money, but are they worth a lot because they are so old?"

Her father didn't speak for a minute. He just stood there rubbing at the coin with his thumb, considering. Then he handed it back to her, tilted his head to one side, smiled broadly and said, "What the hell. Follow me."

He hobbled up the path to Beer Can Falls, then past that, up into an area where rocks the size of large dogs dotted the banks of the stream. She followed along behind, still startled at his having used the 'H' word. Her father never talked that way.

They came to a space the size of a large blanket that was clear of big rocks. At its center was a darkened spot, surrounded by three smaller stones that looked like places to sit. He gathered a very small heap of sticks and lit them to make a fire. It was a very, very tiny fire, but that seemed to be what he wanted.

Finally, he motioned for her to sit on one of the stones, and said, "A hat full of fire. Papa always said that was all any real woodsman ever needed."

"Papa?"

"Yes, Papa. My grandfather. When I was a kid, I lived on this same farm with my parents and my grandfather. My father was a tough man who worked all day, every day, but my grandfather loved the woods and would often take me for long walks in the countryside hereabouts. He constantly pointed out the different trees and flowers to me, and was a great one for poking into every nook and cranny, every crevice or hole in the ground. As I grew older, I came to realize that he was searching for something."

"What was it?" asked Abby. "Coins?"

"One sunny spring day, I finally asked him. I was about 10 at the time. That's when he brought me to this place. He called it the Indian's Rock Garden. He made a little bit of a fire and sat me down. Then, he reached up under this rock here, like so, to where there is a crack you can't see, and he pulled out this."

Her father held his hand low beside the crackling fire, and its orange light danced across the surface of a coin. He flipped it over with an expert flick of his thumb, and there was the woman again. Now Abby could easily read the letters at the top, "E.PLURIBUS.UNUM." The letters were all run together. Below was the date — 1878.

"It has the same date as the one I found," she exclaimed.

"Yeah, I know, and it's the same with the ones the Scouts found. I don't know why."

She looked at the shining coin. "This one looks almost new. It's not scratched or dented at all, and the letters aren't worn down."

Her father smiled. "That's because it has never been lost. It's been tucked in that crevice since before I was born, safe from weather and wear."

"Did your Papa put it there, Daddy?"

"Yes. And, he and I searched for years for the rest of them, but never found a thing. Now all of a sudden every kid who happens to look at the ground is finding them. I just can't figure it out." He shook his head and looked confused.

Abby didn't understand. "How many are there?"

Her dad smiled, "Counting yours there are seven now, but if the story is true there should be a whole bag of them."

"What story is that, Daddy?"

Her father didn't answer immediately. He just sat there with a sort of sad, far away look in his eyes. Abby was half convinced he was close to tears.

Finally, he spoke. "Every time we would go out looking for the treasure, the first stop was always here. Papa would build his hatful of heat, retrieve the coin, and then tell the tale as we sat looking at the firelight dance off of the silver dollar. I heard the story so many times, I can tell it like he was still sitting here himself...

* * *

"When I was eight, me and my family moved to this place. The year was 1883. We spent the spring and summer fixing up the old house that was here even then, and then started clearing the scrub timber from the land, so Pa could get a farm going the

168

following spring. Pa and Mother were always around, and sometimes I would help him, and sometimes I would help her. They didn't mind the work. To them it was a great adventure, and I was happy because they were happy.

"My mother's name was Fanny, and in October of '85, her father died. She went away to be with her kin for a few weeks — to lay the old man to rest, and such — but Pa and I stayed behind to tend to the farm. I was 10 years old that year.

"One night, a huge storm shook the house and slammed the shutters until near dawn, and when I went out to fetch the water that morning, I found the body of an old ragged-dressed man. He was covered with dirt and looked like he had crawled up out of a grave. I was a good deal upset and ran for Pa right away, and then I watched as he rolled the body over and put his ear to the dead man's mouth. Suddenly he sat up, and said, 'He's still breathing.'

"The man groaned with pain when we started moving him, and Pa said it looked like he had got himself crushed somehow. I held the feet, and Pa wrapped his arms around the man's body, and we carried the poor old fellow indoors to my bed. Pa did his best to make the man easy, and then he went for the doctor over to Startown. I was to stay behind and watch over the man. I remember I wasn't scared at all. I was more like sorry for the old guy; he was banged up so bad.

"For over an hour, I sat there in the quiet room, listening to the clock tick, and the cows complain because we hadn't tended to them yet. I was sitting on the bed and sometimes would squeeze a few drops of water onto the man's lips from a handkerchief dipped in a bowl of water. Mostly, though, I just sat still and watched, wondering what had happened to the poor old guy. I had never seen a man so old, never seen a dying man, but I knew, somehow I knew, that the man lying there was not long for this earth.

"It scared me some when the old man's eyes opened, and he started staring around every which way. Finally he saw me, and

169

then he began to whisper something in a hoarse voice I could barely hear. I couldn't make sense of it. It was just a bunch of words — Startown, ambush, deputies, dark trails, bag of coins, heavy, treasure in mine, black man. Then the old fellow's eyes flew wide open, and clear as day, he said, 'The man, the man. Save Jakey.' He said that again and again, and I didn't know what to say — what to do. Then he started pawing weak-like at his pockets, looking for something — looking hard for something. Like he was scared.

"By the time Pa and the doctor got back, the man had slid off, and we never did find out who he was, but I never forgot those words the old guy said just before the end. I practiced them in my mind, so I wouldn't forget them. I told Pa about what he said, but Pa just said that pain would make a man say strange things. He thought the guy was some old oil field Johnny who walked off a cliff in the night and dragged himself up into our front yard to die. Pa said the words were just the ravings of a dying man. I never believed that, but my Pa was not someone who I ever argued with. I never showed him what the man gave me — trusted to me. I had promised. He was gasping for breath; there were tears in his eyes. He pressed it hard into my hand, and cried out, 'Hide it, hide it. Tell no one! Promise!" And, I had promised.

*   *   *

Abby waited for more, but that was all there was. She sat there thinking about the strange, sad story. She tried to think what she would have done, but no answer came to mind. Finally she asked, "Where was the treasure? Where was it from? Who was Jakey?"

Her father snapped out of his reverie and laughed. "Good questions. I must have heard that story thirty times, and at the end of it, I was always fired up to get out into the woods and find that treasure. By the time I first heard the story, Jakey, whoever he was, must have been long dead, but Papa was always a little sad that he had not been able to find and help him."

170

Abby heard something over the hiss of the stream and the scratch of leaves overhead, and suddenly she was filled with dread.

"Daddy, that's the dinner bell. Mom must be home. We had better get up there. The kids have been alone an awful long time."

Abby was surprised when her father did not immediately leap to his feet and tear off up the hillside. Surely, they would be in lots of trouble. The movie must have ended long ago, and who knew what mischief the boys had gotten up to. Why was her dad just sitting there with his eyes narrowed? They had to hurry! Tonight was the fire truck rides, and they had to eat first. They were in enough trouble already. They should be running up the hill instead of just sitting here.

Finally, after what seemed an age, her father spoke.

"Abby, we have got to play this smart to stay out of trouble, but I think I can keep us both out of the hot water. Will you do what I say?"

"Sure Dad, but I think we had better hurry. Mom will be *awful* mad."

He smiled, "OK, but let's hurry smart. You go back down to the dump and get as many of those old things we found as you can carry. Bring them up the trail and meet me at the top, just before it breaks from the woods. Do you understand?"

"I don't understand," said Abby, shaking her head. "How is that going to keep us out of hot water?"

Her father's smile broadened, "Don't worry, Sweet Pea. I know your mother better than you do. Trust me. I'll put out the fire and meet you at the top, and then we'll walk home together carrying the antiques we found."

"Antiques? It's just junk, Dad," exclaimed Abby.

He laughed, "One man's trash is another man's treasure," then he got serious and added, "Look, Abby, whatever you do, don't tell your mother about the coins, or there will be hell to pay. Got it?"

"Yes, Dad. I sure hope this works."

"Trust me," was all he said.

And so she did. As she raced back to the dump, Abby wondered if her father was going to keep saying "hell" a lot around her. It made her feel grown up, but still, somehow it didn't seem right.

She scooped up the saltshaker, eggbeater and the spoons, and then decided she needed more. The radio made for a very large load, but she managed it somehow, and arrived at the top of the hill just as he father limped out of the leafy rhododendrons on the left. He took the radio off her hands, and then, bravely as she could manage, she marched beside her dear father toward the homestead and her waiting mother.

17

Mouse hurried through his homework and then got into his Class A uniform. He was surprised to find that it had been washed. For days now, he had felt as though he was living alone in the big old house, but somehow his mom had found time away from her job, away from the food stand, to worry about how he would look at the fire truck rides tonight.

He was just leaving the house at 4:30, when there she was, coming up the walk, shouldering her books from school and some groceries too.

"Hi, Mom," he said. "Thanks for washing my uniform."

"You're welcome, Mouse. It smelled like smoke, and I didn't think you would like to wear it that way."

Mouse laughed happily, "Especially not to the fire hall. I might have set off the alarms."

She smiled warmly at his little joke. Mouse loved to see her smile.

"Honey, are you getting along all right without me or your father around? I worry that you are alone too much."

"It's OK, Mom. I'm doing OK. I've got to hurry right now though, or I'll be late."

"Go ahead, honey. I have to hurry, too. There are vegetarians to feed up on Main Street. Next week, though, when things quiet down, we'll spend some time together. Can you make it that long?"

"Sure, Mom. I have got to go now, though. See you later. Thanks again for the uniform."

Mouse hurried down Liberty, up across Main to Wood, and then down half a block to the fire hall. The line for the rides was already forming. The three big roll-up doors into the truck garage were still closed tight, so he went in through a side entrance.

Inside, preparations for the evening's events were already well underway. The three trucks that were normally housed in this space had already been moved outside, and the Scouts were in the process of setting up large folding tables in a giant "U" shape. The crowd would slowly walk around the "U" as they waited to board a pumper. Mouse pitched in, and the tables were soon in place. Then, he and the rest of the Scorpion Patrol sat on the concrete floor close to where long rows of fireman suits hung from hooks along the wall. Pig was also a Scorpion, and Mouse sat next to him and watched as Paxton talked to Mr. Ellsworth and a man dressed in a very official-looking, very black uniform.

Finally, Paxton gave a nod, and the two men walked away. Then, he turned to face the patrols seated along the walls. It was a good turn out. Most of the thirty Scouts in the troop were here tonight — a lot more than had been camping the previous weekend. The ride at the end of the night just for troop members was always popular, and the fact that working at the fire truck rides counted as community service for First or Second Class didn't hurt either.

"Patrol leaders, front and center," said Paxton in a loud, authoritative voice. Lee Hamlin, patrol leader of the Scorpions, scrambled to his feet and joined the other leaders around Paxton. The senior patrol leader looked them over, and then turned to face toward where Mouse and Pig sat watching.

"Mouse, you too!" he commanded, and Mouse scrambled up and joined the leadership group.

Paxton looked at him and said, "I know you are not an official patrol leader, Mouse, but we need one more patrol for tonight. Do you think that you and the Mice could handle it?"

Mouse wondered what "it" was, but then figured he and the Mice could probably handle anything short of actually driving the trucks, so he said, "Sure," pleased to once again be trusted with a leadership role by Paxton.

"Good man," said Paxton. "OK, guys. I have just been talking with Mr. Ellsworth and Chief Williams, and here is how it's gonna be. The Wolves are the oldest, so they will help people get in and out of the trucks. There will be two trucks and each load should be about 20 people.

"The Flaming Arrows will handle the sign-in station and look for people who may have special needs. If anything crops up in that line, I want to hear about it.

"The Scorpions will handle the equipment station, explaining how air tanks work and the use of various pieces of field equipment. Mr. Williams will be down there shortly to tell you what you need to know.

"The Porcupines will handle the food and drink station. Make sure nobody gets more than their share. We have a lot of people to feed tonight, so make sure the cookies last. You guys have to keep the drink dispensers full too. When one starts to get a little low, fill it up immediately, so they never run dry at the same time."

John Grubber of the Porcupines asked, "What is it we are drinking?"

"Bug juice, of course. Red Kool-Aid."

"OK, we can handle that."

Paxton turned to Mouse. "That leaves the Mice. You guys are in charge of literature. You'll find stacks of it down at the far corner of the garage. Read it all and pass it out to the people as they come by your station. Got it, Mouse?"

Mouse was disappointed. It was not a very interesting job compared to the rest, but it made sense. His patrol could hardly expect one of the good jobs. The Mice were hardly a patrol at all, just a pickup group from a weekend campout. Oh, well, at least they would be together.

"Yes, we can do that," he said.

"Good," said Paxton. "Now get busy. The doors open in 15 minutes."

As the other leaders returned to their patrols, Mouse realized he did not have a patrol to return to. Pig was with the Scorpions, Beaner and Jim were Porcupines, Bobby Carfield and Pee Wee were Flaming Arrows. Should he get Paxton to call them together? No! He didn't want a nursemaid. It was his job to manage his patrol. That was what leadership was about. He could round them up one by one, but then he would have to explain the situation three separate times. That was way too slow. He now stood alone at the center of the floor, and he was nervous about it, but he knew just what to do. Turning to survey the Scouts, he said in a very loud voice, "Mice Patrol, front and center."

He had calculated his tone to match the way Paxton would have done it. Someone among the Wolves laughed, and Mouse could just guess who that was. He glanced over that way to be sure and found he was right. Chuck was standing among the older Scouts, still laughing, like something was hilarious. Mouse didn't care about Chuck. His cousin wasn't even wearing a uniform, just shorts and a camp T-shirt — some Scout he was! And, he was the only one of them laughing.

Pig came walking over and said, "What's up?"

Beaner and Jim, Pee Wee and Bobby were just a few steps behind, and soon Mouse had the whole crew sorting through flyers and reading up on the information that they contained. There was one on fire safety in the woods, one on fire hazards around the home, something about electricity and downed power lines, and a couple on how to become a firefighter.

It was Pee Wee who rebelled, "This is all good information, but it's sort of boring. We need to do a demonstration to get the people interested."

Mouse knew just what he meant, but he had orders to carry out, and they didn't include any demonstrations. "Sorry, Pee Wee, but this is what we have been asked to do, and Paxton is counting on us to do it as well as we can."

Pee Wee was undeterred, "Yeah, but if we had a good demonstration, people would be more interested in reading this stuff. That would mean we were doing a better job, right?"

At first, Mouse just wanted to tell Pee Wee to be quiet, but then he reconsidered and said, "OK, you're probably right, but what kind of a demonstration could we do?"

Pee Wee's eyes lit up. "We could put some water on the floor and then put a wire in it and..."

Mouse laughed, "No way, Pee Wee. People have come here for a ride, not an electrocution."

"How about a campfire then? We could show them how to light a ..."

"Forget it, Pee Wee. That's as bad as the last one. No indoor campfires, right?"

That silenced Pee Wee for the moment, but Mouse could tell his overcharged brain was still busily working on the problem.

They arranged the flyers on the table, and then Mouse started quizzing the patrol about the information contained in them. When someone missed a question, they had to read the appropriate flyer again, and soon everyone had mastered the material. At the next station down, Mr. Williams, in his impressive fire chief uniform, had just finished teaching the Scorpions what to say about a pile of interesting looking equipment that was stacked up on the table. As he walked back toward the front of the fire hall, he passed by the Mice and smilingly asked, "You boys doin' all right here? Any questions?"

Before Mouse could reply, Pig said, "Could we maybe borrow one of the fire suits to show?"

Pee Wee latched onto the idea like a bird onto a breakfast worm. "Yeah, that could be our demonstration!"

Mr. Williams looked puzzled, "Demonstration?"

Now, Mouse got behind the idea.

"Some of the guys think that the literature will be boring unless we have a demonstration of some sort. Could we borrow a fire fighter's uniform?"

Mr. William considered, and then said, "OK, you can borrow mine, but it will only fit the big guy here. Will that be all right?"

"Yes!" chorused the younger Scouts, and so Mr. Williams went to fetch his fire suit. It was sort of a pea green with reflective bands of orange and green on the arms, body and legs. The boots were black rubber with brick red trim, and they were very tall. The helmet was yellow as a canary, and inside was welter of straps and fasteners. The chief showed Pig how to climb into the suit, and the rest of the patrol stood around watching and listening to his explanation of the process.

"See the way that we keep the pants and boots? It just looks like a pile of stuff on the floor, but notice how the boot tops poke up through the pants. Here step into them. Now pull up the pants, put the suspenders over your shoulders, and you're all set to go. Usually, we don't put the coat or helmet on until we arrive at the scene, unless it's a structure fire."

"A structure fire?" asked Beaner.

"Yeah, a burning house or barn. A structure on fire."

"The helmet seems a little small," said Pig doubtfully.

"Here, reach up behind, where I have my hand. Feel that wheel? Turn that to adjust the size of the helmet."

"Neat," said Pee Wee. "Would it fit me?"

Mr. Williams laughed. "Now that would be a sight to see. If you want to try it though, that's fine with me. You can't hurt it. Just don't lose anything, OK?"

Mouse assured him they would be careful with the suit, and then the man was gone, off to get the bay doors rolled up and the fire trucks rolling.

The fire suit was a great success. When Pig was all decked out in pants and boots, jacket and helmet, he looked just like a real fireman. Then, each of the Scouts took their turn at trying on parts of the uniform. Beaner put the boots on, tried to run and fell down, so Mouse made a no running rule. Pee Wee did manage to get the helmet on, but it was so loose it fell off onto the floor, so Mouse said there always had to be a helper standing nearby, to guard against that accident happening again.

The bay doors rolled open with a throbbing rumble, and the line of waiting people started coming past. For a while, they completely ignored the literature as they surged by toward the fire trucks waiting on the street out front, but gradually the line backed up and then moved by fits and starts past the literature station. Now, a few bored adults were reading some of the flyers, and Pee Wee went into action.

He got up on a chair, held the fire helmet up high, and loudly proclaimed, "Wear the fire helmet! Look like a fireman! Come one, come all. All you've got to do is answer a few fire safety questions."

Mouse and the others caught on right away, and soon they were all passing out flyers to eager youngsters who wanted to wear the helmet or boots. Only the larger kids and adults were given a chance at the jacket, since Mouse thought it would be bad for it to be dragged on the floor.

If the people in the line learned a little fire safety, the Mice became experts by asking the same questions over and over again. They had trouble keeping up with all the takers, and a crowd gathered at the literature station to be quizzed and then try on a piece of gear. Mouse hung back and watched for problems. At one point, he managed to coax a one-year-old into saying "Wah" as answer to the question, "How can you put out a fire?" and then laughed with delight as the little girl's head and shoulders disappeared up into the big helmet.

Moms and dads, boys and girls, grannies and babies all had a crack at wearing the gear, always after first answering a question or two about fire safety. More than one adult paused before leaving to say how good the stunt was, and Mouse himself was pleased. That Pee Wee! He would make a salesman some day.

Along about 9:30, the end of the line finally appeared, and Mouse was surprised to see the entire Grit clan back there. He watched with some nervousness as they got closer, fearing a run in with Simon Grit. Mouse could feel the tenseness growing, but somehow, he didn't quite know why, he was sure that he could face the man this time. Maybe it was because his friends were here, and he was leading them. But, it had been the same on Saturday night, and he had frozen then. Now, though, he felt more confident. Why was that? There was something else, too. He saw Abby Grit back there, talking to her little sisters, and he remembered how she had smiled at him in art class a few days before. He didn't quite understand why, but he suddenly wanted very much to talk to Abby, and to somehow get her to smile that same smile again.

When the Grits were nearly to the literature station, Mouse slid up beside Pee Wee and softly said, "Let me run the helmet quiz for these people."

"OK," said Pee Wee, "but don't make the questions too easy."

Mouse took the helmet and faced around. Somehow, there was Abby, standing right in front of him. He was startled for a second, and then asked, "Would you like to try on the helmet, Abby?"

"OK. What do I have to do?" she asked.

"Just answer three questions."

"OK. Ask away." And, she smiled the smile that Mouse had hoped to see.

Mouse said, "Suppose you wake up, and the room is filled with smoke. What is the best way to get away safely?"

She was quick with her answer, "I would get down on the floor and crawl toward the door, because smoke rises."

"Right," said Mouse, pleased. "Then what would you do?"

"I would make sure all of the children got out of the house, and then I would care for them while Mom and Dad put out the fire or called for help."

"Suppose your mom and dad were not around, and it was just you and the kids?"

Abby thought about that a second, then answered, "I guess I would call for help and wait."

"And suppose you couldn't call for help, because the phone was in the burning building. What would you do then?"

Abby replied confidently, "I'd send George and Pete down the road on their bikes, to Startown, to call 9-1-1."

Mouse was pleased at the quickness of her mind. "You must have been a Girl Scout," he said.

"More like a Grit Scout. Mom and Dad worry about things like fires, and we all know what to do in case of an emergency. When you live on a farm, you have to learn to think for yourself."

Mouse handed her the helmet, and when she had put it on, helped her to turn the wheel at the back to adjust its fit. It made him feel strange to have his hands in her hair, and to be so close to her. That didn't make any sense at all, though. He had known Abby Grit since kindergarten, and always before, she had just been another one of the slimy girls. Now she seemed different. The whole thing was very confusing, and he found that he could think of nothing much else to say. It was OK, though. Her brothers were talking to her about how silly she looked, and her mother and little sisters were adding their two cents. Mouse just took a step back and watched her enjoy being the center of attention.

Suddenly, Mouse noticed Beaner, Jim, Pee Wee and Bobby were bellied up to the table a few feet to his right, staring at Simon Grit. This evidently made the man nervous, and for some reason, he kept shifting his gaze between the boys and his family members making a fuss over Abby.

Finally, Beaner worked up the courage to speak, "Uh, Mr. Grit, we were wondering if you have found out anything yet."

Mouse's eyes widened, and he examined Grit's face carefully in order to gauge the man's reaction to the question. Grit winced and looked almost fearful.

Pee Wee had a question too. "Do you think we will get to keep the silver dollars?" asked the small Scout.

Mouse heard someone gasp, and swung around to see it was Mrs. Grit. All the amusement at Abby's new hat had left her face. She clearly had been shocked by the question.

She faced around to look at Pee Wee, and said suspiciously, "What silver dollars?"

Pee Wee replied casually, "We found some silver dollars below the dump at Bear Run last weekend, and Mr. Grit said he would check to see if we could have them back."

Grit finally found his tongue. His voice had a resigned, crumpled sound about it.

"Don't worry. I'm working on it. I'll call Beaner when I find out." Then he looked toward his wife and children, and said firmly, "OK, let's get going. It's nearly our turn to ride. Abby, give the helmet back and come along."

With that, he marched off. It was obvious they still had a few minutes to wait, and the children were clearly disappointed at not getting a turn with the fire gear. They were a well-disciplined bunch, though, and quickly went to catch up with their father. Abby handed the helmet back to Mouse. Her smile was gone, replaced with at look of concern. She leaned in close and whispered, "Sorry my father got upset," and then hurried off to rejoin her family.

Mouse was a few seconds figuring out what had happened, then he got it. Mrs. Grit had not known about the coins, and now she did. She had been shocked. But, if she didn't know about the coins before tonight, why would she be shocked? Mouse didn't have a clue. Anyway, the coins weren't that big a deal. It was the treasure that was the real trouble, and he was very glad that, in less than half an hour, he would lay that particular problem in his grandfather's lap. Mouse was confident that what he had to say about the location of the mine would help with the solution of the problem — Judge Sweet would be a lot easier to deal with than Grit or the Pennsylvania Game Commission. Mouse's only remaining worry was that Chuck might have removed the treasure and be prepared to lie about it to Grandpa Mike.

Now that there were no new customers for the literature, Mouse sent his Scouts to feast on what was left of the food — broken cookie bits and the dregs of the bug juice. He took the fire gear back to Mr. Williams' hook on the wall and did his best to arrange it to look the same as its neighbors. When he walked back to rejoin the group, Pig handed him two cookies and a Dixie cup full of very red-looking bug juice. "Come on," he said, "I want to see what happens when Chuck meets up with Grit out at the fire truck."

Mouse took a sip of the bug juice. The thick stuff puckered his mouth and overwhelmed his taste buds with an intense taste of concentrated cherry flavoring,

"This stuff is awful!" he said fervently.

"I sort of like it," replied Pig, taking a swig from his own cup.

"Maybe we should warn Chuck about Grit," said Mouse doubtfully. Pig gave him a wide-eyed stare of disbelief, and that finally made Mouse smile. "OK, you're right. This should be good."

They walked out into the night air, to where the last of the public rides was about to board. Chuck and Andy Weston were helping people up onto the truck. It was almost comical to see Chuck turn and see Grit standing there. Mouse couldn't see Grit's face, couldn't hear any words that he might have started to say, but he did see Chuck's reaction — his big, brave cousin simply turned and started walking away, fast. After he had gone 15 feet, he turned his head to look back. When he saw Grit was following, Chuck ran.

Pig snorted. "I figured Grit would recognize him from that day Chuck made him fall. I didn't figure Chuck would just run away, though."

Mouse still had a little sympathy for his cousin. "I wouldn't want Grit after me, either."

Pig gave Mouse an assessing look, and then said, "Yeah, but you would have faced him. You wouldn't have run."

Mouse wondered if that was true.

The high point of the evening had finally arrived. Always at the fire truck rides, the last ride of the night was reserved for the Scouts who had helped out during the evening. Many had gone home already because of the lateness of the hour, but there were still enough and more to fill up a fire truck.

Mr. Williams took the wheel of Pumper 13, the boys scrambled up its steep red and chrome sides to pile together in its bed, and then they all went rolling off into the night. The big truck swung left, around the corner of Eighth and Wood. Someone hit the siren, and Mr. Williams gave the throbbing engine a little more gas. The cold night air cut at Mouse's cheeks, and his eyes watered, but really he was warm enough, piled up with his buddies in the back of the truck. Ten minutes later, they were back at the fire hall, and Mouse found himself waiting beside Paxton to dismount the pumper.

"Good job tonight, Mouse," Brian said. "You seem to have a way with those guys."

"Thanks, Brian, but Pee Wee and Pig came up with the fire suit idea. That's what made things go."

"It was a good idea," said Paxton. "What would you say to making the Mice a real patrol in the troop?"

Mouse considered. "Would those guys want to do that, do you think?"

Paxton gave Mouse the same wide-eyed look of disbelief that Pig had used earlier.

Mouse got the message and smiled. "OK, OK. I think it would be great!"

Brian nodded, "Good. I'll bring it up at the next committee meeting. I bet the Mice will be famous some day, that is if Pee Wee doesn't manage to get you all killed first."

Using various chrome projections as handholds, Mouse scrambled down the side of the truck. When he hit the street, he immediately started looking for Grandpa Mike. He was feeling pretty worn out, but there was still the matter of the treasure to be discussed before he could creep off home to bed.

Mouse found his grandfather sipping coffee and talking to other firefighters in the bays at the back of the engine house. He looked tired too, but this wouldn't take long, since Mouse would be the only one doing any talking — Chuck was nowhere to be seen. All he had to do was tell the story exactly like it had happened, then he would explain about what he had found out at the courthouse. Mouse was pretty sure what should be done with the treasure, but it would be nice to have Grandpa Mike confirm his opinion.

Mike saw him coming and motioned Mouse over to a table at the side of the hall where they could be alone. He was smiling and Mouse was encouraged, working out just what to say. He wouldn't freeze this time.

"Hi, Grandpa."

"Hi there, little Mouse. Did you have a good time of your fire truck ride?"

"It was pretty good. Look, the reason that Chuck and I wanted to talk to you tonight was…"

Mike finished the sentence for him, "…to tell me about a leather bag Chuck and you found out in the woods."

The old man smiled at Mouse's astonishment, and added, "Chuck told me about it while you were out getting your truck ride."

Mouse was speechless. Chuck had snuck back and told Mike his own version of events. Now Mouse would have to convince Mike of the truth — that he alone had found the bag; that Chuck was just trying to horn in on the discovery. His carefully planned speech was useless. What should he say? Should he call Chuck a liar? He didn't even know what Chuck had said. Did his grandfather know what was in the bag? Did he know about the treasure? Maybe the coins were no longer in the bag. Maybe it would be just his word against Chuck's that the coins had ever been in the bag. Maybe...

"What's the matter, Mouse. Cat got your tongue?" his grandfather laughed. The words bit. Mouse hated the expression, so often used by both his grandfather and his cousin. It seemed almost like a magic spell meant to render him speechless.

Mike turned a little softer and said, "Don't worry, grandson. Chuck also told me about your run-in with Simon Grit, and I can understand you being afraid to report the bag to him on account of that. What we decided was that Chuck will call Clyde Swagman, the WCO for that area. That way Simon Grit won't be involved at all."

Mouse was starting to get mad. Everything was decided. They had not even asked his opinion. How could he tell Grandpa it was all wrong?

Mouse gulped and stammered out a question, "What... What did Chuck say was in the bag?"

"Oh, yeah," said Mike smiling in disbelief, "he did say you had some idea the bag was full of treasure, but that you guys had to hide it because Grit was coming, and he wasn't so sure himself. I'd give up on the notion if I was you, Mouse. It's just a dream. In the real world, Boy Scouts don't find treasures."

So that was the story, huh. Well, Chuck hadn't reckoned on the coin Mouse had found in his pocket when he got home from the campout. He had picked it up in the cave, and now it was the proof that would convince his grandfather the bag did contain a treasure in coins. Mouse felt for the silver dollar among the many items that inhabited his pocket — fire safety literature, loose change, half an arrowhead. Then, he felt the weight of it on his fingertips and started to speak, "But, Grandpa, the bag *was* full of treasure, I found it and ..."

Then, a great piercing wail filled the fire hall. Mouse had never heard it so loud, and quickly covered his ears. His grandfather was gone at a run, headed for the line of uniforms, along with every other man in the place. Mouse was amazed at the speed of their return. As the men hurried toward the trucks still sitting outside, Mouse followed along behind to stand beside Pig and watch the men mount up.

"Barn on fire out at Stoney Lonesome Road," Pig shouted. Mouse could barely hear him for the deafening scream of the siren.

Mike wasn't as quick as the younger hands, and so came thumping out of the garage very much at the tail of the line. Mouse didn't speak. The glittering silver dollar that he held up between thumb and index finger did his talking for him. Mouse thought his grandfather would be pleased to see it, but he was wrong. Mike stopped dead in his tracks, and suddenly he was very angry. He shouted close to Mouse's ear, "I'll see the both of you after the parade on Saturday. Either Chuck saw that bag was full of silver coins, or you are trying to make him out a liar. Either way, one of you is in big trouble!"

Mike pulled his head back and stood staring. Mouse didn't know what to say. Mike's face was red and great furrows wrinkled his forehead.

"Saturday, after the parade, do you understand?" he snarled.

Mouse squeaked, "Yes, sir," and then Mike was gone, running clumsily to scramble aboard the truck just as it began to move. Then it was gone, wailing away into the night. Mouse watched mournfully, his ears ringing, his eyes watering, his mind a tumble of fearful anticipation at the confrontation to come.

Saturday! Saturday was three days away. Why couldn't they meet sooner than that? And when they did meet, would Mike be in a shouting mood, like tonight? Mouse dreaded the thought. He knew he would just clam up when faced with that much anger from his grandfather. Then Chuck would say what he pleased, and Grandpa Mike would believe it.

Mouse was sick of both of them. What he needed was someone else to confide in. His dad was gone, his mom was never around, he barely knew Judge Sweet. Who did that leave? Who could he trust?

A voice came from behind, "So what was that about a bag full of silver coins?"

Startled, Mouse swung around and said, "Don't *do* that!" but then suddenly an idea blossomed full-blown in his head, and he smiled at his friend. Pig might make the perfect ally!

18

When they got back to the farm about 10 p.m., Abby scooped up her sleeping 6-year-old sister, Terry, and was carrying her toward the house when the fire whistle went off over in Clarion. It was a good five miles away, but she could still hear it on crisp, clear nights such as this one, and Abby wondered where in the great surrounding darkness the firemen were off to.

Her mother and father walked in front, their arms full of other sleepy children, and they did not comment on the distant alarm. They had barely spoken a word to each other since the revelations at the fire hall, and Abby took that as a bad sign. What was it her dad had said down in the woods that afternoon? "If your mother finds out there will be hell to pay?" Abby wondered just what that meant.

She went up to her bedroom, got into her pajamas and read her history book as she waited for her parents to settle the little ones. First her mother and then her father popped their noses in to say goodnight, and then the upstairs was quiet. Abby put down her book and padded down the hall to the bathroom near the head of the stairs. She washed and brushed and started to return to her bed, but as she stepped out of the bathroom, she could hear voices downstairs. It was not her habit to eavesdrop on her parents' conversations, but the tone of her father's voice made her pause and listen. He sounded like a man pleading desperately to be understood...

"... old man had pressed it into his small hand and begged him, "Hide it, hide it. Tell no one!"

Simon had finished his story. Now, Susan spoke. She sounded tense and upset.

"I have heard all this before, Simon. It's a good story but that's all it is, not something to waste your life on, like your Papa did."

"Papa had a full and good life," was Simon's angry reply. "If he chose to spend his later years roaming the woods with his grandson, that was his right. He earned it. Without Papa, I would have had all the dreams squeezed out of me by my old man."

"You always talk about it like this," said Susan sadly. "To hear you tell it, those times were the best you ever had. But, to hear your father tell it, you two played hooky from the farm and left the working of the place to him."

"Well, consider the source," said Simon bitterly.

"I don't know what you mean by that," Susan said, now sounding prim. "I always found your father a kind and thoughtful old man. He helped us get this farm, didn't he? He worked until his dying day to insure it would be as good as he could make it for us!"

"Yeah, well he mellowed some in his old age, and he always did have a way with women. You didn't know him in his prime. Nothing I did was good enough. No matter what hours I worked, there he was wanting more. Papa was the best thing in my life until he died, and even then he left me the car so I could escape."

Susan sighed, "You and that car. You and your Papa. I thought that was all in the past. Now some boys find a few coins and you are right back at it.

"Simon, I'm worried. I can't run this place alone. You can't go wandering off like you used to. We have a family to raise.

You are not 12 anymore. It's time to put this dream of finding a treasure behind you. It is time to get back to the real business of your life."

"Look, Susan, I don't care what my father told you. Papa was not cracked on the subject of the treasure, and he did not fill my head with unrealistic dreams. Yeah, we did wander around in the woods looking for it, but Papa always made sure our real work was done first. He, unlike my father, knew that all work and no play make a dull, colorless life. It was my fear of ending up like my father that drove me off the farm in the first place."

"I know he must not have been the easiest of men, Simon, but he kept your family together and made the farm pay for over 40 years. Surely that counts for something?"

"Yeah, it counts for 40 grim years for me and my mother. I felt like I abandoned her when I left, but after Papa died I couldn't get away fast enough."

"Well, if farm life is so bad why are you back here doing it now?"

"Because there is more than one kind of farmer, Susan. Papa knew how to make a farm pay and how to be happy at the same time. My father never did. He maybe had more ambition than Papa, but he never smiled, never saw the beauty of the world around him.

"I remember when I was a boy, working with Papa. We might be covered with sweat from weeding or tending fences, and then he would just look at the sky and say, 'That's enough. Tomorrow we do something different.'

"I was always so excited when he said that. Those outings recharged my batteries. They made the hard work worthwhile. My dad never came along, though, and did his best to make us feel bad about going. He might have stopped me going altogether, except Mother would put her foot down. She understood, even if she did stay behind."

Susan responded gently. "So you would leave your father to work and go skylarking through the woods looking for the treasure?"

"We didn't spend all of our time looking for the treasure. Up until the time I was 10, I didn't even know about it, but I still looked forward to those days in the woods. We would march along ancient Indian paths and old disused roads, and Papa would tell me about the trees and plants, rocks and animals that we met up with along the way. He could just about walk up to any creature we came across, and could tell you everything there was to know about every one of them."

"Well, that part sounds fine, Simon. You do the same thing with Abby, George and Peter. I have seen you do it."

"And, do you think the children enjoy living out here on a farm, Susan?"

"Yes, we all do, and that's why I'm so worried about the way you've been behaving this past week. It's like you have some secret you aren't sharing with the rest of us. It's like you are not part of the family anymore," she sounded close to tears.

"Oh, Susan, that's the furtherest thing from my mind. It's just that Papa and I looked so long for that treasure. It would be wonderful to finally find it.

"I still have the map we used to trace the roads and trails. We would get sandwiches, a couple of apples, and then head out. He liked to go down to the Rock Garden, have a look at the coin, spread out the map, and tell me the story. Then we would make a plan and hit the trail. It puzzled him a good deal that we never found the treasure, but believe me, he was not obsessed with it. We found lots of other stuff, you know — ancient horse troughs, old oil wells, bits of machinery, old coalmines. We just never found the stash of silver coins.

"When Papa died, I thought the treasure hunting was over for good, and I set my mind to getting off the farm and away from my old man. Then, last Saturday five coins showed up, and … well, I admit it. I went a little crazy."

"All you've found is a few old coins," Susan asked quietly.

"Yes, but they're the right kind and all of them have the same date as Papa's. I am close to that treasure. I can feel it. If I could just find it before the others do, I would feel I had somehow repaid my grandfather for his kindness to me all those years ago, back when I was a boy."

"Simon! Do you really think other people are after the treasure? Doesn't that sound a little paranoid to you? Who else would even know the story?"

"Yeah, I know, I know," Simon sounded a little abashed. "Maybe I am paranoid. I've spent hours down at the dump this week, digging and poking around. I haven't found a thing, but I have had a feeling that others are looking too. There were those Scouts on the weekend, and then there was a boy in a red car out there one afternoon who ran away when I shouted at him. I just have this awful feeling that someone will steal the treasure, and I will never even know it is gone. If I found out someone else had run off with it, I don't know what I would do. If the thing is to be found, I am the man who will find it."

"That's the kind of talk that worries me, Simon. You could spend years looking, and you would have nothing left at the end of the search except bitter memories of wasted days."

"I know, I know," said Simon sounding contrite. "At first I thought I'd find it right away, but I didn't, and now I'm starting to lose enthusiasm for the search. I feel bad about that, for Papa's sake, but life is busy enough without wasting hours each day rummaging around alone in a mound of trash."

"So why don't you just quit? Your Papa is dead, Simon. If he was alive today, he would point to your children and say, 'There is your treasure.'"

"You're right, Susan. They *are* my treasure. *You* are my treasure. But I have got to keep looking a little longer. It's something that I owe to the memory of my grandfather. I often think of him when I'm in the woods, and if I could just solve this puzzle, find the treasure — my memories would be all the sweeter. Can you understand that?"

"I guess I do, and I'm not against your poking around some more. I do understand what it means to you, Simon. Just remember though, you may never find that treasure, and you have other treasures that require your attention. If you *are* going to look, please let us be a part of the looking. If you are obsessed, please let it be a part-time obsession. And, whatever you do, please, please don't do anything that would endanger your health, your freedom or the welfare of your family.

"Simon, I have never been happier in my life than I have been living on this farm with you. No old stack of coins, no matter how valuable, is worth a tenth of what we have built here together. Please, try to remember that."

"Yeah, you're right about that. Well, one thing is for sure — I am mighty glad that this whole thing is out in the open. Whatever happens, you and the kids are going to be a part of it from now on." Then he yawned. "Come on, Susan, it's too late for farmers to be up. Dawn will be on us in no time. Let's go to bed."

They moved toward the stairs, and Simon continued. "The whole thing will be over with, one way or the other, in a couple of days, Susan. After Autumn Leaf, things will get back to normal."

"That will be good, Simon. Speaking of Autumn Leaf, maybe when I get home tomorrow we should get started on harvesting the roses and …"

Now they were climbing the stairs, and Abby slipped away down the hall to her room. She softly closed the door and turned off the light.

An hour later, she was the only one still awake in the dark house on the hillside. She lay in her bed, staring out the window at clouds fleeing across the face of a red-orange moon — a tumble of worries pattering about inside her head and keeping sleep away.

19

Thursday at 1:30, Mouse walked into History, the final class of the day. The last thing on his mind this rainy Thursday afternoon was history. School would adjourn in less than an hour and would not resume again until the following Monday — it was an Autumn Leaf tradition. For those students whose families didn't flee from the uproar of the final days of the festival, the rest of Thursday would be spent with friends at the carnival and at the food booths that lined Main Street. Nobody in the room was thinking about history.

Mr. Galardo walked in, stood behind his desk, and looked at his distracted students.

"Good afternoon, class. Are you all ready for Autumn Leaf Weekend?"

Most of the class cheered, but some few, like Mouse, looked out the windows and wondered if the rest of the festival would be rained out.

Mr. Galardo noticed and said, "Don't worry, you pessimists. The weather forecast says the weekend will be crisp and clear with sunny skies. Today's storm should be over by midnight."

Then the old history teacher reached into his desk and pulled out a stack of papers. He tilted his glasses to read what was on the first sheet and said, "I see there will be a hula-hoop contest on Fifth Avenue tomorrow. The winners in each age group will receive a silver coin, and everyone who participates will get a large piece of candy, courtesy of the sponsors of the event, the Lions Club."

He looked at the class. "Are any of you planning on competing in that event?"

Mouse looked at the man like he was crazy. The other kids were puzzled too. No one had heard of the contest.

Bobby Spranker raised his hand and asked, "Sir, what is a hula-hoop?"

The teacher smiled. "It is a hoop made out of plastic that is about a yard across, or a meter if you like a more modern system of measurement. You put it around your middle and then wiggle your hips, sort of like doing a hula dance, to make it go round and round."

He looked at the rest of the class, "None of you are entering? No? Well, all right, I guess. How about the hot air balloon rides out on east Main Street, are any of you going to do that?"

The class exchanged more puzzled looks.

"OK, then," continued Mr. Galardo, undaunted. "How about the train rides on the LEF&C? They leave from the train station starting at 10 on Saturday morning. Are any of you going to do that?"

Mouse was puzzled. A train ride might be fun, but for the life of him, he could not remember where the train station was. Did Clarion even have a train station?

Mr. Galardo was beginning to look concerned. "You people surely aren't planning to do much at Autumn Leaf. How about the planetarium show up at the university? No? Well, I am sure that some of you are going to be in the Gong Show right here at the school. What about that?"

Abby Grit held up her hand. "Mr. Galardo, there isn't going to be a Gong Show at the school."

The teacher looked confused, "Did they cancel it?"

"There never was going to be a Gong Show. Student Council never talked about it at all. Where did you find out about it?"

Mouse added, "I don't think there is a train station in Clarion, so how can there be train rides?"

Bobby Spranker piped up with, "I don't think there is any such thing as a hula-hoop!"

Mr. Galardo laughed, held up the papers, and said, "But it's all got to be true. Every one of these events is listed right here in the newspaper."

Bobby said, "Those aren't newspapers. They're just pieces of paper."

Galardo fanned the sheets and turned them so the class could see. "Now, don't they look like copies of newspapers to you, Bobby Spranker?"

Bobby was confused, but Mouse had an idea.

"What date is on them?" he asked.

Mr. Galardo reexamined the sheets, and did a double take. "Heavens! The hula-hoop contest was in 1958. You all missed it!" then he paged rapidly through the remaining sheets. He appeared to be shocked. "The rest of these are from 1978. Where does the time go?"

The class was laughing now, and finally, the old teacher dropped his act and laughed along. When the noise had died down to chuckles, he held up a hand and spoke again.

"The Clarion Chamber of Commerce was started in 1952, the brainchild of three young men — Po Haskell, Leon Hufnagel and Don Stroup. At one of its early meetings, Mr. Hufnagel told of a interesting visit he and his wife, Jeanne, had made to the Coudersport Potato Festival. This started a discussion which eventually led to the idea of an annual festival for Clarion, to be based on the glorious autumn leaves that surround us at this time of year.

"That was nearly fifty years ago, and though some of the many men involved have died, and the rest are very old, their grand idea lives on. What would Clarion be without its Autumn Leaf Festival? It just wouldn't feel like Clarion, would it?

"To you, it probably seems Autumn Leaf is always the same — the Autorama, the carnival, the fire truck rides, Farmer's and Crafter's Day, the parade and then the fireworks to finish off the week on Sunday. What you don't realize is that the festival is a living, changing thing. For the first few years, it was only a single day long; now it lasts for over a week. The parade used to take 45 minutes, now it takes 2 hours. Attendance used to be in the thousands, now it is in the hundreds of thousands.

"It is truly amazing what the seed those men planted has grown into. Those good men made history. Not the kind of history you find in books, but a more local, a more personal kind of history that you can only read about in old newspapers.

"These pieces of paper in my hand come from the Clarion Free Library. You can get copies yourself if you only walk down there, thread microfilm into a machine, and start looking. It's all there, the week-by-week history of our community stretching back for well over 100 years.

"What will you find if you go looking? I can't tell you that. I can tell you, though, that what you read will change the way you look at the world!"

*   *   *

Mouse stood at the school's entrance looking out at the drizzly day, wishing he had brought an umbrella. Students streamed out the doors and off to do the carnival in the rain. The older kids were often matched up boy-girl, but the ones Mouse's age were more usually in large same-sex groups. He knew he could join his classmates, but he had other plans.

Pig would have made a good companion for the mission he had in mind, but Pig had not come to school that day. His family were what some people called "runners." Pig had said they planned to spend the long weekend camping along the lake above Kinzua Dam — far, far away from the horrendous traffic and

198

massive crowds associated with the final days of the Autumn Leaf Festival.

Mouse looked at his watch. They would be well on their way by now. He wished Pig hadn't had to go, but that was just the way it was; some people viewed the festival as a yearly plague, like tent caterpillars or gypsy moths. To them, the great days at the end of the festival were something to be avoided. Mouse grimaced. He just hoped Pig had found time to take care of the business the two had discussed the previous night. It was frustrating not knowing if Pig had gone — absolutely maddening to not know if he had succeeded.

Mouse zipped his jacket up tight, jerked his floppy boony hat down tighter onto his head, and stepped out into the rain. It was only a couple of blocks to Comstock's Coins; he hoped they were open. He shoved his hands deeper into his pockets. The coin was still there in his left, and he rolled it over and over between his fingers, wondering if Mr. Comstock would be able to tell him anything that would help. Mouse had to have as many facts as possible for his meeting with Grandpa Mike on Saturday. The old man liked Chuck an awful lot. He would be very hard to convince.

Mouse walked up Liberty, detouring around the bigger puddles and had just turned toward Main when a high-pitched voice behind called out, "Wait up!"

He turned, and there was Abby Grit some 30 feet behind, hurrying to catch up. She carried a bright blue umbrella and wore a dark jacket unzipped to the waist. Underneath was a snug yellow sweater. She had on jeans that were tight at the top but belled at the bottom, and he could tell by the way she blithely waded the puddles, that her footwear was suited to the day.

Mouse smiled as she joined him, "Hi, Abby. Looks like you're better prepared for the weather than I am."

She didn't seem interested in small talk. "Where are you going, Mouse? I wanted to talk to you about last night."

He didn't know what to say. He sure wasn't taking Simon Grit's daughter to Comstock's Coins, no matter how nice she looked.

"Oh, up through the carnival, I guess," he said bashfully.

"Can I come too? I'll share my umbrella with you."

"OK," he said and slid in underneath.

It was a small blue umbrella, and they had to walk close together to get any protection from the spattering rain. Mouse was nervous that he would brush up against her, but liked being close, even if the subject of their conversation was not the one he would have picked.

"Mouse, were you there when the boys found the coins on Saturday night?" asked Abby.

"Yeah. I was one of the guys that found one."

"What happened then? I keep hearing little things, but nobody has told me the whole story."

Mouse looked over at her. There was no harm in her knowing this part. "Well, we went down to the stream, Bear Run you know, to where my grandfather found a coin twenty years ago and dug around and found a bunch more."

"Were they all silver dollars?" she asked.

"Yeah, that's right, and they all had the same date."

"1878," she said without hesitation.

"Right," he replied. Ahh, so she did know something about the coins. "So, anyway, we were whooping it up down there and still looking, when first my cousin and then your father showed up."

"Your cousin? Who's that?"

"Chuck Wing. You know… the football player."

"Oh, yeah. I've heard about him. He's a jerk… Oh, sorry, I didn't mean to…"

"That's OK. He is a jerk. He's a liar, a bully and a coward, as well."

"Does he own a red car?" she asked.

Mouse didn't understand for a second, but then realized that she must know about Chuck's return visit to the dump on Monday, "Yeah, a red Dodge Neon."

"That makes sense then," she murmured. "So he was there last Saturday night, and my dad was there — right?"

"Yeah, I was just about handling Chuck, when your dad showed up and took all the coins. He said it was because we had found them on State Game Lands. He also said he would check to see if we could keep them or not."

"You guys must have been pretty disappointed," she said, sounding sympathetic.

"Yeah," said Mouse with feeling, "and it seems like he isn't doing anything about checking on them either. The younger guys have been after him about it every time they see him, like at the fire hall last night. I guess they are trying to make him hurry up, but it doesn't seem like it's working."

They had reached the carnival, and Abby did not immediately reply. Regardless of the rain, kids from five area schools lined up for the rides; mobbed around the games of chance; and waited to buy the sweet, overpriced carnival food. Abby and Mouse did a tour of the grounds and said "Hello" to many friends. Mouse was very aware of being at the carnival with a girl and found it made him feel good to be seen with her. Abby seemed to be enjoying herself as well, and talked constantly about the people on the rides, the chances of winning at the ring toss, and how good the food smelled. Mouse was glad she talked so much; he was having trouble thinking of anything much to say.

"Would you like something to eat?" he finally asked a little timidly.

"I could eat half a candy apple," replied Abby.

"OK, I'll go get us one to split."

"Let's go together, and I'll pay for my half," she said.

"You don't have to do that," said Mouse. If she let him buy the apple it would be sort of like a date, wouldn't it?

"I am buying my half," said Abby firmly.

"Are you sure?" asked Mouse.

"I am sure."

So they stood in line, Mouse strangely crushed at the setback, and got a cherry red candy apple covered with nuts and paid the man four dollars for it. They found shelter under the marquee of the old Orpheum theater, where they took turns biting into the sweet fruit, and Mouse's spirits revived somewhat.

After they had disposed of the stick, Abby said, "Let's walk someplace quieter. There is something I want to tell you about my father."

"About your father?" Mouse was puzzled. What was there to know?

"Yes, but you have to promise not to tell anyone. Come on."

They walked away down the alley toward the fire hall and then headed up along Wood. It was much quieter a block off Main, but they could still hear the distant hoopla of the carnival. The sidewalk was nearly empty of pedestrians and ran under immense old trees decked out in vibrant red and yellow leaves that dripped water down onto the bobbing blue umbrella as they moved along underneath. They were both silent for a long time, and then suddenly Abby was telling a story. It was like something out of a book; about a boy who found a dying man and listened to a strange tale of buried treasure that he told. And, about how the old man had pressed a silver dollar into the boy's hand as proof of the tale.

When she had finished, Mouse asked, "Did that really happen?" as he dodged out from under the umbrella to avoid a deep puddle.

"Yes," she said quietly, and when he returned to her side at the end of the lake-like puddle, she put her arm through his and held tight, as if to say she didn't want him darting away like that when she had important things to say. Thereafter they walked arm-in-arm. After wading the first puddle, Mouse's sneakers were soaked, but the closeness of her, and what she said next made it easy to ignore the discomfort.

She spoke more quietly now that he was closer. "The boy grew up, then grew old and never told anyone about the coin. After his wife died, he started wandering the woods in search of the treasure with his grandson. They searched together for many years but never found anything. Then the man died, and his grandson moved away and forgot all about finding the money. He grew up, and when I was just a little girl, he moved back to the farm where he was raised and became a farmer himself."

Mouse got it, "And he was... he is your father, right?"

"Right! And he is not a thief or a liar or any other kind of bad man, but last Saturday night some Boy Scouts found a bunch of old coins, and he went a little crazy. He remembered the story of the treasure and the days he spent with his Papa looking for it, and he just had to find the rest of coins.

"Then this boy appeared at the dump, and Daddy is now convinced he is not the only one looking for the treasure. He thinks others want to steal the money he and his grandfather spent so many years searching for."

"And, the boy drove a red car?" asked Mouse

"Yes, a red car."

Mouse was silent and so, for once, was Abby. They turned a couple of corners and walked back up past the high school again. Mouse didn't know quite what to do — quite what to say. It seemed Grit was not the villain he had thought him to be, but remembering the incident with the deer and the run-in on Saturday night, it was still hard to think of Mr. Grit in any very friendly way. Abby, though... With Abby it was a different story. He debated telling her about his having found the treasure, about his investigations, and about the coming showdown with Grandpa Mike and Chuck. He was sure she would listen, but what would happen if she told her dad? If she promised not too tell, was that a promise she could keep? In fact, didn't her telling him her own father's story show that she was not very good at keeping secrets? But, still… she had told him. He owed her something for that. He could decide about telling her everything later on, but wasn't there something else he could do to show that he appreciated all that she had just said?

They had turned up toward the carnival again, and Abby misplaced a foot and splashed his leg. "Sorry," she said.

Mouse came to a decision and replied, "That's all right, Abby. Look, let's go in here and see what we can find out about this treasure."

She was puzzled for just a second, then smiled and said, "OK," and they walked arm-in-arm up to Comstock's Coins.

20

The house was old, very old. It was made of crumbly brick, had white shutters badly in need of paint, and was covered by a dark gray slate roof. Some few of the slates were askew, their anchoring nails rusted away to nothing. Mouse knew the old house, remembered avoiding it at Halloween when he was younger. It looked haunted by moonlight, and the older kids had strange tales to tell about old man Comstock. Today, it merely looked abandoned and forlorn, but there was an old flaking sign that read "Comstock's Coins" above the entrance and a handwritten placard in the window announced:

State Quarters — Collect Them ALL — MS Just Arrived!

He opened the door for Abby, and a bell chimed somewhere deep within. Mouse wondered if he ought to let Abby enter first, to be courteous, or if he should go first, to face any dangers lurking inside the dim old place. In the end, they squeezed through together and stepped into a shop from another time. Gloomy daylight filtered through the grimy front windows, and a low glassed-in counter went right round the room. It was filled with stacks of yellowing papers, mysterious dirty bags and old decaying boxes of every shape and size. At the far end of the shop stood a very large safe, its six-inch thick doors wide open and its interior full up with thirty drawers of various dimensions. Beside the safe a curtained hallway ran back into the interior of the building, and something or someone could be heard slowly moving down it in their direction.

Mouse and Abby walked on a much-worn patterned rug across the salesroom toward the approaching sound, the wooden floor beneath the rug squeaking occasionally to add still more mystery to the place. It was as if they had stepped a hundred years back in time. Strangely, Mouse was more intrigued than scared. He somehow sensed adventure in the air.

Abby seemed to hug his arm tighter as the noise in the hallway increased. It was sort of a thump and shuffle, thump and shuffle. Mouse wanted to browse the showcases to give himself time to assess Mr. Comstock before talking to the man, but there wasn't a coin anywhere in sight here at Comstock's Coins, and so he just stood still and awaited the slow arrival of the proprietor.

Mr. Comstock crept out of the deeper gloom of the hall. He was an old, old man with a messy haystack of white hair, who looked almost as if he had just awakened. He was wearing a dark suit that hung large from his bony frame. He carried a dark wooden cane and used it to favor his right leg, thus explaining the sound made by his progress down the hallway. Mr. Comstock had forgotten to shave that day, and white stubble stood out on his lean jaw, but his was a good face. His smile was genuine, and the blue eyes danced and sparked as he examined his customers.

When he spoke, his voice was surprising young and energetic.

"Good afternoon, Mr. and Mrs. Sweet. Come to do a little Christmas shopping have you? Here, come over here and let me show you the new quarters album. Your children will love it."

Was the man kidding or did he really think they were some long-ago couple come Christmas shopping? Mouse felt Abby stiffen and tried mightily for some reasonable response to the old man's unreasonable statement. Nothing came and so he silently dragged Abby over toward the counter in front of the safe. He was ill at ease but was also determined to see this thing though, particularly so because Abby was beside him. Right here was where he could redeem his foolish behavior in the cornfield.

The old man stood behind the scratched glass counter, bent down to lean his cane against the case, and as if by magic, his hand came back up holding a large map of the United States. He reverently placed it on the counter, as if it were some rare and precious document. Round holes pocked its surface. Some had bright quarters plugged into them.

Then, Mr. Comstock began his pitch, "This is it! The best possible way to display all of the state quarters. As you can see, the task is just begun. So far, the mint has issued only 16 coins; that's just four dollars worth. The series began in 1999 and the last of the fifty will not be issued until 2008. Think of it! Six more years of fun."

Pointing to the Pennsylvania quarter he added, "Just look at the detail of our own state's quarter, Mrs. Sweet. Look at it closely; see the outline of the state and the keystone symbol? Isn't the picture of Liberty wonderful? And the words, bend down and read the words — Liberty, Virtue, Independence. Aren't those just the words to describe how you want your children to grow up?"

Abby bent down, Mouse thought she was blushing a little. Perhaps she wanted to hide the fact. He glanced up at the old man, who, it turned out, was watching him intently. Their eyes locked, and suddenly, Mr. Comstock grinned mischievously and gave Mouse a broad wink.

The tenseness fizzed out of him — the old man was not crazy. Mr. Comstock was a trickster! Mouse grinned back. Now he knew how to handle the man. He would play along and just hope that Abby would catch on.

Mouse tucked his smile away. Clearing his throat, he said, "This is very nice, Mr. Comstock, but my wife and I were looking for something a little different. Something a little older."

Abby snapped bolt upright and looked at Mouse as if he too was suddenly crazy. Mouse had to struggle hard, but managed to keep a straight face.

Mr. Comstock was enthusiastic, "Surely. Do you have something specific in mind, or would you like me to, perhaps, show you some other interesting items to select from?"

"It's for our oldest, you know," said Mouse casually, "we were thinking of giving him an old silver dollar."

"An excellent choice, Mr. Sweet. What series?"

Series? What was a series? Then inspiration flashed like a bulb in his brain, "Well, we wanted one from the year that young George was born."

Abby had still not recovered her wits, but was busily following the conversation, evidently trying to make some sense of it.

Comstock frowned, "I'm afraid that silver dollars have not been minted since 1935. There were other dollar coins after that, maybe one of those would do. The Susan B. Anthony was minted from 1979 to 1981 and again in 1999, then the Sacagawea became available in the year 2000. What year were you looking for?"

Now Mouse grinned, "1878."

"Ah, your oldest you say," Comstock chuckled. "He must be getting to be a fine big fellow indeed. Let me just check and see what I can find."

Mouse struggled not to laugh aloud as Abby's puzzled look changed to one of wry amusement. "You guys!" she muttered in his ear, and then she elbowed him none-to-gently in the ribs.

Comstock rooted around busily in the drawers of his safe and finally cried, "Ah ha!"

He laid the coin at the center of a square of dark green felt on the counter. To Mouse it looked exactly the same as the one he now fingered in his pocket.

"This is an excellent coin to begin a collection with," said Comstock with enthusiasm. 1878 was the first year they made the Morgan dollars and the series ran to 1921. There are many

208

stories about this particular coin, though — stories that fire the imagination and make it just the thing to introduce a young man to the joys of coin collecting."

"Stories?" said Mouse.

"Tell us some," said Abby, now sounding at ease and very interested.

"Well, first of all you should know that it's called a Morgan dollar because the designer was George Morgan. He asked a schoolteacher, name of Anna Williams, to pose for the face of Liberty on the obverse of the coin. See her there? After the coins were issued, Anna became famous as Miss Liberty all over the United States.

"When Morgan created his design, he must have used a starving eagle as his model for the reverse of the coin. As you can see, the bird looks mighty thin. Some people call it the 'buzzard dollar' on account of that. That wasn't the only strange thing about the eagle either. In Morgan's original design, the eagle had seven tail feathers, but somehow this was changed to eight in the final design. After the coin's release, this caused a ruckus, since it was a well-known fact that eagles have but seven tail feathers. So, the mint stamped over the eight-feather coins it had left and changed the dies to seven feathers for all future coins.

"The series itself has an interesting history and is still widely collected. It all began when the silver barons…"

Mouse listened hard for some clue as to the origin of his coin in the tales that Comstock told; stories of silver miners in Nevada, of the Washington silver lobby, and of the discovery of a hoard of 400,000 Morgans in 1974 that sold for $7.3 million dollars. The old man certainly knew how to tell a story, that was for sure, but none of the tales were of local origin. This wasn't helping. How and why had so many 1878 Morgan dollars ended up in a sack in an old mine in the woods? Mouse decided he would have to show Comstock his coin. Sure, Abby would see too, but a single coin would not give away that much of the secret. Anyway, Abby had trusted him with her father's tale, and Mouse was beginning to think that he should trust her with his.

He took the coin from his pocket, hiding it in his balled up fist, waiting for the old man to run down a little and give him a chance to speak. Odd, but Abby's hand soon lay beside his on the counter, and Mouse was just beginning to speculate as to the meaning of that when her slim fingers opened to reveal a silver dollar just like the one he had found on Saturday night. Now, he slowly opened his hand, showing the coin that he had kept from the hoard in the mine.

Comstock's storytelling stopped abruptly. He took Abby's coin and examined it closely. "Counterfeit, of course" he pronounced with finality, "but a good one in its day. It has been buried in acidic soil."

Then he picked up Mouse's coin, rubbed it with a bony, wrinkled thumb, and peered at it closely. After finishing a close visual inspection, Comstock did a strange thing. Balancing the silver dollar on his forefinger, he gave it a sharp rap with his thumbnail, and sent it spinning into the air. It fell exactly back into the center of his open palm. He had a satisfied look on his face.

"Here, listen to the real thing." Comstock picked up his coin from the felt square and sent it spinning. This time the coin rang like a tiny silver bell while it was airborne.

"Hear the difference? Your coin is counterfeit too, but in excellent shape. Boston Buck probably made the both of them."

"Boston Buck?" Abby and Mouse said together. Now they were getting somewhere!

"Yes, Boston Buck, or 'Boss' Buck, as he was commonly called. Did you ever hear tell of Horsethief Days over in Knox? Well, the original horse thief was Boston Buck and that was what he is most remembered for, but he was also what was called a coniaker. A coniaker is someone who makes counterfeit coins.

"Long ago, the Jones House up on Main Street had a display of some of his coins in a glass case in the lobby. They looked just

210

like the young lady's coin here. I have never seen one as good as yours though, young man. Where did you get it?"

Mouse wasn't about to answer that question, so he proposed another, "The Jones House? Where is that?"

"Burnt down about 1940. I suppose the coins went up too. I haven't seen one of these for years."

"Would they be worth a lot of money?" asked Abby.

"I'd give you, say, three dollars for yours and maybe ten for the young man's."

"How much is a real one worth?" asked Mouse.

"I'll sell you this one for $13," said Comstock with confidence. "That's just about what it is worth."

"So the counterfeits are worth less, even though they are rarer?" asked Mouse.

Comstock smiled and said easily, "Coins are like friends — the ones that are worth a lot are sometimes not half so nice to have as the ones that are interesting."

Mouse didn't comment on this small piece of wisdom. Instead, he asked, "What would a hundred coins like mine be worth?"

Comstock laughed, "Not much. Maybe $100, perhaps a bit more," then he looked closely at Mouse. "You know, it begins to sound like you maybe found Buck's loot. Am I right in thinking that?"

Mouse wasn't going to reply to that one either. Instead, he said, "Buck's loot? What's Buck's loot?"

Comstock grinned, "Seems like every five or six years a guy comes in here with a metal detector on his shoulder, looking for clues as to the whereabouts of Buck's loot. How they get to hear of it, I don't know, but they all tell nearly the same story, so I figure it must be written down someplace in a history book or an old newspaper or something."

He paused a second to collect his wits, then continued, "Seems like in 1885, Boston Buck…"

"1885!" said a startled Abby. "How sure are you of that date?"

Comstock laughed loudly. "Young lady, if I wasn't pretty good with dates, I wouldn't be in the coin business. Dates are like people to me. You look at a coin, see a coin. I look at a coin and see the times and events when it was minted. Coins are my friends, and each one has a story to tell."

"Abby," she said, "Call me Abby, please."

"OK, I'm Gus. Pleased to meet you, Abby."

"I'm Mouse," chimed in Mouse, and he realized then that he was no longer the least bit embarrassed by his nickname.

Comstock solemnly shook each of their hands and mused, "Mouse, eh — quiet and secretive, sometimes clever."

Mouse couldn't think of a reply but was pleased with the assessment.

Abby was impatient, "You were going to tell us about Buck's loot?"

"Oh, yes. Well, anyway, in 1885 federal constables went to Boston Buck's house up north of Fryburg and arrested him on charges of coniaking. They never did get him on the horse stealing, but they had infiltrated his gang and did get evidence on his counterfeiting operation. Evidently though, the arrest didn't go quite according to plan, and the counterfeiting plant was never found. Some of the men who have come in here have said it was in an old coal mine up Lake Lucy way. Supposedly one of Boss Buck's gang evaded arrest, collapsed the mine, and then disappeared with a leather sack that was thought to be full of counterfeit coins. That's Buck's loot, and people with metal detectors and more time than sense are still searching for it."

"And, it really wouldn't be worth anything, even if they did find it?" asked Abby doubtfully.

Comstock sighed, as if this was not the first time he had had to explain the economics of the lost loot. "Well look, if you could travel back in time and pass the money in 1885, and if you didn't get caught, then each coin would be worth about $20 in today's money. If you had 100 coins back then, it would have been like having about $2000 dollars today — not a lot, but nothing to sneeze at either. The problem is that no store would accept a coin that old anymore. You would have to take it to a dealer, and any coin dealer that is going to stay one for very long would spot the coin as fake as quickly as I did. Do you understand?"

"Yes," said Abby thoughtfully.

Mouse's reaction to the news was different. He was elated. It seemed to make all the difference in the world to him that the treasure was worthless. *That* would take the wind out of Chuck's sails. There might be a little glory in finding the treasure, but that would be the end of it. Mouse wasn't sure what Grit's reaction might be, though. He and Abby had to talk this over. Maybe they could figure out something that would settle the whole affair to everyone's satisfaction.

Anyway, it was time to go.

"Uh, thanks, Mr. Comstock, uh, Gus. It was wonderful talking to an expert. Suppose we wanted to buy the real coin for... for George. Would that be possible?"

"Sure," said Gus, "no forms to fill out, no waiting period. It's $13 dollars, like I said. Would you like it gift wrapped?"

"No, no. We'll take care of that."

Mr. Comstock made change for the twenty that Mouse handed him (so much for his dinner money) and handed him the coin.

"Thank you very much. If you or your wife ever want to sell either of your counterfeits, I would be glad to make an offer. Maybe I could go a little higher than what I said earlier."

"A hundred?" asked Mouse jokingly.

"Well hardly that, Mr. Sweet."

21

As they walked toward the door of the shop, Mouse took her hand and said, "George will love this, Abby." He did it impulsively, as a joke, and she did flash a smile, but then, somehow, he forgot to let go as they left the shop. To Mouse, it seemed as though she gripped his hand in return, and again he felt that strange energy that seemed to flow between them whenever they touched. Did she feel it too? He was afraid to ask.

The rain had stopped, and the temperature had plunged during the short time they had been inside the strange old shop, almost as if the receipt of so much hidden knowledge had somehow transformed the world outside.

"Why was he calling us Mr. and Mrs. Sweet?" wondered Abby.

Mouse chuckled, "I think it was just his idea of a joke."

"Yes, I suppose so. And, you went along with him," she accused.

Mouse laughed. "You caught on pretty quickly."

"Yes, but you had me confused there for a minute or two. I thought you had both gone crazy. Why did he name us Mr. and Mrs. Sweet, do you think?"

"I'm not exactly sure," said Mouse, considering. "Do you know Judge Sweet?"

"I don't know him, but I remember Daddy saying that was the man you were with at the kiddies parade. I thought he might be your grandfather."

Mouse sighed. "Things would be a lot simpler if he was. Maybe I looked a little like a Sweet to Mr. Comstock. It could be that I do; Judge Sweet told me he and I are related."

Abby smiled, "Whatever the reason, Mr. Comstock sure knew a lot about the coins, didn't he?"

Mouse thought so too, but did not answer immediately, as they had once again reached Main Street and the crowd at the carnival. They had walked in a great circle, first along empty streets where Abby had shared her secrets, and then into the coin shop where they had both learned so much. It seemed like everything had changed in the last hour and that life was now somehow simpler. He knew that once they left the crowds behind again, he would tell Abby everything, and then together they would figure out just what to do. She was perfect in so many ways.

"Mouse?"

"Yes, Abby?" he said softly.

"I have really got to get over to my aunt's house." She sounded wistful. "I was supposed to be there an hour ago, and they will be worrying about me."

"Your aunt's house? Is that in Clarion?"

"Yes, over on Wilson Avenue, down by the glass plant."

"OK, I'll walk you over — make sure you arrive safely," he smiled.

"Thanks. I wanted to talk some more about the coins."

"Me too," said Mouse. "I think we should each tell everything we know, and then decide what to do. How does that sound?"

"That's fine," said Abby cheerfully, as if she had been thinking the same thing. "You already know almost everything that I do. The only other thing is where I got my coin. I was down at the dump with my dad, looking for curious things among the junk, and I looked down and there it was. When my Dad saw it he…"

215

A loud voice cut her off.

"Well, well, well. What have we here? Little Mouse Monroe holding hands with a girl. How sweet." It was Chuck, along with a half dozen other senior boys — Ace Friedling, Brian Paxton and Andy Weston among them.

Mouse was outraged. Where did Chuck get off mocking him in front of Abby? He wanted to pop him one. Instead, he coldly announced, "Grandpa wants to see us after the parade Saturday about the bag."

"Yeah, I'll be there, little Mouse. Just make sure you let me do the talking, understand."

Mouse's eyes narrowed. We'll see about that, he thought.

Chuck looked at Abby, "How are you doing there, Abigail. You are looking mighty nice today. Why are you hanging with Mouse though? He's all right for a tenth grader, but you could do lots better."

Mouse felt her hand tighten in his. Her reply was quick and biting, "Like maybe you, for instance, Stinky?"

Chuck's buddies laughed. It seemed everyone knew about Chuck's run-in with the skunk. Suddenly Chuck looked nasty. Abby's shot had definitely hit home.

"Maybe I was wrong about you," he said angrily. "Maybe you should stick with little Mouse here after all. Maybe he will put up with your tongue. I sure wouldn't."

That was too much, and Mouse said, "You're some sweet guy, Chuck. If you aren't trying to bully me, you are insulting the girl I am with. Why don't you just take a hike?"

Chuck swung round to face Mouse and grabbed his jacket.

"You better watch your mouth, Mouse, if you know what's good for you," he threatened.

Mouse was unafraid. He was ready to do what he could if things got physical, but Abby had other ideas. "Pretty brave all of a sudden, aren't you, Stinky? The last time I saw you, you were running away from my father. Looks like odds of six against one are more your style."

Chuck's face went blood red. His left hand tightened on Mouse's front and he drew his right back to strike. Mouse set his feet and got ready, watching his cousin's eyes. There were some things worth fighting for.

Then Chuck's companions separated the two of them. Chuck struggled to free himself, and Mouse did the same. It was time they settled this. He might get whipped, but he would do enough damage to make Chuck think twice next time.

Abby seemed unimpressed. She walked a few steps down the street, turned and said, "Come on Mouse, I've got to get to my aunt's house, and anyway something smells around here."

Paxton had hold of Mouse.

"Man, she has a mouth on her, doesn't she?" he said. "You better watch out. Chuck won't forget this. What's with you anyway? All of a sudden, you are like a different guy. If you keep going like this, you're going to get stomped."

Mouse shook him off. "I'll take my chances, Brian. I'm tired of being frightened every time someone says 'boo.' From now on I am going to stand my ground, speak my mind, and let the chips fall where they may."

Paxton laughed, "Where did you hear that, in some old movie?"

A smile twitched at Mouse's lips, but he spoke seriously. "Maybe, but I still mean it."

Paxton walked away to catch up with his buddies, mumbling, "If you don't die, we're going to have to come up with some other nickname for you. Mouse doesn't fit anymore."

"Mouse is just fine," he said to the retreating back and then rejoined Abby.

"Those guys are jerks," she said with feeling.

"Not all of them. Just the one," he replied.

Their hands linked up again, and they walked down Main Street in the general direction of her aunt's house. They were silent, digesting recent events.

Then a very surprised face was peering down at them from inside the Methodist Vegetarian Foodstand.

"Hi, Mom," said Mouse. He was a little nervous but smiled a big smile nonetheless. They slowed down. Mouse wanted to introduce Abby to his mother, but then realized this was not the time or place. The food stand was busy, and that would cause delays and problems, and so he just said, "Bye, Mom," as breezily as he could manage and guided Abby on past the stand and down the street, his mother regaining her wits just enough to call out a slightly confused sounding "Bye, honey."

"That was my mother," confided Mouse.

"I figured that when you called her Mom," replied Abby with a sly smile. Mouse smiled too. Paxton was right. She did have a quick tongue in her head.

Foot traffic was very dense and conversation impossible for the next half block. Mouse used the time to work on a plan for wrapping up the adventure of the lost coins. He thought he saw a way, but needed a little more proof of Boston Buck's involvement. Maybe he and Abby could work on getting that together.

"Will you be in town tomorrow?" he asked.

"Yes, I'm staying at my aunt's until Sunday. Mom and Dad have a stand tomorrow at Farmers and Crafters Day, and I'm to baby-sit the kids at Aunt Ellen's in the morning and then help at the stand in the afternoon."

Mouse was disappointed, "So you will be busy the whole day?"

"Yes, and on Saturday we all go to the parade, but after that I could maybe get free for a while. We won't be going back to the farm until after church on Sunday."

Mouse considered. Not everything was perfectly clear, but maybe he had the beginnings of a plan.

"Look, will your dad be at the parade on ...," and he stopped. Abby had just said something, and Mouse was very sure he had misheard. It had sounded like "Now there'll be hell to pay."

He looked at her with concern, and then snapped his head around to where a truck was stopped dead in the middle of Main Street. An angry man inside yelled, "Abigail Grit, get into this truck NOW!" It was Simon Grit. Mouse's heart sank. The plan. She didn't know the plan!

Did he imagine it, or did she give his hand a squeeze before moving to obey the shouted command? Mouse was suddenly desperate to calm her father; he needed to convince Simon Grit that he was not an enemy.

Grit threw the passenger-side door wide open and Abby scrambled neatly up and in, then he leaned across and glared fiercely down at Mouse, "Listen boy and listen good. You keep away from us or there will be hell to pay. Stay away from my fields, stay away from Bear Run. Most of all, boy, you stay away from my daughter. You can go anywhere in the whole wide world you like, but don't ever come near me or mine again. Do you hear?"

Mouse didn't blink an eye. He was as calm as a sunny day.

"I understand, sir, but let me just expla…"

Grit slammed the passenger door, punched the gas, and the truck burned rubber for ten feet, raising a cloud of blue smoke and a noise like something dying. Mouse watched the truck slide a little at the sudden acceleration and speed away. Abby's last words came back to mind. She had been right.

There would be hell to pay.

*　*　*

That evening Mouse wandered the east end of town looking for some sign of Abby. As he walked, he worked on his plan. It would be good to know more about Boston Buck, but he now knew most of the rest. He understood where the treasure had come from, why Grit was so determined to find it, and who really owned the coins. If he could just calm Grit down long enough to explain, things would be all right, but the last time he had seen

219

the man, he sure had not been in any listening mood. Grandpa Mike was the same way. Mouse was puzzled about what to do. All this anger made planning so much harder. Things would be so much easier if only he was dealing with rational people — like Judge Sweet.

After an hour, Mouse gave it up and walked back to the center of town where he found himself part of a crowd watching Indians dancing in front of the courthouse. Some of them banged on drums, while others hopped and twirled, shook and chanted to the throbbing beat. The monotony of it was soothing, so he just stood there listening and watching the sweat-slick bodies bounce and rotate under the starry night sky. The performance should have been silly, placed as it was in the middle of a carnival, but there was something about it, something about its appeal to ancient Gods, that comforted him. The Indians finished with the Hoop Dance, and then Mouse turned away from the crowd and walked toward home. It had been a good day, all in all. He was feeling less confused about so many things.

Tonight, he would look up Boston Buck on the Internet, and tomorrow would pay a return visit to Judge Sweet and tell him the whole tale — all about the counterfeit coins, Simon Grit, Chuck, Grandpa Mike, Abby, the man in the courthouse, even Gus Comstock. Judge Sweet was the key to it all.

He would ask for Judge Sweet's advice, and then he would act on it.

22

By four in the morning, Simon Grit was up and loading buckets of mums, zinnias, marigolds and cosmos into the bed of the old pickup. Even though the water that sloshed at the bottom of each bucket didn't add much weight, he still had to stow the load just so if the flowers were to arrive in Clarion upright and in good condition. The pavilion tent was part of the load too, and that further complicated the packing.

He pulled away from the barn at 5 a.m., the sky just starting to lighten. It looked like it would be a cool and sunny day, perfect for the business at hand. Susan and Abby were to meet him at the stall site and set up the tent while he returned to the farm for a second load — more cut flowers and the dry stuff: straw flowers, statice, Indian corn, gourds and the last of the honey. It should be a good Friday, perfect for Farmers and Crafters, but his mood was grim, and his thoughts were often of his traitorous daughter. What was to be done with her?

He had been worried a little the previous day, when she was late arriving at Ellen's house, but had supposed that she had lost track of the time, what with the carnival and all. Driving down Main Street, looking for her, he had been shocked to see her walking hand-in-hand with a boy. Then he had recognized the kid, and in an instant, mild annoyance had gone to full-blown, all-consuming rage. What had the girl been thinking?

Abby had been silent as they drove away toward Ellen's. That had suited him just fine; he was way, way too angry to talk. Once started he would lose control, would say things he'd later regret, would impose punishments that Susan would later argue against. All because of that lousy, sneaky Mouse Monroe.

As they had neared the house, Abby had looked at him sadly and said, "Daddy, …"

He had cut her off with a curt, "Shut your mouth." Abby had gone silent, tears slowly trailing down her cheeks. Even Simon had been surprised at how harsh and bitter he had sounded.

Susan was there when they got to Ellen's and had looked surprised when he ordered their oldest to the bedroom. He had told Abby to stay out of his sight, and she had, until hours later when he had left for the farm to tend to the chores and get ready for this morning's early start.

Even this morning though, he was still mad as hell at his daughter.

When Simon got to Clarion, cops at barricades already blocked normal traffic from Main Street, but they saw the flowers and let him pass with no trouble. He drove up to the old Orpheum Theater, and there they were, standing under the marquee, just as planned. They looked drab and unhappy in the dim morning light.

Susan gave a wave and greeted him, "Good morning, Simon. You're right on time."

There was something missing, though, and Simon somehow doubted the day would be a very happy one, no matter how many flowers, gourds, jars of honey and ears of corn they sold. Beyond a small nod, he ignored Abby, but did make an effort to speak cheerfully to his wife.

"Hi, Susan. Let's get unloaded, and I'll get back to the farm for the second load before traffic picks up. They'll chase the trucks off Main at 7:30."

The girls took the pails as he handed them down and carried them over under the marquee of the gaudy old movie house, where they would be out of harm's way until the tent was erected. The off-loading went swiftly, and 10 minutes later Simon was ready to pull out for the farm again, leaving the women behind to set up the lightweight tent and begin arranging the goods for sale.

As he waved a hand in farewell, Susan came over to the truck window and said, "Bring the antiques you found, too. I cleaned them up a bit, and they might spark a little interest. They're in a box on the kitchen table."

"Right," he said and pulled away, very depressed.

He thought about it all the way back to the farm. Somehow, the sweet girl who had been his confidant two days before, the girl who had helped to pull the wool over his wife's eyes with this business of the "antiques," this same girl had turned on him and walked hand-in-hand with that Mouse. It just didn't make any sense. There must be more to it than he knew. She must have had some girlish plan to win the boy's confidence, some amateur scheme to weasel information out of him. Maybe that was it. But if that was her plan, why hadn't she told him? Then he smiled grimly. Well, he guessed he hadn't given her much chance to explain. Maybe things weren't as bad as they seemed. Maybe she was on his side after all. Maybe she had found out something.

By the time he got back to town with more flowers, a bushel basket full of gourds, a box of honey and the suspect antiques, Simon's mood had improved. Abby was gone of course, gone to spell Ellen with the younger children, so Susan's sister could spend the morning enjoying the crush and bustle on Main Street. Susan was there though, and as they packed in the remaining goods, he looked around and thought the booth looked just fine. He would move the truck down behind Hufnagel's and then walk the block and a half back to begin the business of the day. It would be just the two of them then, just like old times. Suddenly he felt better. It might be a pretty good day after all.

At 10 a.m., he was finally able to say a few words to Susan. "Things are going great, aren't they?"

"You bet, honey," she said, looking just a bit frazzled. "We have never sold so much so fast. At this rate, we'll be cleaned out by 2 o'clock. Do you think you should run back over to the farm for a couple of more buckets of mums?"

"I guess I could manage that, but maybe we had better wait until Abby gets here at noon. You two can hold the fort while I'm gone, and then we can each sneak off for a bite to eat."

Susan frowned a little doubtfully. "OK, but are you going to be all right around Abby? Last I heard you two weren't talking."

"Yeah, it will be all right," Simon said reassuringly. "I think maybe I ought to talk to her anyway, find out what she has to say about this Mouse business."

"I guess it was a big shock for you seeing them together like that."

Simon's laugh was brittle, "I guess you *could* say that." He might have known the two women would have talked things over by now.

"So what's changed?" asked Susan.

"Aw, I don't know. She's always been the best girl in the world. I guess I don't think she could suddenly change into some sneaking, conniving hussy."

Susan laughed a knowing laugh, as if she wasn't quite so sure. "She is a teenager now, Simon. She is going to change; get used to the idea. Always remember though, deep down inside she will never change at all. At heart she will always be our little girl; on the surface, though, we are in for some interesting times."

"Oh, joy," was Simon's ironic reply and then they parted to explain to new customers the best plan for making the flowers last, and the virtues of gourds and corn as seasonal decorations.

Abby was there on the last clap of the courthouse bells at noon. She was looking considerably more chipper than earlier and lit up even more when Simon gave her a big "hello" and said how nice she looked. Shortly after that, he headed off down the street to get more mums. The sidewalk was jam-packed, but he smiled happily at the throngs of people he passed. Somehow it was exciting to be a part of the busy crowd.

He had gotten to Fifth and Main and was about to turn away down Fifth, when he heard a deep voice boom out, "Simon Grit, you old son of a bitch. How the hell are ya?"

Thirty feet further on Odell Pinkus was motioning for Simon to join him. Now Simon really smiled — Odell Pinkus at Farmers and Crafters Day? Talk about unlikely.

"Odell, what are you doing here? And, you have a booth! What are you, a farmer or a crafter?"

"I ain't much of neither, I guess," said Odell with disgust. "Here, stand up on this chair and look around and tell me what you see."

Simon humored him and was soon standing shakily on the frame of a lawn chair that had seen better days, Odell steadying him with a hand on his belt. From up there he found he could see most of a block in either direction. The stalls stretched away both ways, as varied in their colors as they were in shape and size. The sidewalks and streets were positively packed full of meandering shoppers, browsers and people just having a good time.

"So, what do you see?" prompted Odell.

"I see people, lots and lots of people having a mighty good time. I see colors, every color that God ever invented. I see long lines of booths and a mighty fine day."

Odell was immune to the poetry of the remark, "Yeah, yeah. Now tell me what you don't see."

"Don't see?"

"Yeah, what's missing from your mighty fine day?"

"What's missing? Rain clouds? Snow banks? Lots of things."

"What's missing is men," said Odell with bitterness. "I spend all this time, all this money to bring my collection of hubcaps and most of the junk in my dad's basement up here, and there ain't nothing but women to buy the stuff. Hell, they won't even stop and *look* for God's sake."

Simon hopped down from the frayed lawn chair, and Odell promptly plunked down into it. Simon looked him over. He was wearing a less-than-clean looking T-shirt and sucking on some beverage out of a bag. What could the man be thinking of?

Then he surveyed the crowd close at hand and realized Odell was right. There were easily five women for every man, and whereas the women browsed and poked, compared and considered, most of the men had a long-suffering air about them, as if they were not there from choice — "You *will* go to Farmers and Crafters, dear," a resigned shrug and hubby answers, "Yes, my sweet."

"Well, you know this isn't a lawn sale, Odell."

"Yeah, well now I do. I'm going to lose a wad of cash on this deal," grumbled Odell.

"So, it's not going too well?" asked Simon with some sympathy, even though he felt more like laughing. Odell at Farmers and Crafters? What could be stranger than that?

Odell fixed him with a hard stare and said, "Women, as a general rule, aren't very interested in hub caps, even if they are prime undented hub caps. Then there's my old man's junk. It's beat up, but mostly it still works. I've got his radio, an old metal detector, a two-slice toaster, and pretty good oscillating fan. I even got a fuel pump for a '64 Chevy. These women ain't interested in any of it. All they want is flowers, cute little knickknacks, and crap like that. Who'd want that stuff?"

Simon *had* to laugh now, "Well, our flowers are selling pretty well."

"Yeah, yeah. Rub it in," growled Odell. Then he looked at Simon hopefully. "Could I maybe interest you in a fuel pump? It's in prime condition. Or, how about a radio?"

"I've got an old radio already, Odell, and I don't own a '64 Chevy so I don't suppose I need a fuel pump for one. Tell you what though; I'll maybe take that metal detector off your hands if it works."

Odell brightened, "Yeah, she works. I tried it out this mornin'. What'll you give me for it? It's probably worth $60."

Simon considered. He'd only need the thing a couple of hours, for one last visit to the dump. He'd scout around the edges and see what he could turn up. It was a long shot, but he still itched to find that treasure. Then he had an amusing notion and laughed. In return for the metal detector, he'd teach Odell how to sell his junk.

"Tell you what, Odell. I'll give you a T-shirt and a basket full gourds for the metal detector."

"What kind of lame deal is that? I got a T-shirt, and I don't know as I need one gourd, let alone a basket full. Get real, Si! What will you give me for it in hard cash?"

Simon was still chuckling as he said, "Look, Odell, if you take my deal, I'll tell you how sell a lot of this other stuff. What you need is a marketing plan, and if the one I give you doesn't work, you can have the gizmo back next week, and keep the T-shirt and the gourds besides."

Odell looked very doubtful, muttered "gourds" with distaste and then slumped in his chair with a resigned air. "I guess I'll take your deal. I sure ain't doin' too well the way I'm goin'."

Simon was suddenly all business, "OK. Give me the metal detector. Here's a twenty. Go over next door there and buy yourself an Autumn Leaf Festival T-shirt and put it on, then use the T-shirt you're wearing to polish all this stuff. It's got to look clean and shiny."

"OK, I'll do it," grumbled Odell, "but I don't see what difference all this spit and polish will make."

"You will once you get the gourds going. Oh, and lose whatever is you have in that paper bag. You can't drink beer and be an effective salesman. If you're thirsty get yourself a Coke."

Simon took the detector and hustled off toward his truck. When he returned 40 minutes later, he was wobbling along

227

carrying four buckets of fresh flowers and a small basket filled nearly to the brim with gourds. Odell was busy polishing the fuel pump, but gave that up to paw through the gourds.

"Hey," he said, surprised. "These things are pretty neat. Seems like they're all different. How'd they grow that way?"

Simon didn't have time to chitchat, "Look, Odell, here is what you've got to do. You listening? Put down that gourd and listen!"

"OK, OK."

"What you do is you watch the crowd until you see a man and wife coming your way, and then you start yelling, 'Gourds, get your gourds here, only 50 cents each!' Don't yell too loud, but make sure the woman hears. Do you understand?"

"And you say that's going to sell the rest of this stuff?" asked Odell doubtfully.

"I think it will," said Simon with confidence. "See, what the wife will do is stop to look at the gourds because they cost a dollar or two dollars everywhere else, and she knows it. Because they are all different, she will take a while picking through them to find the ones she wants. While she's doing that, you go to work on her husband. Remember, he's been wandering around behind her for hours and is good and ready to look at something hard and shiny. Get the idea?"

Odell was smiling now. He liked it. "I do believe I do, Simon. You always were a clever son of a bitch."

Simon winced, "Odell, you have got to talk right, too. No 'hell's or 'son of a bitch'es. Talk to these people like they were your grandparents."

Odell looked confused, like maybe he had learned to talk the way he did *from* his grandparents, but finally the point sank in and he muttered, "OK, keep it clean. Like in school. Got it."

"Good luck," said Simon, and he picked up the flower pails and made for his own booth half a block away. He dearly wished he could stay and watch old Odell play the role of merchant huckster, but he had to get back. Susan and Abby would be waiting.

Two hours later, it was just him and Abby running the booth. They had sold all the honey and most of the dry flowers, but there was a constant stream of customers who had put off buying the fresh stuff until they were about to leave, so he and Abby didn't get much chance to stand around and chatter. That was probably for the best, Simon figured. Though they were now on more cordial terms, they both knew there were things to hash out between them. Monday would be soon enough, though, thought Simon. Life would return to normal then. He was happy now, and he was content to wait. It had been a good day after all.

"Daddy, do you have change for a fifty?"

"Sure, Sweet Pea. Is it for those folks over there pawing through the roses?"

"Yes. It's the woman doing the pawing, though. The man has some sort of ugly motor or something, and he just keeps looking at it and smiling. It's weird."

Simon looked over and caught a glimpse of the man and the object he was holding. Then he started to laugh, and the laugh swelled and grew, until Abby had to laugh too.

She saw it was what the man held that was the cause of the merriment, but she didn't understand. "What is it Dad? What's he got in his hands?"

Simon gasped the sweet fall air, steadied himself against a tent pole, and exclaimed happily, "Unless I miss my guess, Sweat Pea, that is a fuel pump for a '64 Chevy."

23

For the fifth time that lonely Friday spent among crowds, Mouse climbed up into the dark recesses of the Hahne Building, to where Judge Sweet kept his office. He padded down the hall, knocked at the door, tried the knob and turned away. He was not surprised at all.

Mouse had been searching for the judge since 8 a.m. that morning. His office had been empty all day, but the streets were thronged with people, and so Mouse spent most of the time wandering around in hopes of seeing the man who was the key to all his plans. He tried phoning and visiting the judge's home, but no one was there. There wasn't even an answering machine. Was Judge Sweet away or was he somewhere among the tens of thousands of people jumbled up in downtown Clarion?

Mouse felt as if he had visited every one of the 300 booths along Main Street. He had looked at pinecone and popsicle-stick crafts, smelled the potpourri and scented candles, and heard a hundred different wind chimes. He had puttered around the carnival stalls, gazed up at the screaming rides and checked the lines at the food stands. He had even looked inside the courthouse. Judge Sweet was nowhere to be found.

Now it was late afternoon, and he was reluctantly coming to the conclusion that he needed another plan. The day had been wasted with fruitless searching — now he would just have to come up with something on his own. Mouse headed down Main again, thinking hard. If he could just bring Grit and Grandpa Mike together, maybe he could tell them everything he knew and get the two talking. Maybe then they could iron out the mess with the treasure even without Judge Sweet. It sounded like a long shot, but it was the best he could come up with. To pull it off, he'd need guts, facts, and luck — lots of luck.

He was on the other side of the street when he passed by the Grits' stall, and paused to peek in that direction through a screen of bobbing heads and moving bodies. Abby was there now, and she and her father were laughing about something. Mouse was very glad to see that Abby had survived her father's very different mood of the previous day. He doubted the smiles would last long, though, if he sauntered over to join them, yet he had to talk to Abby or get a message to her if the scheme he was brewing was to succeed. Mouse shrugged. He would come back when he was done at the library and figure out how to slip her a note.

Now he moved to walk down the middle of the street, and he noticed right away that the foot traffic was thinning. Yeah, people were heading home. Earlier, Main Street had felt like an immense outdoor mall; now it was a road again. He was not at all surprised when a pickup truck came very slowly from the other direction. That would be the first of the vendors getting ready to pack up. In an hour, the exodus would be complete and Main would once again be full of cars and trucks. He had to hurry. He had to find the information and get it to Abby quickly, along with a note of explanation so she could get her dad to show up at the right place, at the right time.

The used book sale in front of the Clarion Free Library was still in full swing and, here at least, the crowd had not thinned. Lines of tired shoppers still idly pawed through the boxes of books and flipped through the curious old volumes. What Mouse wanted was not out here in the sun, though. What he wanted probably only existed on a piece of film in a quiet room inside.

Up the old gray stone stairs, through the large front door and into the quiet, quiet interior of the library, he went. There seemed to be no one around, but that was OK. He had seen the machines before; he knew where to go, what to do.

Mouse went to the room marked "Local History." It was empty too, but that was all right. There were the microfilm machines; there were the cases full of microfilmed copies of old newspapers. He would manage.

His Internet search the previous night had turned up Boston Buck quickly enough, but most of the information had been about horse stealing, not counterfeiting. One of the Web pages, though, had referenced three dates in the *Clarion Democrat* as its source of information — October 15, 1885, October 22, 1885 and November 12, 1885. Mouse had written the dates down and now hoped the newspapers of those dates would have more to say about Buck's loot and what had become of it. Anyway, copies of the actual newspaper articles would convince Grandpa and Grit better than any printouts from the 'Net could. Anybody could put anything on a Web page.

He found the right reel of film, with some difficulty threaded it into the machine, and then fiddled and fussed with switches, reels, lenses and sliding plates until, after a quarter of an hour, the image of an old newspaper appeared on the screen.

It was from January 1885, so he turned the fast-forward knob and watched the film race past into the future. When he stopped it again, he found that he had overrun the dates he wanted and was now in early 1886, so he rewound at a much slower pace, stopping frequently to check his place in time.

The pages of the 1885 *Clarion Democrat* were old and strange, much different from the papers he had seen in Mr. Galardo's history class. There were ads for Shallenbergher's Depot for Dry

Goods, for Grayson and Sykes Carriage Manufactures, for lush farmlands in Wyoming, and for disease remedies of every description. What was pyaemia? What was scrofula? What was a liver regulator, or Brown's Iron Bitters or Ayer's Sarsaparilla? Mouse wanted to stop and investigate, but this was not the time.

Then the banner running across the front page said it was November 12, 1885, and Mouse started scanning the image closely. A list of county office holders, borough officials and lawyers was printed at the left side. Scanning this he saw a familiar last name:

Jacob Sweet, Attorney-At-Law, Clarion, Pa. Office on Fifth.

That was interesting. Some early relation of the judge's no doubt, and Mouse suddenly realized, some early relation of his own as well. He poked the print button and out came a white-on-black copy of the screen. He'd ask Judge Sweet about the man.

Examining the reverse image printout for readability, Mouse was startled to see that they had had poetry on the front page back in those days:

Patience

Have patience heart!
That were no rose that were not first a closed
    bud.
How comes the day? Not with the noonday
    sun overhead,
But slowly stealing up the east, in faintest red.
Have patience heart! Whit so thine own life's
    dawning good.

He didn't understand it, but there was something there, something that seemed to speak to him. No time now though.

HANK HUFNAGEL

Where was the part about Boston Buck? That's what he needed to find, and find fast!

Rapidly he finished scanning the first page. Nothing. He touched the control to move forward. Zip went the mechanism, and there was the old man himself looking out of the page at him!

Clarion Democrat — November 12, 1885

"Boss" Buck.

A BRIEF HISTORY OF THE VETERAN "CROOK"
AND THE GANG HE LED.

During the past month few names have been brought more prominently or frequently before the reading public in this section of the State than that which heads this sketch, nor during the past quarter century could any man in this section of the country for shrewdness, cuteness and alleged cussedness lay claim to a more brilliant record than this same distinguished individual.

234

Mouse read it closely and was unsurprised to find much he already knew from the Internet. Boston "Boss" Buck had been born in 1817 in Centre County, pretended to be a horse dealer and trader, was six foot two inches high, and weighed about 230 pounds. This was good stuff, but not what Mouse was after.

Then, most of the way through the long article, the writer turned to Buck's abilities as a counterfeiter. Mouse's mouth went dry and his heart quickened; this part had been missing from the Internet account:

> None of them could make it like him. He used a composition of antimony, block tin, bismuth and glass, which to compound in the proper proportions must have been the result of long years of careful experiment and study.
>
> The money was coined in plaster paris moulds, and the counterfeiter's den, was a cabin eight miles from Marienville, and five miles from any habitation, in the wilds of Forest county. The guardian angel of the sacred spot was a trapper who lived by his gun in the forest. He was in Buck's house the night the old man was captured, but had mysteriously disappeared, though he was supposed to be there when a search was made for him. His escape prevented the capturing of the counterfeiting apparatus, which was so arranged that every evidence to coniacking could be destroyed in an hour. The old sly trapper is in all probability still engaged in the innocent occupation of shooting squirrels, without the least suspicion that a pair of iron bracelets are sighing to encircle his brawny wrist.
>
> Old Boss Buck was arrested about 11 o'clock at night. He came down to the door in answer to the officer's knock, holding an open knife carelessly in his hand, as though for no purpose.

"Are you Mr. Buck?" asked the detective, who had previously made his acquaintance in the guise of a book agent.

"I am," said the old man, looking suspiciously at this visitor.

"I have a warrant for you! Come out and get in the wagon."

"I want you to read that warrant first," replied the "old Boss," drawing back.

The officer, with one eye on the paper and the other fixed on the old man, who stood threateningly in the doorway, read the warrant. As he finished Buck took a step forward and raised a knife with an angry gleam in his eye, but quick as lightning the officer's right hand seized his wrist, and his left grasped him firmly by the arm, and an assistant appearing at that moment, the king of counterfeiters was on his face in an instant and his hands were secured by a pair of iron cuffs. He knew that it was all up with him, yet when raised to his feet, and afterwards placed in the wagon, he never said a word, but a sigh, so deep that it was painful, shook his frame, and he remained silent, after giving expression the one remark: "I have no counterfeit money."

Pay dirt!

Mouse quickly made two copies of the article, rewound the film, replaced it in its box, shut off the machine and impatiently waited to pay for the copies at the front desk. A passing staff member, her arms full of used books, finally took notice of him and relieved him of his money. Then he was out the door and down the steps as fast as he could go. It was no good though; he knew it the minute he saw the cars and trucks driving on Main Street. Farmers and Crafters was over. The Grits would be gone.

He tramped the carnival, examined the groups around the street musicians, visited the art show. After dark, he hung around the teen dance in front of the courthouse in hopes that Abby would somehow miraculously appear.

One of a group of girls asked him sweetly, "Where's Abby, Mouse?"

He stammered that he was looking for her and then blushed as they walked away giggling. Stupid girls!

The dance ended and the crowd faded away. A few die-hard enthusiasts still hung around with the carnies, but the day was over, and Mouse resigned himself to yet another failed search and dragged himself on home.

With trembling fingers, he dialed the number he had found in the telephone book. It rang four times, then an irritated voice answered, "Grits. Simon speaking."

He had hoped to get Mrs. Grit or Abby. He should have guessed it would be Mr. Grit who would answer the phone, should have planned what to say. Mouse was tired to death of failure. How could he start this conversation with Mr. Grit? Should he ask after Abby? No, that would just stir the man up, better to come to the point immediately. OK, so what should he ....

"Jerk!" snarled Simon Grit, and the line went dead.

Mouse looked at his watch. It was nearly midnight. What was he thinking of, calling someone at that hour! He would not try again. Tomorrow would be soon enough — tomorrow when he was fresh, tomorrow when he was supported by his grandfather. He'd find a way to set up the meeting tomorrow after the parade. But patience was hard. He wanted to do it now, do it before he went to sleep — do it so he *could* sleep.

Patience. The word sparked a memory and he dug around for the poem from the 1885 newspaper and puzzled over the verses, then turned off the reading light behind his pillow, and five minutes later, he was sound asleep.

Patience

Have patience heart!
That were no rose that were not first a closed
bud.
How comes the day? Not with the noonday
sun overhead,
But slowly stealing up the east, in faintest red.
Have patience heart! Whit so thine own life's
dawning good.

Have patience heart!
Seek not at morn to make the day as bright as
noon.
Force not the bud before its time, to be a rose.
How slowly, when we watch the sky, the
daylight grow.
And yet, for all, the sun goes down too soon.

24

The rooster's shrill crow woke Simon Grit just before dawn. Half an hour later, he was frying a couple of eggs and marveling at the strange quiet of the house. It made an interesting change, but even after just two days, he missed the bustle of the rest of his clan. Ah, well. He would see them soon enough, and maybe it was for the best. After he tended to the livestock, he planned to spend a couple of hours in the woods with his new gizmo. Susan might understand or she might not — best if she didn't know. If he didn't find anything this time, that would be the end of it. What were the chances, anyway? The treasure had been lost for over a hundred years.

An hour later he stepped into the woods, the metal detector slung over one shoulder. He carried a flashlight in one hip pocket and a small garden shovel in the other. He had tested the detector on a couple of quarters, and sure enough, it worked to a distance of about 8 inches. That should do just fine.

He walked down the hill toward the stream and the dump beyond, and he was curious to see that frost lay everywhere on the ground down here in the woods. This would be a fine sunny October day, but he could see his breath and knew colder mornings weren't too many days away. That would be fine. Life would slow a little; the mosquitoes and horseflies would disappear; they'd make some maple sugar, sled ride, and maybe he'd take the boys along hunting. The treasure seemed insignificant next to all that; hell, the treasure probably didn't even exist anymore. He'd give it another hour and then drive over to Ellen's, hook up with his family, and then they would all walk up to see the parade. He looked forward to it, but this last little experiment with the metal detector would be interesting too.

Simon turned on the machine and began waving it back and forth as he inched down the path toward the big fallen tree below the dump. He hoped to find a trail of coins that would lead somewhere and at first was excited by the constant squeals of the detector. Time and time again, though, he dug down only to find a nail, a lug nut or some other small metal object. Once he found an old-fashioned key of curious design, but he never turned up a coin.

When he got away from the dump, the detector quieted down a good deal, and he made much better time. At the end of half an hour, he had reached the fallen hickory with nothing much to show for his efforts — certainly no trail of coins leading away to treasure. Fine. He'd scramble up to the top of the ravine and scan back along the top. If that didn't turn up anything, he'd trail on home, get cleaned up and head for Clarion.

Simon was content; another failure this morning wouldn't bother him. He'd just turn those coins found by the Boy Scouts over to Swagman on Monday, let the kids know he had done it, and then get on with his life. It was the right thing to do. The search for the treasure had brought nothing but frustration and heartache for a week, almost like the thing was jinxed. He had had enough of it. He was ready to move on to something more productive; maybe next week he'd do a little work on that weak section of fence at the upper end of the high pasture.

Simon turned off the detector, slung it across his back and wormed his way up through the rhododendron that covered the

240

steep slope. He felt a small stab of pain from his wounded thigh and consciously took it easy. The thing was healing OK, and he didn't want to tear it up again with a fall. He came level with the root ball of the downed tree and stood resting and surveying the pretty valley below. He eyes glided down the stream with the churned up water and came to rest on the crown of the hickory lying on the hillside opposite. The trunk of the thing made a pretty good bridge across the ravine and he turned to see how easy it would be to get onto at this end. That's when he saw the hole. His heart leapt a mile, and he went hot and shaky, suddenly filled with anticipation. This *had* to be the place!

He hugged the metal detector to his chest and slid down the slope into the mine on his rump. His wounded thigh complained at the rough treatment, but he ignored it. This must be the old mine in the story, and the footprints in the dirt at its entrance had told him he was not the first to find it.

He got to his feet, fished out his flashlight and pointed its yellow beam at the rock walls and dirt floor of the place. Clear as the morning, he could see a set of tracks going deep into the mine and returning — tennis shoes — it was one of the kids for sure. He followed along and found a flashlight lying on the floor at a place where the ground was disturbed. He tried the light. It was broken. He examined the ground carefully. There were tracks and parallel lines in the dust that showed the kid had been trying to gather up something in the dark, after his light had broken. Then, four feet off to one side, where it had rolled in the dark, he saw what the kid had been collecting. He picked it up, and it was perfect, so round and real, not a trace of corrosion. The treasure had been here, and now it was gone.

He limped back along the way he had come and then stopped to examine the coin again in the dim light that filtered down into the mine from outside. Sure enough, it was an 1878 silver dollar. He was not at all surprised, but he was sad; sad that he and Papa hadn't found the stash; sad for the young thief who had stolen it away. The taking of such a thing from state lands could not be ignored. He hated to turn the kid, whoever he was, over to the tender mercies of Swagman, but what else could he do? If the finder's intentions had been pure, there would have been some notice by now; Simon would have heard about it at Autumn Leaf or there would have been something in the papers. No — the kid meant to keep the treasure and that he could not allow.

Simon heard a scrape above and realized someone was up there. He pressed himself tight against the wall and waited. There was more scraping, but no one came down the slope into the mine. Gently Simon laid aside the metal detector and then quietly crawled up toward the daylight. Three feet from the top, just under an old rotten beam, he saw the soles of two tennis shoes and the cuffs of a pair of olive drab Scout pants. He heard un-Scout like swearing. The voice was deep. Who could it be? Why had he come back? Why was he on hands and knees, and faced away from the entrance to the mine? It didn't make sense. It didn't matter. He would soon get answers to all his questions.

Simon crawled upward a few more feet, cautiously reached forward, and then quickly grabbed the kid's left foot. He yelled, "Gotcha!" and began pulling the stranger down into the mine. For a second the idea worked. He heard a wail, and could tell his opponent had grabbed at something to keep from being dragged down into the dark. That was OK. Simon just pulled all the harder. The kid started flailing around with his free foot at the hands dragging him underground. He was strong, seemed strong as a man, but it didn't matter. There was no way Simon would let go. Then it happened. The kicking foot hit the rotten beam and something moved. Earth began to slowly fall from above and then the whole entrance of the cave seemed to sag downward. Simon never let go of the kid's shoe, but suddenly that was all it was, an empty shoe. He hurriedly rolled back into the mine to avoid being buried under the tons of earth that were now settling down to close the entrance to the mine forever. All was darkness.

He felt for his light and was relieved when he flicked its switch and the beam sprang obediently to life. He examined the wreckage of the entrance, then gulped and yelled, "Hello!"

By the third "Hello", he knew that no one was going to answer. That's when he started to get mad.

It was a good thing he had the little shovel and the light. He wouldn't need much of a hole, just enough to worm out through, and he started to dig just above the remains of the wooden beam. And, he kept at it. Hours passed, his hands were scraped and bloody, his leg was on fire, and he could tell his thigh wound had pulled open and was bleeding freely again. Through it all, his rage grew and grew. What kind of a person would leave a man to die a lonely death in a collapsed mine? The kid had not gone for help. The accident had been no accident at all. Simon's assailant had meant to do murder, and now he would pay.

It was near noon when the first speck of daylight showed, and what a cheering sight that was. Twenty minutes later, Simon wriggled free of the earth and started sliding painfully down the slope to the trail by Bear Run. He knew where he would find his man. He had been dressed as a Boy Scout, and that could only mean he would be marching in the parade with the rest of them. If he didn't show up, people would ask why. And anyway, it would make for the perfect alibi.

Simon hobbled grimly up the trail toward the top of the hill, his truck, and the Autumn Leaf Parade. He was dizzy. He was furious. With one hand, he tried to slow the flow of blood from his thigh. He'd have to get that looked at again, but first things first. The single soiled tennis shoe he clutched in his right hand was proof of the attack. He had business in Clarion.

25

Shortly before noon, the first of the marchers in the *Clarion Hospital Autumn Leaf Festival Parade* stepped off down Wood Street. The parade was as big as its official name implied, and the last marching units would not take step one for yet another hour. Troop 51 was slated to walk somewhere about the middle of the grand line of participants. The Scouts idled away the time by helping themselves to some of the candy they were to throw to kids along the route, and by chattering among themselves about the bands, floats and twirling girls that marched and rolled by their position on Grand Avenue. Finally, the parade marshal gave a wave of his hand, they fell into rough marching order, and the hike along the mile-long parade route began.

Mouse walked near the center of the troop surrounded by Beaner, Jim, Bobby and Pee Wee. These guys had heard about the plan for a permanent Mice Patrol and wanted to stay close to their new leader. The patrol was already famous for its exploits of the previous week, and many a young Scout kicked himself that he had missed the Clarion Camporee, where it had all begun. Now these same young Scouts were doing their best to get into the new outfit. Mouse was proud of the stir the Mice had caused, but his thoughts today were of other things.

Grandpa Mike had arrived, panting and adjusting his neatly pressed Class A uniform, just as they started to move. Mouse glanced back to where he now walked at the rear of the troop. He looked calm enough, and he was wearing the neckerchief slide made from the old coin. Maybe that meant something, maybe it didn't; Mouse couldn't tell for sure, but he fervently hoped his grandfather was in a good mood or there would be big trouble at the end to the parade.

The troop had to walk a couple of blocks along Wood Street and then up Seventh Avenue to get to Main, where the real crowds would be waiting. Still, even on these back streets, people in lawn chairs lined the sides of the road, and youngsters waved and yelled at the Scouts to throw them candy. The younger guys responded enthusiastically and most of their supply disappeared before the parade was even fairly underway. Mouse knew better and threw his sweets one at a time, rather than by the handful. As he walked along, he constantly scanned both sides of the route, looking for Simon Grit, looking for Abby.

It was a very pleasant day for a walk and the marching gave Mouse the opportunity to enjoy the spectacle of the crowd as it, in turn, enjoyed the huge parade wending past.

The troop turned left onto Main Street and then Mouse saw the real crowd that had come to watch the event. If the parade was large, the crowd was immense. Children sat in front on the street curbs; behind were mothers and grandmothers looking very comfortable in every style and type of portable seating ever invented by man. Behind the seated folks, the standers were stacked five deep, arranged roughly by height, with here and there a young son or daughter perched on a dad's shoulders. Every high point along the route had been scaled and filled with teenage boys. Every upper story window of the stores and office blocks along Main Street was wide open and filled with bobbing heads and pointing fingers. Mouse was appalled. There might be 50,000 people in this merry crowd. How in the world would he ever spot Simon Grit or Abby among the throng?

"Mouse, could I borrow some of your candy?" It was Pee Wee, holding up an empty bag. "I'm all out. We should have brought more, maybe in a wheelbarrow or a pickup truck."

Mouse smiled; he would use the Mice to find the Grits. "OK, Pee Wee, I'll give you some of mine, but get the other guys over here for a minute first, would you?"

Pee Wee scurried about and soon the Mice walked as a tight group at the center of the troop. Mouse did the best he could to equalize the remaining candy among them, and then warned them to slow their rate of fire so what they had would last until the end of the parade. Then he changed the subject. "Do you all remember what Mr. Grit looks like?"

They nodded, looking none too happy at thought of the man.

"OK," said Mouse, "I'm hoping to get my grandfather to talk to Mr. Grit at the end of the parade, but first I have to find him. Will you guys split up and help me look?"

"Split up?" said Beaner doubtfully. "We can't split up; we have to stay in the parade."

"Well, that's right. What I meant to say was, would you split up your eyeballs," said Mouse, struggling to make himself understood.

"Split up our eyeballs?" said Pee Wee with mild alarm.

"Yeah, what I mean is, Beaner will look high to the right, Jim will look high and to the left; Pee Wee and Bobby will check the crowd at street level to left and right. Get the idea? If you see Mr. Grit let me know."

That brought a chorus of agreement from the Scouts and Mouse added, "Watch for Abby Grit, too. She will know where her dad is. Do you all know what Abby looks like?"

"You mean Abby Grit, your girlfriend, Abby Grit?" said Bobby with a sly grin.

"Where did you hear that?" asked Mouse in surprise.

"Aw, everybody was talking about you and Abby being together at the carnival Thursday. Is it true?" Bobby sounded just a little bit shocked.

Mouse didn't quite know how to answer so he said, "Look, just keep an eye peeled for either of them, OK?"

Pee Wee went away muttering about "split eyeballs" and "peeled eyes," but Mouse was pleased to see he and the others were now watching the crowd intently for any sign of the Grits.

Each band, float and twirling squad had to pause briefly in front of the reviewing stand to be looked over by the judges, and this caused the parade to move by fits and starts. During one such pause, Mouse found they were standing at the corner of Fifth and Main, near to the park and directly below Judge Sweet's office. He looked up and his heart leapt when he saw that all four windows of the old place were wide open, little kids hanging out to peer down at the passing celebration of fall. He could see adult hands resting on small shoulders to protect against a plunge, and in the background, he could see the dim forms of other adults moving around the room. The judge was in!

Mouse wanted to run upstairs and convince him then and there to come along to the end of the parade, but he knew that wouldn't work. After the parade, if he could just manage to get Grandpa, Grit and the judge together, then all would be well. As he thought about how that could be managed, he tried to throw the last of his candy up through the second story window and into the judge's office. He managed to do it a couple of times, too, before the troop had to move on. Mouse shrugged and moved along with the rest. He'd just have to play it by ear, figure out something later on. Anyway, where in this vast multitude of cheering, waving people was Mr. Simon Grit?

They marched past the reviewing stands, where people filled five rows of rented folding chairs, and the parade judges watched closely to evaluate every tootling band, every crepe-paper-clad float, and every troop of flashing twirlers. The crowd packed the courthouse steps, and adventurous boys sat insecurely in the trees overlooking the judging station. The public address system was going full tilt and added to the cacophony created by the cheers of the crowd, and the screams and rock music from the nearby carnival. The place was bedlam. The place was wonderful!

Once past the reviewing stand, the parade speeded up and it seem like no time at all until they turned the corner onto Second Avenue, the demobilization point just a block away. Mouse had pretty much given up on finding his quarry in the parade day crowd when Bobby waved and yelled "There's Abby" and pointed to a group of people in the front yard of an old white house on the corner. Mouse immediately broke ranks and ran over to her.

"Abby, where's your dad?"

The whole family group turned to look at Abby, who seemed as confused by Mouse's behavior as by his question. She rallied quickly.

"We haven't seen him. Why? Do you know where he is?"

"No, but if you could get him to come to the end of the parade, we could all talk about the treasure. My grandfather will be there and I have it all figured out now. If your dad isn't here, could you come up there anyway? There is something I've got to show you."

Abby looked at her mom, who looked doubtful.

"Mom, this is Mouse Monroe," said Abby by way of introduction.

"I know Mouse, dear," replied her mom, "but I am not so sure your father wants *you* to know him."

"Mrs. Grit, could you let her come?" pleaded Mouse. "I promise it's important." Then he looked around. The troop was getting away. "I've got to get back to the parade. Please let her come."

Mouse raced to regain his place, passing by his grandfather who gave a glare that said, "What do you think you're up to?"

The last half block went quickly, Mouse's eyes darting everywhere. Yes, Abby was following. That was good. Yes, Grandpa was still back there, irked but still back there. Pretty good. Up ahead, off to the side, Mouse caught a glimpse of cousin Chuck. Chuck did not look good at all. He had a worried, almost a scared expression on his face, and there was something wrong about the way he was dressed — Clarion Bobcats T-shirt, white shorts, white socks and shiny black dress shoes. Why in the world was Chuck wearing dress shoes? Why were his knees so dirty?

Then they reached the demobilization point, and the marching units dissolved into chaos as the members of the various groups headed off to waiting busses, back downtown to the carnival, or to their homes for picnics and barbecues. The troop flew apart, and most of the Scouts could be seen heading back down Wood toward the center of town, where they would see the tail end of the parade and meet up with their waiting families. Mouse went the other way, over toward the open area on the corner where Chuck stood, looking lightning-struck. Something was very wrong.

To his left, Mouse could see Abby politely making her way through the mob in his direction, and a glance back showed Grandpa Mike just behind. Mike would have seen Chuck too, would be wondering why his favorite grandson had not shown up to march in the parade. There was no Simon Grit though. There was no Judge Sweet either, but at least Mouse knew where he could find him. Mouse struggled to find the best way to say the things that needed to be said. This was no time for the old frozen Mouse to reappear. This time he would be ready... And then he saw Simon Grit.

The man came out from between two houses where he had no doubt been waiting, but this was not a Simon Grit that Mouse had ever seen before. This was not an irate farmer, a zealous state employee or a protective father. Mouse had nerved himself to deal with those men. This Grit, though, looked like something completely different. This Grit looked like a madman. He was covered from head to toe with dirt. His hair was matted flat and encrusted with mud. His whole left leg was covered with a wet slick of what looked to be blood. He was limping badly, pulling the leg along like some monster lunatic in a horror film. And, oddest of all, in his right hand he was carrying a dirty white

249

tennis shoe. Mouse paused. Was he ready for this? The man looked beyond reason, like a bomb about to explode. Mouse swallowed hard and stepped forward.

Chuck was between them, watching Mouse and the others approach, completely unaware of the danger to his rear. When Grit's hand closed around his neck from behind, Chuck spun reflexively to escape, but in a twinkling, Grit had him by the arm and the two were standing nose to nose.

"Try and kill me, will you, you little thief," said Simon Grit.

Chuck tried to back away, but Grit was having none of it. "Want your shoe back, boy?" he snarled, and with that something in the man seemed to snap. He swung at Chuck's head with the shoe. Chuck dodged, but the quick backhand caught him unprepared and the shoe cuffed him a ringing blow on the ear.

Mouse had expected Grit to come at *him*. Why was the man attacking Chuck? Mouse moved forward, trying to think what to do, then Grandpa Mike shoved past and inserted himself between the Chuck and Grit.

"What the hell are you up to?" Mike shouted as he broke Grit's grip and pushed him away. Grit glared at Mike and seemed about to answer when his gaze dropped, and he saw the coin that held Mike's neckerchief neatly in place. Grit's hand shot forward, grabbed at the coin and held tight. Suddenly, Mike's neckerchief had become a noose, and Grit used it to shake him back and forth. Grandpa Mike seemed disoriented.

Simon Grit screamed, "You son of a bitch. It was you who put the kid up to it. It was you who stole the treasure — can't even do your own dirty work, got to get your children to do it. You're lower than a snake, slimier than a cesspit. I'll see you in jail for this."

Mike's face turned from white to red. He grabbed at the hand at his throat and, using a two-handed grip, leaned forward. Suddenly Grit went down, but that was not quite good enough. Even as he fell, Grit held tight to Mike's neckerchief and pulled the older man down with him. The two rolled in the grass, Mike trying to free himself and using his fists to do so, Grit hanging on for dear life and crying out, "Help! Police! Murder!" at the top of his lungs.

Mouse scurried around the pair thrashing on the ground, "Grandpa! Stop fighting!"

Abby was beside him, "Daddy, let go!"

The men didn't hear, locked as they were in their own strange world of battle; Grit determined to let go of neither the shoe nor the coin, and Mike just as determined to get away from the madman.

"OK, you two," came a heavy voice. "Stop that and get up!" It was a very large police officer, and Mouse saw that two more were moving to join him.

The officer spoke again, more calmly, "Mr. Wing, stop struggling. We'll get him off you."

If Mike heard at all, the words didn't sink in, and he continued to whale away at the defenseless Simon Grit, whose left hand held the neckerchief and whose right still clutched at the tennis shoe.

Mouse took it all in; saw what would happen; knew what he had to do. The cops would put a stop to the wrestling match and haul both men off to jail, that was for sure. None of them were going to listen to his fancy story about treasure lost and found. They would only be interested in the fight and the murder Grit was still screaming about. Anything Mouse might say would be ignored. He was just a kid. Only one man he could think of had the authority to stop this thing before it got completely out of control, and that man was at this very moment peacefully watching the tail end of the parade from his office windows perched high above Main Street.

Mouse turned to Abby, "Come on. I know how to save them."

"Mouse, we've got to stop the fight," said Abby, tears running freely down her cheeks.

"The cops will stop it," said Mouse coldly. "We've got to stop what will come after."

251

She just looked at him, confused.

Mouse said, "They will both be hauled off to jail."

Abby was surprised and frightened. She hadn't thought that far ahead. "What can we do?"

"We can talk to Judge Sweet. He can fix it. Come on!" and he pulled at her hand, and she started to move.

"Are you sure?" she asked, reluctant to leave her father.

"No, but it's the best shot we've got."

They ran from the fight down Wood, wormed through the crowd at the park, bolted across Main at the reviewing stand through a squadron of zooming miniature cars driven by crazy men in funny hats, sprinted across the courthouse lawn, blurred past an ambulance waiting for disaster to strike at the corner of Fifth and Main, and darted into the dark and quiet of the Hahne Building. Mouse took the long flight of steps two at a time and then thought to wait for Abby at the top. They walked, panting, down the dark hallway to where happy 'oh's and 'ah's came from the open doorway that led into the judge's office.

* * *

Theo Sweet stood by the window looking over his grandson Johnny's head at the Zem-Zem drivers down at the reviewing stand. He smiled with satisfaction. Those guys were truly crazy, with their figure eights and their two-wheel turns. It was a wonder any of them stayed on the road and out of the crowd. Johnny squirmed to get further out the window, but Theo tightened his grip to let the little fellow know that he was quite close enough to falling already. Johnny loved the zooming cars, and somehow that let Theo see them again himself with the eyes of a child. Though he made a point of getting out of town on Farmers and Crafters Day, he would not have missed parade day for the world. This was Clarion at its liveliest.

He wasn't aware of the arrival of more guests until his wife said, "Theo, there are a couple of young people here to see you.

252

You had better go talk to them. I'll keep Johnny from plunging to his death."

Theo smiled as he turned away. Maggie still had an amusing way with words.

He smiled again when he saw who the visitors were. "Hello, Mouse. Have you come to watch the parade from the best vantage point in town?"

"Hello, sir." The kid was covered with perspiration, out of breath and very serious. "This is Abby Grit."

Theo smiled. "Glad to meet you, Abby. Did you see Mouse's mighty toss when he threw the candy through my window earlier?"

"No, sir," said the girl shyly. She had been running too and looked greatly distressed; she had been crying.

Theo tried to soothe her, calm her down. "Would you like to join us? My daughter and her sons are here from Pittsburgh. The boys are loving the parade, and tomorrow night, I'm taking them to the fireworks over at the stadium. We'd be glad to have you both join us."

"No, thank you, sir," she replied, looking more watery about the eyes, quivery about the mouth — better get them out into the hall and find out what this was all about.

Once they were all seated on folding chairs in the lobby, Theo said seriously, "OK, Mouse, what's up?"

Mouse's answer was quick and to the point. "My grandfather and Abby's father have been arrested."

"What in the world for?" asked Theo, surprised. Mike Wing and Simon Grit? He could hardly think of two men less likely to be in trouble with the law.

"They got into a fight down at the end of the parade," said Mouse. "Mr. Grit was calling Mike a thief and a murderer, and he grabbed Mike, and that's when it started."

Abby didn't deny it, but she was quick to add justification for her father's actions. "It was the coin, Mouse. He grabbed him

253

because of the coin he had on his neckerchief. That's why he called him a thief."

"What is this about murder?" asked Theo very seriously.

"I don't know," said Mouse.

Abby said, "Daddy was supposed to meet us before the parade. He never showed up, but he was at the end, and he was all dirty and bleeding, like he had been in an accident." She looked very miserable, stifled a sob and then added mournfully, "He had a tennis shoe in his hand. I don't know what happened or why he had the shoe."

"Chuck had on dress shoes," said Mouse suddenly, as if this one fact somehow explained everything.

Abby looked startled. Theo was confused, "Dress shoes?"

"Yeah," said Mouse with confidence. "Chuck had on dress shoes because Mr. Grit had one of his tennis shoes."

Theo still didn't get it, but he noticed the girl look at Mouse and nod her head as if the statement somehow made sense.

This was too complicated a puzzle for a Saturday afternoon. He would call Hamm and get the official description of events. Then he would see what he could do to help.

Judge Theo Sweet took out his cell phone and dialed the well-remembered number of the chief of police.

26

It was Sunday afternoon, a little past 4 o'clock, when Mouse's mom tapped at the door of his room, "Mouse? Can I come in?"

"Sure, Mom," said Mouse, laying aside his algebra book and turning to look toward the door.

"Hi, honey. I decided to take a little break from the veggie stand to talk to you for a minute. Are you all right down here by yourself?"

"Yes, I'm fine. I'm just getting ready for a test tomorrow."

She smiled, "That's good, honey. Do you think you could spare an hour to go up to the park and talk to your grandfather when he gets off work at five?"

Mouse frowned, "I don't know if I should, Mom. We are all supposed to meet with Judge Sweet tomorrow afternoon, anyway. Won't that be soon enough?"

"You told me about the meeting, but your grandfather stopped by the booth just now. He's still thinking a lot about what happened yesterday, about his argument with Mr. Grit and all. He seems to think you can help him understand why it happened, and wants to know everything he can before the conference with Judge Sweet."

"Grandpa doesn't have any reason to worry," said Mouse. "He didn't do anything wrong. He was just unlucky. I've been trying to talk to him for a week, to explain everything, but he has been too busy to listen."

"Yes, I know, and he told me he's very sorry about that. Now he wants to hear everything that you and Chuck have to say."

"Chuck will be there?" asked Mouse, a little surprised. "I thought Chuck was grounded for life on account of having buried Gri... Mr. Grit."

"Your grandfather told me that Chuck's parents are letting him out for an hour to talk. Daddy, I mean your grandfather, really wants to talk to both of you though, and it seems to me that Chuck might not tell quite the whole truth unless you are there too.

"Mouse, I really think it would be a good idea for you to go."

"OK," Mouse relented. It didn't really matter all that much. "Will you be coming too?"

"I'd like to, honey, but I really should be at the stand at closing time. We have to knock everything down and store it away until next year, and you know I'm in charge."

"That's OK, Mom. I can go alone."

His mother looked hard at him; she was puzzled. "Mouse, you somehow seem different. You used to be so nervous around your grandfather and Chuck. Now you seem so calm. You're not on drugs or anything are you?"

Mouse laughed, "No, Mom. I'm not on drugs. It's just that Abby and I told Judge Sweet the whole story yesterday, same as I told you last night, and he believed us. Now, I trust him to settle the thing. It doesn't really matter what Chuck tells Grandpa. It's what the judge thinks that matters."

His mom smiled, "You are probably right about that, Mouse. I know Judge Sweet is just the man I would pick to settle a dispute. Still, you do seem different, as if somehow you are no longer so terribly afraid of confrontation. What has happened to you, Mouse?"

Mouse smiled wanly, "Lots and lots happened this last week, Mom. Chuck had his own version of events last weekend, and I thought Grandpa was ignoring me in favor of him. You were busy and Dad was away, so I had to solve the problem for myself. I ended up talking to so many adults about so many strange things that, somewhere along the line, I just stopped being afraid. Now I have this idea that adults are just kids too, and knowing that helps a lot."

Nancy Monroe smiled doubtfully at that, evidently thinking it a cracked theory, "I'm not so sure that is a very good way to look at things, honey. Adults have jobs, responsibilities, authority — a hundred things kids know nothing about."

Mouse smiled, "I guess you're probably right, Mom, but I do have a job as a student, I have the responsibility to do well at my schooling, and I have at least some authority as the leader of my patrol in Boy Scouts. If you think about it, most of the things I do mimic things that adults do, so I guess you could say I was a small adult."

"Good, honey. You are a young adult, and I am very proud of you, especially after the way you have handled this whole business with the coins. But, don't you see, saying you are a young adult is a lot different than saying adults are old children? I don't think that's true."

"But adults are kids," said Mouse positively. "This past week I met a man who was bullied by a woman just as mean as any tough eighth-grader. I met another man who was as obsessed with old coins as any kid ever was about Star Wars or Magic. Even Grandpa Mike is so focused on his own interests that everything else is unimportant, just like the kids at school who live, eat and breathe football."

Mouse could tell by her expression that his mom was not convinced. They would have to talk some more about this, but if he was going to meet Grandpa, he had better get moving. He did think of one final argument, though, and so he grinned a wicked grin and added, "I better be getting up to the park, Mom. Let me get my jacket, and I'll walk you back to your lemonade stand."

She burst out laughing and gave him a hug.

* * *

Walking up Main toward the park, Mouse could see that Autumn Leaf was finally winding down. The crowd was thin, and there was a worn out air about the people on the street. It seemed to be just the diehards now; people out to buy one last Momma's Best Caramel Apple, one final Genuine Original Stromboli Sandwich. Even the weather seemed tired of all the excitement. Light gray clouds made a low ceiling overhead, and the air moved not at all, as if the giant machinery that kept the weather going had been turned off for the day. Mouse hoped it would clear up later, when thousands of people would turn out one final time, for the *Allegheny Power Fabulous Fireworks* over at the university stadium. This afternoon though, the *Northwest Savings Bank Antique Tractor Show* was a gray and sparsely attended affair, mostly a quiet day of only local interest that gave everyone a chance to rest up for the final splash of fire that would conclude the year's festivities.

Mouse liked the old tractors. The men standing beside them looked proud and capable, and the machines, unlike the cars at Autorama, were not pretty toys. These tough old workhorses had plowed fields, baled hay and threshed wheat for farm families all over the area. Mouse smiled at the worn but still well cared for machines; they were like old plow horses given a well-earned day of companionship with others of their kind.

Chuck and Grandpa Mike were sitting on the steps of the monument in the park. They seemed as drab and worn as the day that surrounded them.

"Hello, Grandpa. Hi, Chuck."

Chuck just glowered, evidently unhappy that Mouse had showed up. Mike, though, leapt to his feet and his reply was quick and sharp, "High time you got here, Mouse. Let's get this show on the road; it'll be dark in a couple of hours."

Mouse followed along beside Chuck, who seemed terrified and hung very close to Mike's side. They clambered into the front seat of Grandpa's red truck, Chuck in the middle. The old man revved the engine and sent the truck hurrying down the road.

"Where are we going?" asked Mouse, but he already knew.

"Bear Run, where do you think?" said Mike.

Chuck whined, "Grandpa, I don't want to go to Bear Run. If Mr. Grit's there he'll kill me."

"Shut up, Chuck. Show some spine. Anyway, Grit's in the hospital. I guess I did a pretty good job on him yesterday," replied Mike with grim satisfaction.

Mouse had been there, seen the fight, knew better. Grit was exhausted and bleeding at the start of it. Who did Grandpa think he was kidding?

"Grandpa," said Mouse, "Chuck's right. This isn't a good idea. We should wait till we talk to the judge tomorrow."

"He's not a judge anymore," said Mike, with a satisfied smirk. "Now he's just an old busybody. Him and his office full of law books. He gets more cracked every year. I'll get to the bottom of this without any help from that pompous old fool."

Mouse was shocked. "But, he's your cousin or uncle, isn't he?"

"Yeah, Mr. Golden Boy Lawyer. My dad used to tell about what he was like in high school — a bookworm, timid as a mouse and not worth a damn at football. That'll be the day I trust to Inky for justice."

"Inky?" asked Mouse. More nasty nicknames? It must run in the family.

"Yeah, Inky Theo Sweet, the teacher's pet."

"Why did you call him Inky?" asked Mouse.

Mike laughed gleefully, "Ask him some time."

Mouse didn't have to. He knew the answer would somehow involve ink and someone named Wing. Mouse shook his head and made more room for Chuck, who was prodding him in the ribs with a sharp elbow. Kinship could cut both ways, he realized. It could bring two boys closer together if they were much the same, or drive them further apart if there were differences. He had seen brothers like that in the Scout troop. Some were allies and pals; some were vicious mismatched enemies who just happened to live under the same roof.

The truck roared down the dirt road and pulled into Bear Run Camp. It was a damp, foggy day down in here. Most of the fine gold and scarlet leaves of the previous weekend now lay on the ground, and the ones that remained in the trees flutter tiredly, trying to break free and float to their final rest on the forest floor. The place felt like a dying thing, and Mouse didn't like it, but he was curious too. Curious as to how this little drama would play out. Had Pig successfully completed his mission? Had his pal come through for him?

Mike practically dragged Chuck down the hill to the uprooted tree. Mouse followed along behind, more-or-less ignored and forgotten. He was amazed at how thoroughly the entrance to the mine had been erased. All that remained was a mound of loose dirt, rock and forest clutter, with a man-sized hole poked into it that led steeply downward into blackness. Mouse looked closely at the root ball of the felled tree, and was pleased to see half of an arrowhead tucked into the crotch where two of the largest roots met. He smiled. Good old Pig!

Mike peered down into the hole and spoke to Chuck, "This is where you tried to kill him?"

"I wasn't trying to kill him," whined Chuck. "Don't say that! I was just trying to get away. He had hold of my foot and was dragging me down. It was like some monster had me. It was his fault. The mine never would have collapsed if he hadn't been trying to drag me down."

Mike didn't believe it, "Yeah, right. So, tell me again, why were you out here in the first place?"

"Like I said, I came to get the treasure to give to you," said Chuck, but there was weakness in the words.

"Yeah, I just about believe that too," said Mike acidly. "You were going to bring it to me, the guy you had told there was no treasure, just an old bag."

Chuck was silent, looked away.

Mike wasn't through. "OK, so after you buried him, why didn't you dig up the treasure?"

Chuck had a better answer for that one. "I was scared. I left, went home, changed clothes. Then I went to meet you after the parade, to tell you what happened. I didn't know what else to do. If I dug him out, he would have killed me. I could hear him yelling, so I knew he wasn't dead. I wanted you there when he got out."

"Yeah, well look how well that little plan worked," said Mike bitterly. "Instead of you, he tries to kill me. Instead of you, it's me ends up being collared by a cop and dragged off to the District Justice. Great little plan, Chuck."

Mouse was tired of this. "Grandpa, what should he have done? It seems to me Chuck had a reasonable plan. Anybody would have been afraid of letting Mr. Grit out."

"Shut up, Mouse. I'll get to you later," said Mike sharply.

Chuck glared up at him too, and Mouse read the silent sneering message, "I don't need any help from you, little Mouse."

OK, OK. He'd shut up. They'd both be talking to him soon enough.

Mike turned back to Chuck, "So where is this fabulous treasure of yours? Let's see it."

"I buried it here, deep under the roots."

"Dig her out of there, then."

Chuck got to his knees and started clawing at the earth. Mike pressed in behind to watch, and Mouse found himself, once again, ignored. He backed quietly away up the hill, but he could have been whistling "Dixie" for all the more attention his grandfather and cousin paid him.

When he reached the top, he headed upstream. Things had not played out exactly as he had expected, but he hadn't been far off last Wednesday when he suspected Chuck would return to the dump site a second time, to remove the leather satchel or substitute something else for its shiny contents.

261

Mouse tramped along the path to the clearing where the string burn had taken place during the camporee; man, that seemed like a long time ago. Then he mulled over the last words he had heard Chuck say, "I buried it here." No mention that it was Mouse who suggested the idea or that it was both of them who did the digging. Mouse smiled. That was all right.

He walked confidently to the circle of disturbed earth, all that remained to mark the site of the Mice's famous oily fire. It looked just like the others, but Mouse was not fooled. Pig would have taken pains to make it so. He picked up a short stiff stick and dug at the center of the circle. The thing was only four inches down, just where he had asked Pig to hide it the previous Wednesday. Mouse grabbed hold of the strap and hauled it out into daylight. Propping it against a foot, he opened the old leather bag.

The inside was a jumble of silvery coins. He wanted to dump them onto the ground; to lay them out in long rows; to stack them up into piles. He wanted to count the coins; to savor them while they were still his. There just wasn't time for that, though, and so he just shook the bag gently from side to side to hear them clink, and to see them settle lower. Then he notice something inside, embossed in faint gold on the leather of the satchel. At first only the tops of the letters showed, but when he tipped the bag forward, he could make out the whole of the faint inscription. He smiled as the last piece fell into place, then he closed the flap, picked up the bag and started walking back to where Chuck would be scratching his head over what had become of the treasure. Now Mouse would have his say. Now they would both listen. If they believed him, fine. If not, well, the judge could sort it out tomorrow.

The bag was heavy, a good 25 pounds. Mouse slung it over a shoulder by its strap and headed back toward the dump and the downed tree. He was just to the road when, as if by eerie magic, Simon Grit rose out of the weeds by the side of the path.

"I'll take that," he said. His voice was cold, cold.

Mouse was startled, "Mr. Grit! They told me you were in the hospital."

Grit gave a very small smile, "I figured you would think that, so I discharged myself this morning. I've been sitting here in the goldenrod since just after dawn, waiting for you, and this time I came prepared."

He didn't touch the handgun, didn't have to. It hung like a noisy threat at his hip. Mouse doubted he would use it, but the man was not well, and where the treasure was concerned, he might be capable of anything. Why chance it?

Mouse unslung the bag and handed it to the man. "What are you going to do with it?" he asked, pleasantly as he could manage.

"I'm going to take it to Clarion and give it to Judge Sweet. Come tomorrow, we'll have our little meeting, only it'll be me that brought in the treasure, not a bunch of thieves claiming innocence. Then we'll see who keeps the coins and who gets in trouble with the law."

Mouse was puzzled, "Didn't Abby tell you about what she and I found out?"

Grit paused in the act of turning away, "No. I haven't seen the girl to talk to since we closed the booth on Friday. What has she got to do with this?"

"She was worried about you. She told me about you and your Papa…"

Grit's face turned ugly. "She shouldn't have done that. I'll have to teach that girl a lesson about loyalty…"

"She's as loyal to you as she can be," said Mouse firmly. "Let's just sit down and talk for five minutes. You'll see it's true."

Grit's face cleared a bit.

"Well, all right, maybe I'll listen, but not to you — not now. I'll listen to her, after this bag is safe in Judge Sweet's hands." Then, he turned away and limped down into Bear Run ravine on the path beside the dump.

Mouse watched him go, very glad that Judge Sweet was already in possession of the facts of the case. Then, he sighed. What came next would not be pleasant.

He found them still digging. The hole was laughably large and very, very empty. As Mouse slid down the slope to join them, they looked around.

"Where were you?" ask Mike sharply.

"I went to dig up the treasure."

"Chuck says the treasure is buried here, under these roots."

"Yeah, it was until Thursday morning. After what Chuck said on Wednesday at the fire house, I figured he might come out here and mess with it, like he tried to do on Monday when Mr. Grit scared him away."

Mike looked at Chuck with scorn, then returned his hard gaze to look at Mouse's empty hands. "So where is it? Where is the treasure? Up at the truck?"

Here came the hard part. Mouse waited, expecting the freezing sensation that would tie his tongue and blank his mind. He was surprised, almost smiled, as he realized his angry grandfather no longer held that kind of power over him. Somewhere, sometime in the last week he had outgrown the man. Now he saw Grandpa Mike for what he really was — just a larger version of his bullying cousin, Chuck. Either of them could no doubt whip him, but that was just the way life was, and if they did, well, Mouse would just deal with it.

Mike still wanted an answer, "What's the matter, Mouse? Cat got your tongue? I asked you a question."

Mouse replied, "Yes, sir. I had the bag full of coins, but now Mr. Grit has it. He's taking it to Judge Sweet."

Mike's face turned pale, "Grit's in the hospital."

"He *was* in the hospital. He spent the day waiting for us up above, near where we parked the truck. He said he knew we would come."

Now Mike's face shaded to pink, "He said that, did he! Well, why the hell did you give him the bag? He's going to make us all out to be thieves caught in the act. At the very best, we're going to look like fools. Why didn't you just run? He couldn't have caught you with that gimp leg of his."

Mouse considered explaining about the gun, but quickly decided to let that rest. Why add fuel to the fire? He settled for a simple reply, "Mr. Grit wanted the bag very badly, so I gave it to him."

Chuck sneered, "You wimped out again, didn't you, Mouse? I would have been running like a deer the minute he showed up."

Mouse looked at Chuck appraisingly, "I can believe that, Chuck, but I didn't run. I talked to him, and then I gave him the treasure. It sort of belongs to him anyway."

Mike had had enough, "What a pair you two are — a coward and a weakling. Well, I'm neither. We are going to get that bag back and take it to Sweet ourselves. That'll make us the guys who saved the treasure, and Grit the thief who tried to steal it away."

Mouse shook his head, but Mike was wound up, "Where is Grit now?"

"He was headed back to his farm, but..."

"OK, here is what we are going to do. Chuck, you go try to catch him, slow him down. Mouse and I will take the truck around to his place and meet you there. Get moving!"

Chuck did not look enthusiastic about his part in this plan, but he nevertheless started working his way down the hill. Mouse took a few steps down that way, too, and whispered in his ear, "Careful, Chuck. Grit's got a gun."

That short statement slowed his cousin's progress to a crawl.

Grandpa Mike screamed down at him, "Get a move on, Chuck!" and then he turned to scale the steep hillside.

Mouse was at the top long before the old man. He looked back down and smiled at Chuck, who seemed to be running Grit to ground in slow motion. When Mike finally did crest the lip of the valley he was panting heavily, and the pair slowly made their way to the red truck parked on the leaf-spattered green of the campsite. It was getting dark as they mounted up. Mike gunned the engine for the Grit place.

As he bounced about on the seat, Mouse looked over to where his grandfather wrenched at the wheel. Mike's face was grim as death, and Mouse heard him mutter, "I'll kill the bastard!"

27

Abby sat in the worn lawn chair, staring away to the far horizon where the last of the light pinked the sky. Stars were beginning to appear. It would be a clear, moonless night, and she knew that on hilltops all around Clarion other families would be sitting out too, watching and waiting for the distant fireworks in Clarion to begin.

"Where will it be, again?" asked her little sister, Nancy.

"I've told you twice already," her mother said, a little sharply. "Look for the courthouse tower. The fireworks will be just to the right of that."

Abby could no longer see her mom's face in the twilight, but even without that, she could tell she was worrying about Dad. When would this end? He had not been at the hospital when they went to visit after church, and so they had hurried back home. His old truck was here all right, but Dad himself was nowhere to be found. Abby's mother had been fretting ever since.

Abby was worried too. If she could just see him, just tell him what she knew, then everything would be all right. She had checked the barn and the fields, checked the dirty old dump, and checked the Indian's Rock Garden. Nothing. She didn't know where else to look, and so here she sat in a tattered lawn chair on the hilltop. Her mother sat in another of the same vintage, and between them was a third, the one reserved for Daddy. The four small fry were cozy under blankets at their feet and fretting about when the fireworks display would begin; Abby was fretting too, but her concern was for her missing father.

When the sound came, it sent Abby racing down the dark hill toward the farmyard. She couldn't see the truck from the hilltop in the dark, but she would have known the grind of its starter anywhere. Daddy was down there, and he was leaving, but not without her. She had to see him; had to tell him the truth about the treasure.

She ran, knees high, down through the pasture, quickly scrambled over the gate, and panted into the farmyard just as her father finished turning the truck to point down the lane. She sprinted as it started to move forward, reached out, pulled the passenger door open, and flung herself inside.

It was her father all right. He looked very alarmed as she sprawled head first into the accelerating truck, almost as though he was expecting someone else. When he realized who it was, he started slowing down.

"Get out, Abby. This is no business for little girls," he said sharply.

Abby untangled herself and rolled to sit bolt upright in the passenger seat. She wasn't going anywhere. Her hand brushed a hard, metallic object on the seat between them.

"Daddy," she said with alarm, "there's a gun here. Why do you have a gun?"

"Just in case. I don't expect I'll be needing it now," he sounded defensive.

The truck was still moving, rolling slowly between dark fields full of shadowy corn. Suddenly Abby was very angry. What was the man thinking!

She spoke sharply. "Good, nothing but trouble comes of trying to solve your problems with a gun. You told me that." With that, she quickly rolled down her window and pitched the gun out into the black ditch at the side of the road.

"Hey!" yelled her father.

"What?" was Abby's angry response. "Wasn't it you who told me all the stories about angry, drunken fools with handguns?"

"I am not drunk," said her father, deeply offended.

"Well, that's something, anyway," said Abby primly.

He looked over at her in the dark. "God, girl, you sound more like your mother every day." He sounded just a little awestruck.

He did step on the gas, though, and the truck picked up speed again. Evidently Abby was going along after all. She could tell that the severity in her voice had done the trick, but decided that sweetness would get her further in the long run, "Where are we going, Daddy?"

"Clarion. I've got a little present for Judge Sweet. I took it off your boy..., that friend of yours, Mouse."

"With the gun?" she was shocked and scared. Had Mouse been shot?

"Naw, he was real reasonable, said it didn't matter anyhow." He paused, fighting for control of the truck, as they plunged through a water-filled pothole, sending high wings of water up on either side. When he spoke again, it was almost as though he was talking to himself, "Funny thing about that kid. Last Saturday when I caught him in the west field, he seemed almost stupid — scared out of his wits. Today he was completely different, ignored the gun on my hip and just talked to me man to man — not afraid at all."

Abby smiled but said nothing. She guessed she knew which was the real Mouse. He was brave enough for anything.

Off to the left, headlights stabbed through the trees as a vehicle came around a turn and approached the place where the farm lane intersected the Bear Run-Startown Road.

"Looks like we've got company," her father growled as he gunned the motor so as to be first at the intersection. He pumped the brake hard at the end of the lane, and the rear end of the truck drifted around, just like in a movie, to point straight down the rural road. Without hesitation, he mashed the gas, and the old pickup spun dust and picked up speed.

Abby looked behind. She saw two bright headlights bobbing in the cloud of dust they were throwing up. Someone was trying to catch them. "Who is that, Daddy?"

"That old fool, Mike Wing. He was down there with the two boys, come to steal our treasure away."

"It's not our treasure, Daddy. It belonged to a man named Boston Buck. Mouse found some stuff in the library, and he and I talked to a man at a coin shop in Clarion too."

Her dad was distracted by the driving, but managed to say, "Yeah, Mouse said you could tell me about it. It doesn't matter who owns it right now, though. Right now what matters is to get the thing to Judge Sweet's house. After that, there will be time enough and more for explanations."

Abby felt the hard lump of the bag at her feet. She reached a hand down to explore it in the dark. It was hard and stiff, covered with gritty powder. She found a flap and lifted it, felt around with her hand inside. Her fingers touched a cold pile of smooth round coins. Somehow two of them fell together with a clink.

She looked over at the man who had been so bedeviled with finding this bag. He was concentrating hard on his driving and on the rear view mirror. She looked behind and saw that a large dark shape behind glaring headlights was attempting to pass. She glanced at the speedometer. They were doing 75, but she trusted her father's driving. They went tearing around a sharp bend in the road, and their pursuer lost ground, but then came a long straight stretch, and the truck behind quickly roared up again to hug their back bumper.

"The guy can't drive worth a damn," muttered her father, "but his truck can go some."

The truck was still hugging their tail as they roared through the sleepy hamlet of Startown. Abby noticed the horizon off to the west, where the last of the light was just leaving the sky. Now it was full dark. Another mile would bring them to the stop sign at Route 322, where they would turn left for Clarion. The road was country blacktop now, and the turns were not so sharp. The truck behind was having no trouble at all keeping up, and Abby knew they could not escape.

"Watch out at the stop sign, Daddy," she said, feeling compelled to do so, but unsure how he would take her driving advice.

"Don't worry, honey," he chuckled, very sure of himself. "I'll take it fast, but I'll take it safe."

He took it fast all right, but when the truck briefly went up on two wheels in the turn, Abby had cause to doubt the part about taking it safe. Still, the wheels thumped safely down, and then they were accelerating down the big four-lane highway, headed for the long bridge over the Clarion River.

She looked back. The truck behind took the turn much more cautiously and lost a lot of ground. Abby glanced at the speedometer again. It read 105. She watched the road ahead. They were passing everything in sight, but funny, it didn't feel like they were going any faster than they had been on the back roads.

The bridge flashed past and they started up the other side. The speedometer dropped to 85 as they climbed the steep hill that she knew led up into Clarion. Almost there. At the dangerous Barracks Turn near the top, her father let the truck slow to 55. It was just as well he did. Suddenly, just around the bend, they were bearing down on the tail end of a long line of backed up traffic.

Her dad pumped the brakes and swung to the right, onto the berm, to avoid rear-ending an SUV packed with kids, "What the hell is this about?" he demanded of no one. Then he remembered, "Oh, yeah, the fireworks."

Abby looked back. She was just in time to see their pursuer come around the Barracks Turn. He had not slowed down nearly enough, and suddenly there was the sound of tires screaming in the night. Somehow, he just managed to get it stopped in time to avoid colliding with the SUV.

"Idiot!" exclaimed her father, who had also turned to watch. Then he hit his blinkers and started moving slowly up the berm at the right of the road, passing car after car full of startled people.

"What are you doing?" asked Abby with alarm.

"I'm just going up the side of the road here until I get to Liberty, then I'll pull across these two lanes of traffic and shoot down Liberty to Judge Sweet's house," said her father, evidently pleased with the plan.

"Liberty is a one-way street!" exclaimed Abby.

"Yeah, well you can't make an omelet without breaking eggs," said her father in a tough-guy voice. "By the time that old fool behind stops shaking and decides to follow, we'll be sittin' with the judge on his front porch, sippin' lemonade and counting the coins."

Abby had a sudden thought, "He won't be there!"

"Won't be there? Who won't be where?"

"The judge. He won't be at his house," replied Abby. "He told us yesterday. He's taking his grandkids to the fireworks at the stadium."

Her dad considered for a moment then chuckled oddly, "Even better. Witnesses!"

Abby looked over at him with concern. What should she do?

They continued up the side of the road until an irritated looking young man in uniform stood in their path and held up an officious hand.

Grit killed the engine, grabbed the bag, and with a quick, "Come on!" started limping toward the entrance gate to the stadium. Behind, a loud voice yelled, "Hey! You can't park here."

Her dad ignored him, but Abby glanced back to see if he was following. No. Instead, he was walking toward the bright red truck that was just pulling up behind theirs. She heard his outraged voice.

"Hey buddy, you can't park there!"

Abby turned to hurry and catch up with her father. Up ahead she could hear a loud rock band. Her dad quickly paid at the gate, and then they walked onto the field and started looking for Judge Sweet. Abby kept close to her father as he wound through the hundreds of families and couples resting on blankets, waiting for the fireworks to begin. Abby looked everywhere, searching just as hard as her father for Judge Sweet. In a few minutes, Mike Wing would come running up from behind to intercept them, and if that happened before they had handed the bag to the judge, there would be hell to pay.

Up ahead the noise of the band swelled loud as a final minor chord was struck. Then, the sound slowly died away.

28

Theo Sweet slowly took his hands from his ears. He looked down to examine them. Good. It only *felt* like his ears were bleeding. He brought his hands together to clap wanly as the *Rock Babies* took a bow. The rest of the crowd cheered wildly. Theo looked over to check on his grandchildren, sandwiched tight between their mother and grandmother. They were smiling happily and looking expectantly at the sky, waiting for the first of the fireworks to light up the heavens. Theo shook his head in wonder. Was he the only one who disliked the wall of sound that the band's oversized speaker system sent crashing into their eardrums? As far as he was concerned, the noise they created was best compared to an explosion in a music store.

A scruffy looking young man stepped up to the microphone and shouted enthusiastically, "Let's all give it up for the *Rock Babies*," then he stood to the side and clapped his hands. Give it up? What was that supposed to mean? Then Theo understood. The torture was over; the musical portion of the program was complete. Now he clapped and cheered with the best of them, but soon decided enough was enough. He shuddered. It would not do to cheer them too much. What if they were persuaded to do an encore?

Shortly the master of ceremonies for the evening walked to the microphone. Theo saw it was Mr. MacFarlan, the roly-poly talker from the Boy Scout campout a week ago.

"Good evening, ladies and gentlemen," the man said happily, and then he looked around expectantly.

Theo groaned inwardly. Didn't the man have any sense?

MacFarlan did not.

"I can't hear you," he said pleasantly. "Good evening, ladies and gentleman!"

There was a subdued response from the crowd this second time, but of course MacFarlan wasn't through. Perhaps it was just that his style of public speaking always called for three repeats of the greeting.

"Good evening, ladies and gentlemen," he said it again. To Theo it seemed the crowd did little better the third time around, but MacFarlan was satisfied and launched into the body of his remarks.

"It's a lovely night for a fireworks display, and I want to personally thank the *Rock Babies* for entertaining us this evening. We will all be enjoying the fireworks in just a few minutes now, but before we get to that, I would just like to say a few words of thanks to the many volunteers that have made this year's *National City Bank Autumn Leaf Festival* such a great success.

"Let me begin with the *S & T Bank Autorama*. Work on organizing this year's huge car show began shortly after last year's festival completed, and it was through the diligent efforts of...."

Theo tuned him out — this could take a while. He figured it would be about five minutes before MacFarlan's blather drained away the good will of the crowd, and then the shouting would begin. Theo didn't really like attending the fireworks down here at the stadium. The place was too noisy, the speeches too long, and when the fireworks finally did begin, he would get a crick his neck watching them. Next year, he would insist they go up to the cemetery. There they could sit and lie on blankets arranged among the old stones, the rock music would be but a thumping noise in the distance, and with any luck at all, they wouldn't even be able to hear the long-winded speeches. Yes, and he would just sit quietly beside his father's grave, maybe reach over and touch the stone, and think about the old fellow and the many times they had watched fireworks together.

MacFarlan's voice intruded. "Now let me say a few words about the *Eighth Annual Clarion University and Community Cultural Night*. This is the eighth year that the university...."

Theo looked around. The crowd was silent, still listening. How long would that last? Then he noticed the courthouse lighted bright in the distance. He had noticed again on the way to the stadium how the dormers, gables and the white Queen Anne molding above the clocks on the tower seemed to make a cheerful face. It had seemed to him as though the old seat of government was smiling its approval of the people of the community coming together to celebrate this special time of year. Since he was a boy, he had occasionally noticed that smile on the old building. He wondered if he was the only one who saw it. Surely there were others; the courthouse had stood for well over 100 years, doing its part to protect and serve the people of the county. How many such enthusiastic gatherings of gentle people had it smiled down on in that time?

Mr. MacFarlan was not showing any signs of running down. "Now we come to *Colony/Commodore Homes Farmers and Crafters Day*. Planning for this huge event required many hours of devoted..."

Theo was sure he heard a groan this time. The patience of the crowd was nearing an end. Just saying the names of the events seemed to take forever. The new titles were silly, but Farmers and Crafters itself was a good thing, part of the glue that held Clarion together as a community, just like other big events had back when he was a kid. Right here, where they all now sat on this crisp fall night, there once were the wooden grandstands of a huge racetrack. He still remembered the excitement of watching the horses, and in later years, the stock cars as they went round and round in a big hurry to get nowhere. The crowds had been immense, the smell of the horses and auto exhaust nearly overwhelming. He smiled at the memory; people didn't lie around on blankets back when the horses ran. You really had to watch your step.

MacFarlan had finally come to the events of the previous day. "The *Clarion Hospital Autumn Leaf Festival Parade* was glorious this year, but did you ever stop to think how many people..."

Now there *were* murmurs. The man had run on too long. Another minute and the crowd would start to shout its displeasure at the incredibly talkative man.

Theo glanced over to the right. Yes, he loved that smiling building. The courthouse, the one great constant in his life...

Then his gaze dropped, attracted by movement among the people out on the field. A limping man was going from blanket to blanket, evidently looking for someone. Just beside him, a slim girl easily kept stride, and she too was searching all about. The man carried some sort of satchel hugged to his chest. Suddenly Theo realized who they were. Then he knew what was in the satchel and just who it was they were looking for.

He stood up and started stiffly down the stadium steps, peering out to see how to best shape his course to intercept the pair. Then, behind them, Theo could see two more figures break from the standing crowd at the edge of the field. He shook his head grimly. This could be bad. The girl had seen him now, was pointing. The injured man saw him too, and hobbled quickly toward the grassy area in front of where Mr. MacFarlan stood at the microphone winding up his speech. The crowd had finally had enough speechifying, and there were now scattered cries of "Fireworks," "Enough talk," and "Let's have the fireworks!"

As Theo stepped to the ground and Simon Grit moved toward him in the light, MacFarlan concluded his remarks.

"Now it is time to say good-bye to Clarion's Autumn Leaf Festival for another year. Since 1953, we have enjoyed this wonderful autumn week, and with the continued support of the community, it will outlast us all.

"Sometimes you hear the expression, 'What will it matter in 100 years.' The Autumn Leaf Festival is something that will matter a century from now. It is the successor to other celebrations all of which helped to make Clarion the place that it is today, a place full of smiling and good people, all hard at work keeping their community alive and vibrant, a safe place where people live in harmony with one another, and with the natural world that surrounds our fair town.

"So I say, good-bye, Autumn Leaf. We'll see you again next fall.

"And now…. let the fireworks begin!"

* * *

Mouse caught hold of Mike's arm, "Grandpa, let him go. The judge knows what happened, he…

"Like hell I will," Mike interrupted, whipping around to sling Mouse into a nearby family group lying on a blanket. Mouse stumbled and fell on top of a stranger, said a quick, "Sorry, sorry," and hopped up again. He ran to catch his grandfather, knew he would be too late, and so yelled, "Grandpa, don't!"

He watched with despair as Mike ran up beside Simon Grit, grabbed hold of the bag the man hugged tightly and attempted to wrench it away. Grit may have been surprised at the sudden assault, but his arms were firmly clamped around the old satchel. He tried to shake off his attacker, but could not, and so the two spun round and round in a slow circle, fighting desperately for possession of the treasure. Grit seemed to be having problems with his balance.

Mouse saw Judge Sweet arrive.

"Stop this unseemly display," commanded the judge. "Give me that satchel."

Neither of the angry men seemed to hear, so focused were they on their spinning struggle to secure the bag.

Then the stadium lights went out. Strings of firecrackers crackled and popped. Rockets spiraled, whistling, up into the night, where magnesium bombs exploded to strobe the circling men with a pulsating white light and lend a surreal air to their contest for possession of the treasure. To Mouse, it looked like the fight was somehow taking place in slow motion.

Mouse saw Judge Sweet reach out a jittery arm, and suddenly he too had become entangled in the whirling battle. That lasted for just a few seconds, then Grit's leg crumpled and the trio fell to the ground. As they fell, the top of the bag came open and half a hundred silver coins flew out to sparkle on the grass under the winking fireworks high above. And, even on the ground, the three still struggled for possession of Buck's loot.

Abby and Mouse were together now, just out of reach of the twisting bodies and thrashing legs. What could they do to stop a fight among grown men?

Others standing nearby saw the coins flashing under the glittering streamers overhead, and moved forward, ready to take part in any souvenir collecting that might develop. Abby saw them, felt compelled to protect the treasure, and knelt to rake in as many coins as possible before it was too late. Security officers came running from the ends of the stands, but their movements seemed to encourage others to do the same. People skittered down from the stands, either for a closer view or in hopes grabbing up some plunder. Overhead the sky was lit with huge expanding spheres of scarlet red, emerald green and phosphorescent white.

Mouse saw the crowd closing in, saw the three men still rolling on the lawn, and saw Abby's determined attempt to collect the scattered treasure. If something wasn't done, and done quickly, things were going to get very ugly.

Mouse didn't plan it, didn't think it through, but suddenly he knew what he had to do.

He walked quickly to where MacFarlan still stood, open mouthed, before the microphone. Mouse saw immediately where the cable from the microphone connected to the amplifier. He bent down and spun the volume knob clockwise until it stopped, then moved to stand beside the microphone. He took a deep, deep breath, and tried vainly to think what to say. When it came, it was but a single word — "STOP!"

The electronics of the rock band's amps took hold of that short word, amplified it a thousand times, and sent it screaming into the night. It was the loudest thing Mouse had ever heard. It bounced off the people in the stands, ricocheted over the heads of the crowd sprawled on the grass and sped away into the night.

The impact of the word stunned the crowd to silence. The fighting men paused in their struggle. The approaching mob of coin collectors hesitated. All was quiet; all was suddenly still. Then, from far, far away, somehow bounced from the tall tower of the courthouse, the echo returned — "STOP!"

It was as if the town itself had spoken. Heads swiveled in surprise, and high overhead a huge red, white and blue star burst open and swelled to fill the sky. It was an awesome moment, and all was quiet for five seconds. Then, the noise from the stands increased, and the approaching mob began to inch closer once again.

Mouse saw that no single word, no matter how powerful, was going to stop the commotion.

"Stop!" he said it again, not so loud this time, but loud enough to carry to every pair of ears in the whole vast place. This time heads turned his way, fingers pointed and men started moving in his direction. He needed to do more, needed finally to tell the whole story of how three respectable men had come to be rolling around on the grass, like kids fighting over a shiny coin found in the dirt.

"Do you see the three men on the ground?" he asked the crowd.

"Do you see the coins scattered around them?" he paused and it seemed that all heads turned to look at the coins winking on the ground as the fireworks banged and flashed overhead.

"Do you see the people who are coming to steal the treasure away? They don't know that the coins they want so badly are counterfeit. Even worse, they don't know that the owner of those coins is Judge Theopholis Sweet, one of the men on the ground over there. Think about these poor people. What kind of fools would steal counterfeit coins from a judge while 800 witnesses watched?"

Mouse waited a second, let it sink in, and was pleased to see the opportunists slowly start to back away, trying hard to look innocent of bad intentions. Good, but he was not done yet. No longer would he trust to luck or powerful men to bring this adventure to a close. No longer would he wait for men always too busy to listen. He would settle this mess himself. He would stand on his own two feet; he would tell the world the truth. This time they would all have to listen.

He cleared his throat. When he spoke, his voice was calm and sure.

"Long, long ago, a man named Boss Buck owned a farm in Clarion County. He always claimed to be a horse trader, but his neighbors and the police thought he was a horse thief and a counterfeiter. For over 25 years, Boss Buck carried on his illegal activities. He became so well known that if people found you were from here, they called you a 'Clarion County Horsethief.'

"For years and years, the police could not seem to prove anything against the man, but that all changed in 1885, when he was arrested for making counterfeit silver dollars and sent to jail.

"The night Boss Buck was arrested, one of his men escaped with a leather bag packed full of the counterfeit coins. I found that bag a week ago. The coins were still in it, and later I discovered a name engraved in gold letters on the leather inside. The name was 'Louis B. Sweet.'

"The three men wrestling over there are a respectable farmer, a retired judge, and my own grandfather. Let me tell you how they ended up here tonight. It is mostly my fault."

Then, as simply as he could, Mouse told of how he had discovered the missing loot and of his efforts to discover its origin and proper owner. If he didn't mention Chuck, it was more from kindness than any desire to deprive his cousin of credit. If he didn't speak of his grandfather's indifference, that too was a kindness.

The fireworks finally ended with a short burst of fire and sound, but Mouse kept going. By the time he finished, the wrestling match was over, and the three men stood watching him and listening intently.

Abby was at her father's side, holding his hand and providing support for the sad and battered man. Mouse was very happy to see she looked at him with pleased approval. They had done it. The troubles with the treasure were ended.

Grandpa Wing stood alone. He was not smiling, but there was something in his expression that made Mouse think his grandfather, too, approved of his speech.

The last of the three, Judge Theo Sweet, stood near the others, rubbing at his hip, and at the dirty satchel he now held.

Distant though he was, Mouse could still clearly see the man's smile.

EPILOG

Clarion News — October 16
Lou Sweet's Legacy
By Theopholis Sweet

Last Sunday, my family and I attended the fireworks display at the university stadium. This event marks the end of our yearly celebration of fall — the Autumn Leaf Festival. If you were there, you know the fireworks were not just up in the sky that night, and that I was involved in a dispute with two other men over a bag filled with silver dollars. The grass was covered with loose coins and a crowd was beginning to press forward for a better view, or perhaps in hopes of getting a souvenir, when a young man stepped to the microphone and spoke. His name is Albert Justin Monroe, called Mouse by friends. As I lay in the grass clutching at the old satchel, I listened and came to realize that the satchel itself meant much more to me than the coins it had carried for over 100 years. By the time Mouse concluded his impromptu speech, I was on my feet again and peace had been restored. I am proud to say that Mouse is a distant cousin of mine. Without him, the situation might well have resulted in arrests and legal difficulties for the participants. I don't propose repeating what Mouse said on that occasion, as that information can be found elsewhere in this edition of the *Clarion News*. However, I would like to write about what has become of the coins and to relate some further information pertaining to my ancestors that may prove of interest to the readers of this newspaper.

As near as we can tell, the bag containing the coins lay in a long hidden mine on property that has been in my family since about 1842. Since the name "Louis B. Sweet" is stenciled inside the bag, I believe it belonged to my great-great-grandfather. The coins, as Mouse so persuasively argued, are counterfeit and thus have little intrinsic value, however, a small number of them have been divvied out to the people who had some share in their discovery, as keepsakes of an exciting week. These people include a number of resourceful Boy Scouts, Simon and Abby Grit, Mike and Chuck Wing, and, of course, Mouse Monroe. Some few coins were found on State Game Lands and these have been turned over to Mr. Clyde Swagman of the Pennsylvania Game Commission. The remainder of "Buck's Loot," as the cache of coins is now called, has been donated to the Clarion Historical Society where it will be on display shortly.

The treasure was of minor importance to me as compared to obtaining the bag belonging to my forbearer, Lou Sweet. The discovery of the bag and information provided by Mr. Simon Grit have filled a blank spot in my family's history, something I would not have thought possible a week ago.

Since the fireworks, I have also verified everything that Mouse Monroe related on that night. Furthermore, by consulting old journals and letters in the possession of my family, I have, I believe, been able to piece together a bit more of the history of the people involved. It is an interesting tale.

* * *

BUCK'S LOOT

If you cross the river below Clarion and head up Toby Creek, you soon see a small stream that comes tumbling in from the left. This is Bear Run, named after one of the early industrialists that called this area home. Bear Run has been occupied by humans for thousands of years. Long ago, it was the summer camp of long-forgotten Indians who left arrowheads and other flint tools as the only mark of their occupancy. In historic times, Bear Run has been the home of a large lumber operation, an iron furnace, gas wells, oil wells, coal mines of various shapes and sizes, and finally of the few farms that now occupy the uplands.

Today, Bear Run's lower valley is a very pleasant place, more woods than meadow, and mostly used for hunting and camping. Its delicate waterfalls and rocky glens are a joy to both eye and ear. The land itself gives away little of the doings of earlier, more active days, and you might think the old times are past and gone. You might think the past has little bearing on the present. You would be wrong.

It was to Bear Run that Louis and Elsie Sweet, and their infant son Jacob, moved in 1829. Lou worked as a mine foreman for the Empire Furnace Company, owned in part by his uncle George Bear. Elsie washed and cooked for the men of the company, and brought Jakey up to value the acquisition of property and wealth. From her letters home to Lancaster County, we can tell that she was a hard woman, the perfect frontier type, but much motivated by the desire to see her husband and son succeed. She seldom writes of her husband after the early years, except to say that he greatly enjoys hunting and is often absent from home. Reading her many letters, one can understand why the man might have wanted to get away from this increasingly bitter and driven woman.

Ten years passed. Lou was injured in a mine collapse in which he saved his uncle's life, but he ever after walked with a limp. The furnace closed, and the Sweets came into

285

possession of part of its old lands as repayment of monies owed them on the failure of the great enterprise. These lands became the Sweet Farm, or Sweetlands as Elsie designates them in her later letters. Farm life did not bring the couple more closely together. Lou was increasingly absent on hunting trips, and in 1845, he disappeared completely, though there is some evidence to suggest that he continued to send money to support his wife and son for years afterwards.

The son, now called Jakey, was 22 years of age in 1852, when he inherited some money from his maternal grandfather. Using these funds, he and his mother moved to Clarion, then a new town of just a dozen years and but 700 souls. Elsie opened a boarding house and Jakey studied law with Thomas Smearcase, an eccentric and litigious lawyer of the town. The old records show that Jakey became what was once called a plunger. He entered into many partnerships, fought many lawsuits, and at that early period, was a difficult man on his way up. He seems to have been spurred on by his equally ambitious mother.

In 1867, when Jakey was 39, his mother succumbed to cholera. She was 67 the year she died. Within 6 months, Jakey had married Arabella Hahnfeld, a former resident of the Sweet boarding house whose family had large timber interests in Highland township. Jakey's star continued to rise for many years, and if many thought him a hard and devious man, he was also thought a very successful one.

In 1883, when he was 55, Jakey invested nearly all of his capital in an extensive sawmill near the mouth of Toby Creek on the Clarion River. Sadly, his partner in the enterprise neglected to pay the insurance premium during a period of further expansion, and when a tornado and fire leveled the immense enterprise in January of 1885, Jakey found himself nearly destitute, with an extensive family and an extravagant way of life to support. All that was left of his fortune was some $9,673 and Sweetlands, which could not be sold as title remained with his long absent father, Louis Sweet.

Sometime during the summer of 1885, Jakey decided to make a bold stroke to revive his fortunes. He would drill for oil on Sweetlands using the last of his funds. The small oil boom town of Slam Bam was just a mile to the northwest of the farm, and so Jakey thought the gamble one worth taking. As the well was punched down toward the oil bearing sands far below, Jakey worried constantly about the success of the project and often stayed at the old, ruined Sweetlands farmhouse to oversee operations and urge speed from the drilling crew. The night of October 15, 1885 was one such night — one that in some mysterious way changed Jakey's life forever.

I can tell you very little more about Jakey's father, Lou. If the man wrote letters, they have not survived. In light of recent revelations, it seems fair to say that Lou probably did what he loved best for most of his life. He roamed the wild places and associated with wild men. In some unknown way, he was connected with Boston Buck, the famous Clarion County horse thief and counterfeiter whose story is told elsewhere in this issue of the *Clarion News*. On the evening of October 15, 1885, Boston Buck was arrested for counterfeiting, and on that same "dark and stormy night," Lou showed up at Sweetlands with his saddlebag full of counterfeit coins. Lou hid the coins in one of the old mines on Bear Run, but evidence found by Mouse Monroe and the family traditions of the Grit family of that area seem to point to a tragic meeting of father and son that same morning. The meeting evidently ended in disaster, and Lou died a few hours later thinking himself responsible for his son's death.

In fact, Jakey survived.

Early in the afternoon of October 16, 1885, the Sweetlands well came in. Crowds shortly gathered as the drilling crew attempted to deal with the huge flow of oil. About 3 p.m., a solitary figure staggered from the woods and came hobbling toward the scenes of so much excitement. That excitement redoubled when it was seen that the man was none other than the owner of the well, Jakey Sweet. No one could ever adequately explain just what had happened to the man. He was covered in dirt from head to foot, and was "somewhat crushed" as a newspaper of the time states. His recovery was slow and lasted many months, but he did recover.

In the years after his accident, my great-grandfather was called Jacob, not Jakey. You might think this merely a sign of respect for his advancing age, but my grandfather, who loved to tell the tale, always claimed that after his accident Jacob (his father) was a changed man. He was much kinder, much more thoughtful and became a well-regarded benefactor of the community of Clarion. Most strange of all, Jacob became an avid outdoorsman and preached the benefits of the natural life to one and all. He was an early supporter of the Boy Scout movement and lobbied hard for the creation of state parks to preserve the woodlands in our area.

It is of great interest to me to now know at least part of the reason that transformation took place. Why? Think about it. A tragedy in the woods, 100 years ago, changed the course of one man's life. How exactly it happened, I don't know. It is as though an appreciation of the outdoors and of his fellow man was a legacy somehow passed from father to son on that fateful day. Exactly how that happened, what words might have been spoken, will remain forever a mystery, but it is certain that the change in Jacob Sweet did occur, and that it also affected those near and dear to him. Jacob's sons and daughters grew to see the world in a different way, a point of view that they in turn passed on to their own children, and that still reverberates down to this day, when I, an old retired

Scoutmaster, still enjoy a sunny weekend out with the Boy Scouts camping at Sweetlands.

Hardly anyone finds a treasure such as Boston Buck's lost loot. Not many get to stand up to a crowd and stop a riot. No doubt, such adventures would change a person, but take a look at Jakey's time on earth. In his later years, he lived a quiet and exemplary life, and the good deeds of that period echo still.

A quiet, well-lived life just as surely changes the future as any grand discovery or great accomplishment — especially does such a life affect the lives of our children. Some don't believe this. They shrug their shoulders and mutter, "What will it matter in 100 years?"

Well it will!